Mai at the Predators' Ball

MARIE-CLAIRE BLAIS

Mai at the Predators' Ball

MARIE-CLAIRE BLAIS

Translated by Nigel Spencer

ANANSI

First published as *Mai au bal des prédateurs* in 2010 by Les Éditions du Boréal
First published in English in 2012 by House of Anansi Press Inc.

This edition published in 2012 by
House of Anansi Press Inc.
110 Spadina Avenue, Suite 801
Toronto, ON, M5V 2K4
Tel. 416-363-4343
Fax 416-363-1017
www.houseofanansi.com

Distributed in Canada by
HarperCollins Canada Ltd.
1995 Markham Road
Scarborough, ON, M1B 5M8
Toll free tel. 1-800-387-0117

Distributed in the United States by
Publishers Group West
1700 Fourth Street
Berkeley, CA 94710
Toll free tel. 1-800-788-3123

House of Anansi Press is committed to protecting our natural environment. As part of our efforts, the interior of this book is printed on paper that contains 100% post-consumer recycled fibres, is acid-free, and is processed chlorine-free.

16 15 14 13 12   1 2 3 4 5

Library and Archives Canada Cataloguing in Publication
Blais, Marie-Claire, 1939–
[Mai au bal des prédateurs. English]
      Mai at the predators' ball / Marie-Claire Blais ; translated by Nigel Spencer.

Translation of: Mai au bal des prédateurs.
Issued also in electronic format.
ISBN 978-1-77089-005-3

      I. Spencer, Nigel, 1945– II. Title. III. Title: Mai au bal des prédateurs. English.

PS8503.L33M3413 2012   C843'.54   C2011-908576-3

Library of Congress Control Number: 2011945344

Cover design: Bill Douglas   Cover image: Carmen Moreno Photography/Getty Images
Text design: Laura Brady   Typesetting: Erin Mallory

We acknowledge for their financial support of our publishing program the Canada Council for the Arts, the Ontario Arts Council, and the Government of Canada through the Canada Book Fund. We acknowledge the financial support of the Government of Canada, through the National Translation Program for Book Publishing for our translation activities.

Printed and bound in Canada

MIX
Paper from
responsible sources
FSC® C004071

ANCIENT FOREST ™
FRIENDLY

For Francine Dumouchel, a friend to animals and a woman of courage and conviction

Many thanks to Sushi, a remarkable artist.
— M.-C.B.

What Dieudonné the Haitian might have said to Petites Cendres was this, love, my friend, love before every last bell has tolled for you, but perhaps he said nothing after all being the discreet friend and doctor that he was, and what else could he have said that Petites Cendres didn't already understand, yes there were bells ringing out for the fast and shameless life he led, bells heralding the ecstasy of love that was sure to come his way, not deathly bells whose tones fell leaden through the air, no, jubilant ones rejoicing in the pleasures of this earth, and Petites Cendres would always be sated and content now that Yinn, the new owner of the Porte du Baiser Saloon, had come on the scene, and Petites Cendres found himself cradled in the respect and protection that Yinn and his husband Jason afforded him, never to be humiliated, rejected, or abased again, this was the sacrosanct patron that stood watch over Petites Cendres, Yinn girl and boy, goddess of shining days, the completeness of night that crept up on Petites Cendres, prince of Asia, on those fiery nights when he took Yinn in his arms, or was that just vain dreaming too, standing in for all the nights spent waiting for Yinn in the green pool of the sauna, Temple of Obscure Divinities, a calming, breathless dream that would not allow a cell in his body to sleep, yes you've got to fight said Dieudonné, and which demon should I take on first asked Petites Cendres, indolence replied Dieudonné with a hint of evasiveness, aware he was already neglecting Petites Cendres for the other patients in his infirmary, not a second to lose my friend he said, and if I were you I'd stop everything, really, the hash, the cocaine and I'd stop it tonight, Yinn was working his way through the lines asking if anyone had seen Fatalité today or yesterday, long and lean Fatalité their greatest star, nope haven't seen him these past two nights, that's way too long said Yinn, I haven't seen him for two nights either since he went out roaming the sidewalks advertising the show with ribs you could see beneath the street lamp as though he'd melted into the folds of his robe, that's two nights Yinn said, way too long and he doesn't live far from here, maybe one of you should go and see, last time I saw him he was headed that way over to the second-floor veranda, his skinny legs going slowly up the steps, come on somebody, say you will said Yinn, I told him I didn't want to, hell no and why me, Fatalité, no way uh-uh can't do it, then Yinn said Jason should go, two nights, nope way too long, we're brothers aren't we, yes we are I told Yinn, the ineffable look of those slant blue eyes asking if I'd seen Fatalité, where and in what shape, okay so where then, nothing like this weirdness has hit the Saloon for so long I don't really want to know, still I could see him walking and walking, and where to with that strange gait and his crown of pink feathers reaching up high from strands of brown hair into the night sky the way it always did, Jason, that's who I'll send, Yinn said to Petites Cendres all wrapped up in himself, inside that emaciated body inside a black curtain, a fan of plumes

waving from his head thought Petites Cendres, so perhaps
Dieudonné said only this to Petites Cendres, love, my friend,
love before every last bell has tolled for you, and asked him
if he'd ever seen his friend Timo again, no never saw him, not
ever, see my dear friend Dieudonné, as the Reverend Ézéchielle
likes to say, impenetrable are the ways of the Lord, undeci-
pherable too, but his ghost drifts through my mind all the
time, starting at the Saloon and going all the way to his door,
up the steps to the veranda with a measured pace, one at a
time, and there's Fatalité's apartment shining in the raw light,
always lit day and night, his perch from time to time, you
might say, Yinn had designed Fatalité's outfit, same as everyone else's, a flamboyant display each evening, strong legs
under velvet garters, and Yinn caressed their round butts, here
a split skirt, there a hint of a breeze on their backs, saying it's
cool, but step outside to the waiting limo so they can see you
all over town, flamboyant display in swishing lingerie, incredible outfits brushing skin the better to reveal Yinn's creations,
sitting in the limo recalling Fatalité upright in one too like a
gigantic flower waving to passersby and lobbing necklaces
perhaps a little too indifferently, that detached-looking hand
waving by itself, no smile surfacing on the hollow cheeks,
Yinn and Jason married at last, I could make Yinn my wife
too and no one would know thought Petites Cendres, steal a
ring and, well two husbands, that wouldn't be overdoing it,
I'd tell him no more hashish and no more cocaine if I were
you Petites Cendres said Dieudonné, you and your flighty
friends, said Reverend Ézéchielle, don't suppose you at least
pray once in a while in those saloons and dives of yours, pray
for your brother Fatalité eh, why not, a candle in the wind,
they say that at two in the morning there was no waking him
up any more, one of the best girls, honest Reverend, Jason
was the one who told us over at the Saloon, Fatalité, Fatalité,
she won't open her eyes, she won't wake up, oh my God
she's going, call an ambulance, no way Fatalité's going out in

a body bag, no said Yinn's male Jason, we'd heard him singing in the saloon, those very words, *you'll see, a setting sun's going to shroud us all*, we should have listened to what he said, Yinn's husband his man, one candle, two under the golden coat of the setting sun, gentle, really gentle and asleep, I've got to say, at two in the morning, Fatalité, well no more sunlight for him, whatever, Fatalité's never waking up again. Mai thought about all those fathers and daughters in all those ballrooms, so glad her father wasn't one of those fawning predators perched on the soft necks of their girls, each in her white dress with a white rose in hand, listening to her doting father's breath stifled in devotion, hysterical with rage against modern culture, these girls free and wild, no they mustn't, not his child's freedom, they were called debutante balls, balls of abstinence and purity, eleven to sixteen and here they were under grotesque trusteeship, bare-shouldered dresses, nascent throats beneath fathers' swollen lips exhaling chaste predatorship, for them these treasures of virtue, these little girls enshrined as virgins in medallions to which they alone possessed the key till their wedding day, and their very own right up to that night, each small body firmly gripped by a fatherly hand, oppressed, intact, scattered numberless about the ballroom with mothers and uncles all elegantly conspiring, waltzing with Daddy, tomorrow's squeaky clean generation, culture and chaos laundered out of them from head to ovaries, then with their taboos relaxed, the young turned themselves into pathetic offerings assorted with words like *condoms* or *Viagra* never to be breathed by their fathers, themselves slaves to unutterable desires while their daughters lick their ice cream desserts ready to zero in on anyone who can comfort them after the ceremony, the roses, the good wishes, Papa I'll always be pure Papa, what good fortune, what a privilege that Mai's father was not one of them, taking part only as far as writing to denounce such stultifying control and scandalous rites in the ballrooms of the sacrosanct, clubs of forced abstinence that stunted their very growth, nor would these be the first to grow up inside the bubble of a lying fable invented by cowardly fathers preferring not to see their daughters reach full bloom or be breached by pregnancy or sexual diseases, what else had he told Mai, he told her once that each of us had her own destiny including her, did she recall Lola in the hobo's sleeping bag, though her father saw in Mai only his Mai, not what she truly was, he loved his kids too much to see anything else, yet never could he have been one of those ballroom dads at the rituals of purity and abstinence he hated so much, for our kids' lives are not ours to own he said, just look at how they up and leave like Samuel to New York or Vincent to Boston, already starting his medical studies, and you my little Mai, you too will be far away in college soon, oh no our kids' lives are beyond our control, and what a mirage it would be to hold on to them, Mai thought how little her father knew her as she listened to him, really no more than the ballroom fathers as they loomed protectively over their daughters' virtue, contemplating the pure lines of their faces and thinking nothing would ever change their offspring, fixed and expressionless under the stiffness of their necklines, Mai's face of course lied every bit as much as theirs in angelic retardation, out here on the highway you could hear the humming of the engine, Papa I want those jeans with stars stitched onto the pockets, I want them Papa, Mai said, remembering the nightmares of the night before, nighttime in the dream as well, and she wondered what she was doing at home with her parents and someone knocking at the door, him, the man from the cemetery, his huge shadow sliding over the walls, a white hen beneath his cape, and saying *you remember me, don't you, He-Who-Never-Sleeps, see this hen, I can snap its head off with my thumb, and those white pigeons were my doing too,* all in a dream, the pigeons cooing and the hen dying, when she awoke, she thought she was alone in an empty house, but what was she doing back here at home, and where were her parents anyway, it was a lie, she must still be dreaming, the shadow of He-Who-Never-Sleeps with his straw hat sliding across the wall, a fifteen-year-old doesn't yell for Daddy, so don't tell anyone but I hate both of them, Marie-Sylvie de la Toussaint and her brother, why couldn't they just go back to Haiti, a girl that young just has to keep quiet about such things, Jason I phoned him a few times and Fatalité's cellphone had this echo to it, just kept on ringing, and this echo, hello, it's me Fatalité, hey Fatalité it's me, do you want to get together tonight, hey hello Fatalité a night you'll never forget, hello, this is Fatalité speaking, Fatalité's laugh, fatal grating music, hey guys, it's me Fatalité, just leave me your name, Fatalité for the love of fate, destiny and Jason this was his cellphone and his words, Fatalité Fatalité who here is gonna want me, battered cream-skinned girl, I'll go listen to you sing Fatalité, yes I saw you with your hand on Yinn's hip, you're in love, boy what a dolled up corpse you're going to make, cream everywhere, yes I saw you two, you're in love, and the more I look at you Fatalité, the more alone I feel, it didn't use to be that way but experience wears you down, kills you, here I'm leaving you a syringe, you'll see, g'night Jason and g'night Yinn, what they do with what's left of us, you'll have to pay 'cause I'm broke Yinn, I know you told me always to have some cash on me just in case, just in case, Fatalité is what I am, look I don't like to ask but will you leave my lamp on 24/7 so people won't forget me, I'm sorry Yinn but you'll have to dip into your savings too, I love you brother, adieu Yinn, that's what he left on his cellphone, words coming in rushes, broke . . . I haven't got a thing . . . then nothing as though he just ceased to be, hello, it's me Fatalité, Dieudonné confirmed it was all over, Fatalité confided to him only yesterday, the epidemic's back and they're all ignoring it Doctor, but you know Dieudonné, you see the plague victims every day, in the office and the infirmary, they just don't want to know, Doctor, you'd have to yell and scream and still they wouldn't listen, I really liked this kid, Dieudonné said to Petites Cendres, are you taking your meds Petites Cendres, by everything that matters, don't ever forget we have no one to care for us but ourselves, don't bother looking round, there's no one in charge but you, okay Doctor, I don't need telling again, I'm fine, don't worry about me, replied Petites Cendres feeling hounded on all sides, with Fatalité's last words engraved on his brain, Dieudonné was leaving bag in hand, I've got to be up early tomorrow to drive the girls to school, not staying out all night like you, see Petites Cendres, Fatalité's shown you where it can get you, yeah, yeah Doctor, say no more was his answer, I do most of my work at night, that way customers don't see the spots on my face, why don't you just go and sleep my friend said Dieudonné, any sleep you can get is good, so Petites Cendres tried to change the subject by complaining that Yinn had to pay for all this, but that was all he could say about what he felt except that Yinn was so kind it tormented him, beauty and kindness, probably irreconcilable, or perhaps Yinn's beauty was only inside and spilled out all the brilliance of his spirit on us all, his indefinable blue gaze, so much so that next morning Petites Cendres felt he'd seen Yinn act like a leader after being so feminine onstage the night before, pink-sequined bikini under a long navy blue fake-fur coat like a dressing gown, a majestic queen in high heels, now a tough guy, practically a brawler, onstage at the cabaret telling everyone what to do, repeating what Jason had said down there on the dock, when we get there it will be sundown, it doesn't matter we'll walk right to the end in special groups, walk even if it gets dark early in winter and we'll still all be there together, his voice thickening when it pronounced Fatalité's name, his sister will be there, he had a sister you know, and she'll be there, and they'll step forward into the streets together, Petites Cendres thought to himself, with Yinn in the lead, this time dressed with restraint as a boy in a red vest, cargo Bermudas, and sandals, the bouquet of orchids with round bulbous flowers he held to his chest would surely be as heavy to bear as any crucifix, we'll go right to the end of the dock, Yinn with Fatalité's sister — nobody even knew he had one — crying for her big brother, no, none of us knew, and yes the bouquet of orchids for a cross, ashes beneath them, walk said Yinn, let's walk, his voice firm, the show has to go on again at ten, and Fatalité wouldn't want us to let people down Yinn said, I wonder thought Petites Cendres, does he remember bathing Fatalité that same day when he said laughing, you'll see, Yinn, I'll be there for the show tonight, no promising I'll stay till dawn like the rest of you of course, but you'll see, Yinn, I'll be there, oh so you're soaping my back with gloves on to protect your artist's hands, eh Yinn, eh, go on my friend, I'm that infected kid from Africa, I'm Rosinah Motshewwa and I'm twenty-nine, and you're from some humanitarian association in South Africa bathing me, washing me, Rosinah, and my two brothers are unemployed, I have one small child, that's right it's me, do you see those lesions beneath my staring eyes, and you're holding my head so I don't give way to panic, you see it in my eyes, on my trembling lips that hurt so much, I actually saw Rosinah in a newspaper and I thought how alike we were, she and I, you and your rubber gloves bathing me, washing me, go ahead my friend and don't think for a moment I won't be there with you tonight, and Yinn, leading the procession, knowing the sun was hidden behind thick February clouds, was revisiting the scene of Fatalité's bath, eyes wide with panic as Fatalité took on the name of Rosinah Motshewwa, twenty-nine — better rest, you're hallucinating, Yinn helped him stretch on the bed, maybe a beer would do you some good, Jason could bring you a cold one, then just have a nap, I'll be right here with you tonight; Fatalité's my name, Fatalité, and I'm twenty-nine, Yinn there at the head of the procession, and what was he thinking, walk, keep walking, we've got a show advertised for ten and tonight we're taking up a collection, nobody realized how flat broke he was, can you believe it, Yinn in a red vest and orchids pressed against his chest heavy as a crucifix thought Petites Cendres, Yinn told them all as they walked along, remember those songs he loved, and Yinn sang them into the teeth of the February wind, *I want a perfect body, a perfect soul, I want* then *I am loving angels instead*, why, why does this time have to come at all thought Petites Cendres, the time for loving angels and nothing else, what was the point of a perfect body only to have it tripped into infinity, *yes I want a perfect body, a perfect soul*, and *oh baby don't go breaking my heart*, Petites Cendres joined in too while passersby respectfully greeted Yinn at the front, *oh baby*, it was him, it was Fatalité, her body once more shrunk back into our cradle in the shadows, on this earth though, oh on this earth I did find some peace, Yinn sang beneath her breath or perhaps it was only a lamentation, no way to know for sure, *perfect body, perfect soul, I want, I want* he sang, in the cabaret when Fatalité danced and sang all night, burlesque send-ups, off-colour jibes at the audience, that's what got all the shameless laughs, she partied and never once tripped running up the steep stairs to the stage, *love me, hug me, kiss me* she sang, our secret intimacy that said all the things that shouldn't be said, her spiteful jokes, vodka in hand, let's party, *love me, hug me, kiss me*, when vengeful love shakes itself free and us with it, he loved his songs, tunes with no meaning at all, *love me, hug me, kiss me*, a perfect body and a perfect soul now atrophied and unrecognizable, with only the angels to love, thought Petites Cendres, and Dieudonné buzzing in his ears, you see the rings around your eyes, the sad expression, see that's what happens when you spend your nights out on the sidewalk or in the sauna at the Porte du Baiser instead of at home asleep, Dieudonné looked at him wondering what could be done with such simple candor in the face of utter collapse and destruction all around him, Christ what can we do with you when you just won't

listen the doctor said, okay look, I've got to take the girls to
school early for their morning gymnastics, no idea what it
takes to be a father, have you Petites Cendres, well it's one
joy you're never going to have, are you, no straight and narrow for you either, Porte du Baiser Saloon, there it was right
on Petites Cendres' vest lettered white on black, WHERE REAL
MEN COME TO PLAY, trust me, rushing up and down the stairs like
that, Fatalité had to be on speed, speed and all that other crap,
your beautiful sinister Fatalité, that's what did it, you know
that don't you, *I want a perfect body, a perfect soul* sang Yinn,
the wind snapping the flags along the street, hail to you
Fatalité he said, through the circle of fire, your soul be at
peace in a world where no one else's can, Fatalité, we love
and kiss you, *hug me, kiss me* Yinn sang, oh Fatalité was loved
as she deserved, so loved, thought Petites Cendres walking
with the others to the dock shoulder to shoulder with Robbie
who was going to do the evening shows instead and who was
a half-breed like Petites Cendres himself — though twenty
years younger — a new recruit he thought, money tucked into
the laces and frills down his front, a cruel spectacle of ruined
youth, and legs that would get him through anything, so hard
to see, Yinn's heart was his without begging, years piled on
years he said thoughtlessly, that's what's waiting for us, shut
up said Petites Cendres, you snotty kid, Petites Cendres felt
like asking him why he needed rubber dildos and the answer
would have been that it caught guys' eyes when he was dancing, so you just shove those things anywhere anytime under
that micro-skirt of yours Petites Cendres would have shot
back, with all your talent I wonder why, though obviously,
twenty years younger, nothing was off limits to Robbie, vulgarity was all part of the show Robbie said tonight as he
untangled his thick hair, curling and uncurling it at will, he
was in for a long reign as the tempestuous, desirable, dam-
nable animal of all night-time prowls, oh no this picture was
too much for Petites Cendres to bear, galling how much

imagination these new recruits had . . . Yinn dressing Robbie
up in wilder and wilder outfits, modelling him to his own
taste, slipping his arm around his waist, cozying up to him
saying you know, everything, I mean everything, looks so
fabulous on you Robbie, she'd say beneath the docks where
you could hear the students on break manhandling the boats
as they smacked into the waves, should've yelled at them to
quiet down, Yinn still leading the procession, orchids clutched
like tiny weights across his chest, Petites Cendres brushed
shoulders with Robbie, far more muscular than he even in the
tight dress he wore to troll the sidewalks at night, the same
scorpion tattooed on it as Jason, Yinn's husband, yes husband,
and just as muscular, let's take a pause and pray, we're already
by the sea so do we really need to pray as well said Robbie,
I mean do we really have to pray after all this walking especially in these shoes, do you really think Fatalité would want
all this performance, she was just a simple sex-obsessed girl
after all, it's about respect said Petites Cendres, and you're
only wearing those party shoes for show anyway, Yinn's the
theatre whiz shot back Robbie, look at him strutting it like the
ocean is his backdrop, bumming around and looking for
excitement, hell, even he doesn't know who he is, do you or
me or any of us have any idea where he's from, Christ my feet
are killing me and we really have to pray as well, that's why
Fatalité did this in the first place, to save us all this trouble,
I'm telling you she knew Yinn would be lost without all this
showboating, he's loving every minute of it, the crowd by the
sea under an overcast sky, the basket of rose petals and
orchids for everyone, just so Yinn doesn't get bored, because
God knows Yinn mustn't be bored, when she's bored she lifts
her skirt and does pirouettes in the street like a spinning top,
all kinds of crap just to be provocative and why, because she
can't stand being bored, anything's better, even obscene provocation, goddammit my feet hurt and the wind's so strong I
can't hear a word of Jason's prayers anyway, I mean death is

the greatest thing that can happen to a person so no way should it be boring, right, and while Robbie gossiped away, Petites Cendres standing right next to him saw a flash of about fifty young men tied up on a Thai beach all looking like Yinn and staring at him in a way he just couldn't define, soon after being refused sanctuary they would immediately reboard their makeshift boat to go home again and drown on the way, never mind their being as young and handsome as Yinn, they were condemned to die at sea, their hands tied behind their backs, trussed like parcels and knowing they would die on board those rickety sieves, and that was the way it should be, out of sight out of mind, for the authorities, Cambodia and Laos didn't want them either, so into the deep with them — Gulf of Siam, Andaman Sea, whatever — leave those sneaky illegals to the silent muddy waves out of sight, and with them the mystery of Yinn's birth told to Petites Cendres this way, so here I am the only one left alive because I broke free, that's how come, broke the chain and the rope with my teeth, my servitude along with them Petites Cendres, and Fatalité had her story too Robbie chimed in, a sister from Arizona for instance, we never even knew she had one; when they got near the water, Yinn reminded them they had to be back at the saloon before ten, it was still a night like any other, drama over Fatalité or not, Robbie said, things have to stay on the rails, that's Yinn, order through and through, and he makes no secret of it, he has a mother somewhere too, he conceals nothing but confides nothing said Petites Cendres, the Gulf of Siam, the Andaman Sea, all lost in the silence of water said Robbie, a Korean mother, a military father, two brothers in California yet he reveals so little said Petites Cendres, a goddess in the Temple of Obscure Divinities he thought to himself, well he wasn't going to confide in that blabbermouth Robbie, so another numbing monologue comes out of him, better pray as Jason asked for the peaceful repose of Fatalité's soul, but none of it means anything said Robbie, I mean what

does any of us know about it right, this is a big deal considering Fatalité liked such simple things, like eating and drinking,
a helluva big deal, I bet if he knew he'd never have left
Arizona, really just food and drink anywhere, even the sauna,
leg up to get some attention, remember that Petites Cendres,
Yinn's mother, Mom or Mama Yinn, used to say bow slightly
when talking to a lady and be polite, oh she wasn't happy
about his marriage to Jason, just a worthless scrap of paper,
what a pain and Yinn with his heart broken three times already
she'd say over and over, three boys, three hurts, and this dissolute Jason drinking too much on Friday nights, immoderate
in his sense of order and justice though, Yinn's idea was to
treat everyone, rich or poor, to a meal on Sundays, but not
every night for God's sake said his mother, what on earth is
he thinking, marriage for love and being sad next day because
he's fooled around on you, now is love really such a good
reason, she asks her son some days, he's forgotten about his
soldier father who dumped me with three boys and a pittance,
Yinn learned to sew because I had to make all their clothes,
he even designed them for his dolls, and his older brothers
just laughed at him; and even as a kid he had those long eyelashes over that special blue, like his father's eyes, not really
blue or green or grey but his own colour, oh those eyes, and
what eyes to cloak his soul and shield him from everyone
when he set about dressing and undressing his dolls, and I
always kept a lookout for fabrics and cloths I could find inex-
pensively in the stores — already a makeup artist, he had to
be powdering, adding glitter to the cheeks of his dolls, outlin-
ing their long lashes — and I told him don't listen to your
brothers, you've always been the sweetest, the most gentle,
so don't listen to them my Thai prince, you are so very gifted,
and don't ever forget we have nothing, that your mother does
sewing for the rich, nothing, we have nothing at all, between
us our work will get us through this, and now here he is getting married to Jason, I mean of course love may be a good

enough reason, you are going to get hurt, and what will I do my exile boy in your pain, we never complained of our hunger, looking at me in silence with those eyes suddenly downcast in that way you know so well, not at all like the other boys, more distant, removed from an ancient civilization that no longer survives, and now he wants to please Jason whose wife he is, femme fatale in jeans that fit too tight and crush all that nature has given him, knee-high boots, a black bra and a white vest over it, knotted at the stomach, all just to please Jason, forgetting perhaps how he used to dress, a true prince though we may have been poor, no, love alone is not enough reason to get married, that's what I'm always telling him, this was how Yinn's mother went on about her cabaret-star boy as she stitched his clothes for the show, stringing pearl necklaces, guiding him as she once had much earlier in his costume designs, tiny next to him, a bee and a deer, sometimes stinging Jason, he's going to hurt you so badly you'll never get over it and then who's going to bind your wounds when you're so all alone, because I'm not always going to be here, so trust in my mother's instinct, I won't always be here, believe in my mother's instinct, who is going to bind your wounds when I'm gone and you're all alone, I can barely see now, you need glasses Mama that's all, Yinn would reply, and when I buy them for you, you refuse to wear them Mama, oh no I'm not going to start complaining like all those old ladies who fall in love with you in your shows said Yinn's mother, if their sons were like you they'd be so worried about the future they'd never notice time passing them by, what's going to become of him that pirouette of a son of mine, what's going to become of him they'd say, one day this way, one day the other, a pirouette from boy to girl with beautiful shoulder-length black hair, with no concern for rules of any kind, no oh no they'd be preoccupied with him all the time, time passing them by, and all those strange women, you let too many women caress you, yes Yinn's mother would say, I'm in

perpetual combustion, that's why they come to me Yinn
would say — boys and men I can understand, but so many
women as well — there for a night and then gone, do be
careful son, the split that vents our passion is always there,
wide open, so do be careful, especially if you want to marry
that Jason, his mother remembered him barely starting out as
a delinquent, first admiring that shiny sewing machine she
could not afford in the shop, then him setting it up in their
modest apartment, you've got to take it back where you got
it, I'm worn out with worry about you, do you want to get us
thrown out of this country, delinquent, thief, and no father to
protect you, just gone off with the first woman to wander by,
and the shiny sewing machine in the shadows, sew, Mama,
sew, suture, so the needles no longer hurt your hands, you're
going to take this right back or you're going to prison she had
told him, the shininess of the machine lighting their misery, it
was for you Mama so your fingers would stop bleeding, that's
what the child said pirouetting around and around with my
dresses and jewels on, the little there was left over from times
past, no more jewels and dresses, I had to work for rich
people and I took him along with me and kept an eye on him
so he wouldn't lift anything, sewing machines in rich people's
houses, always keeping an eye out and putting back whatever
he'd taken, do you want to get us thrown out of this house,
out of this whole country, out on the street with all three of
my sons, is that what you're aiming for Yinn, always this
obsession with sewing machines, even in the masters' houses,
a woman brings up her kids by herself, worried sick at seeing
him grow up with a hankering for silks and fabrics, and when
will he ever have enough of this stuff, and us having nothing
at all or so little, his father running off with the first woman
he cast eyes on, and this was how she spoke of him to Robbie
on the wharf as the wind whipped their faces, and he in turn
said to Petites Cendres, remember how much Fatalité loved
this song *You know I am no good but love me anyway*, how

are you supposed to be worth anything in this world anyhow, Robbie asked, I'm gonna be cute, with long blonde hair over my own, and I'll dance so good before and after the show that people on the street will stop and shower money on me, 'specially Fridays and Sundays, so how are you supposed to be worth anything in this world when nothing's worth much anyway, eh Petites Cendres, what do you think his favourite song was, he just loved it, none of us really take up much space at all do we, short orbits, that's all we have, just like Fatalité, oh I know I'm not worth anything, nothing at all, but while I'm passing through, boy am I gonna cause a splash, 'cause you've got a chance at that at least, here's the Reverend announced Yinn, standing near the edge of the sea, now the Reverend will speak, Reverend Stone, where'd they get him Robbie asked Petites Cendres, Fatalité didn't even believe in religion, first a reverend then prayers, Christ it's like being in church or some kind of religious meeting with everybody respectfully gathered round him like that, or maybe we just never realized he had faith in something all along, what do you think eh, Fatalité liked simple things, life, a bit of pot, what else . . . dear friends, intoned Reverend Stone, let us pray for our travelling companion Fatalité who always followed his own road, a fanciful one perhaps, but everyone has theirs, the one that has to be followed, straight or twisting and turning or whatever it may be, but God receive him in his charity just the same, and each of us is welcome into the house of the Lord as Fatalité is, for you know my friends, Fatalité was a believer, a true and fervent believer, and sometimes he said to me the Lord lead me where He wills, for I am but the smallest wave on the ocean, yet we must have some enjoyment on this journey of ours, a journey now over, suspended, the passageway now bricked up, the ocean we hear swell so loud Robbie said to Petites Cendres, and you know when Yinn was young he hid his share of sewing machines just so his mother would no longer ruin her fingers with needle points, but she just had to keep taking them back to the stores and reason with the owners, explaining that he was obsessed with making clothes with the shiny machines standing in the shadows of the rich people's houses where his mother worked for so long as a servant, and obsessed as he was he would one day be an artist, let it be known by all the shop owners or masters of the houses where she explained he really wasn't a delinquent at all, no thief, just a marvelling, passionate child, nothing more, and that was how he managed to stay out of corrections halls, though she constantly reproached him for it of course, the same way she complained of his marrying Jason, a reverend among us, that just doesn't fit Robbie told Petites Cendres, but for all that it was well said just the same, Fatalité's way was his own, and do you think with all these speeches we're gonna be in time for the ten o'clock show, I mean a reverend with prayers and all, I just didn't expect all that coming from Fatalité, Robbie said, God I hope they don't do all this when my turn comes, like when I'm a hundred, I mean I'm not croaking any time soon, and the rose and orchid petals are floating on the waves, it is late and the cocks are still asleep, time for us to go home too, walking in silence, yup time for the ten o'clock show Robbie said. Papa usually writes for an hour after our weekly visit to the library, so if he takes me for a ride in the car instead I'll wonder why; must be so he can talk to me, but what about, Mai thought, he knows everything all the time, certainly whatever Mama's told him, but he's not one of those intruding fathers, no never, but he'll never say anything, he dared ask me one thing though on that foggy road: this Manuel, you've known him for quite a while, haven't you — no, he didn't say the business about the Mercedes and you in the car with him, it did happen didn't it — no, not one of those intruding fathers, you were only eleven then, true he didn't dare to say that, but here I am next to him in the car and it's for no good reason, I brashly ask how his book is going and he says it's not a story but

something that really happened, in fact they always are real
events he said firmly, it's Nora's story he says, completely
absorbed in her so I can't keep his attention on me, I dislike
my dad's heroines because they always take him away from
me, and there's something suspicious about that that he won't
admit to, and why has he taken his writing time to go for a
ride with me, maybe it's so I won't go out dancing, he doesn't
like that, so I couldn't compare him to those possessive fathers
with daughters in the abstinence clubs, purity clubs, who have
a few drinks and watch their little ballerinas dance for them
in their huge tutus, then waltz with them, black dragons in
tuxes, one waltz for Daddy, smooth music especially for this,
and a song rises in the adolescent throats, chanting your love
Papa and your faith are my shield, and I will always be your
baby, yes Papa, always so small and so confident and willing
to sing whatever they're told, nothing's too stupid, then the
exchange of roses and vows between fathers and tiaraed
daughters devoted to total purity for Daddy's sake, more than
a vow, an oath, I will be forever faithful Daddy, your baby girl
entwined in an embrace with Daddy as the vain tears well up,
always faithful Daddy dearest, this is how the purity balls turn
out, so even if my dad isn't anything like them I'm still suspicious about why he wants me to go for this ride, yes of course,
you've known Manuel for years, I remember he says distract-
edly, yes of course, he doesn't want me to open the door too
suddenly, his suspicious reason is that he wants to talk to me,
that we both talk, sort of like a vow between us, and he'll
promise not to tell Mama, but he's still not thinking of me but
of Nora, she is his true inspiration, no dogs to walk so we can
talk freely, no dogs to muddy up the car seats or lay the
weight of their large heads between us or leap on me so hap-
pily, and Papa has absolutely no ulterior motive in speaking
to me or me to him, you see Mai he now said, Manuel and
his father have a pretty bad reputation, like those discotheques
of theirs where you and your friends go dancing, bad, really

bad he said, coming back to Nora, the muse for his book, maybe with a little more nuance, I'd say deterioration or slow degradation, which of course can happen to anybody, Nora is special, the opposite of Ibsen's character you understand, you are too hung up on this woman Mai returned, implacable, besides she's married, I was talking about my book her father replied, then in another tone, it's dangerous for kids like you, but I'm no longer a child Mai said, and Manuel and his father are pimps, but he did not actually say anything, it is just in your head she thought, you are too hung up on this Nora said Mai again, plus you cut your own hair, and badly too I might add replied her father, smiling so he could interrupt the suspicious conversation while letting him be distracted by Nora, the one he was writing about, at the very moment when he should be at his work table, the fog's fallen all of a sudden he said, I didn't realize you'd known one another for so many years, I repeat, sweetheart, this boy has a very bad reputation, I know Papa, I know, you already said that Mai interrupted, but her father returned to it, I didn't realize it he said without smiling, there are two things I don't like about you Mai replied, you write books and you play golf like some sort of old man, and at this very moment she wanted more than anything else for her father to be less suspicious, that she be out from under this interrogation, and that he stop searching her out with those charcoal eyes and brows that had been greying for a while now, the fathers of the purity club in turn made their vows after dinner and a waltz, vows that they too would be pure in their lives as men, husbands and fathers owned forever by their little girls, then went out onto the terrace for a smoke, choking on the lies and posturing, and one of them with a cowboy hat recalled that he'd had ten kids by seven different women but now it was time for vows of purity, and he had three daughters in the room, one only ten years old swearing to Dad that she would remain a virgin until marriage, though she didn't really know what it meant except that tonight she had lived a fairy tale with her father, pretty lies, all of it, and afterwards he'd smoked his cigarette, gone back inside to admire the charming little things, his own and others', a private flower garden, who would all remember this night when each had offered the treasure of her heart to Daddy, when, Daddy, when are we going to sail to Panama Lou asked her father, in spring Ari replied, when the winds are gentler, now the boat was called *Lou's Boat,* no longer *Lou's Camper,* which would have been silly considering she was older now, and it was tied up at the Club Nautique as Ari polished its sides, listening to the sound of the waves while Rosie and Lou played on the bridge with greasy french-fry fingers the way she did at her mother Ingrid's, brought up so badly he thought, and at times they darted down into the cabin with laughter spilling over, greasy french-fry fingers, and it annoyed him that she didn't share his vegetarianism, eating their disgusting hot dogs, so make yourselves useful, help me polish the boat at least with all that grease of yours, if we want to make it to Panama she's got to be watertight he told Rosie, who cast admiring looks at Lou, I'm the one who's going to pilot just like Ari showed me, she knew by now how much it annoyed him to be called Ari and not Papa anymore, she'd heard it spat out and filled with ominous threat in her mother's house, I'll never speak to your father again, and you won't be seeing him so often either, this *won't be, won't be* could only rankle coming from his daughter, who surely felt his exasperated stare, it's Ingrid who talks that way, am I right, and Lou also called her mother by her first name, not Mama, speaking to both parents as though they were strangers, Ari, sad to see his daughter was no longer his or her mother's, as though insolence were something to be prized now, all you are is old grownups, Ingrid and Ari, two old folks I wish I could do without, but I'm still growing so I'm stuck with you, I've just got to put up with it for now, oh yes she told an admiring Rosie, I'm the one who's piloting us to Panama,

because there *won't be, won't be* anyone in charge but me,
Lou's boat, is it true Rosie said, twice a week a bus comes for
you and the other gifted girls, that's what they call you, and
why couldn't I be one of you Rosie asked with anxious modesty, why, I mean I like drawing too and music, and they say
you learn all kinds of things that we don't in class, yes, well
that's because it's only for us gifted kids Lou answered, but
why not me too Rosie's nervous little voice queried, not satisfied with the abrupt reply, only gifted, and you aren't one,
you're still stuck in the middle of your reader, in fact you're
behind like those black kids on Esmeralda, the ones that really
drag behind the others in school, and she knew full well this
would offend her father as she went on whispering in Rosie's
ear, pulling her hair till she cried you're pulling my hair out,
then Lou calmed down, rejoicing in the sense of power that
her exasperated dominance over the younger girl brought her,
I mean she had to, didn't she, lord over these little idiots with
her all-knowingness, and besides they can retake the exams
during the summer and so can you, thought Lou more kindly
all of a sudden, after all you do have to get some people to
like you, don't you, and she felt her father's gaze settle on her
seeming to say be nice with Rosie, though her father wasn't
thinking of her, it was too vague and dreamy for that, Lou was
more and more certain her father had another woman in his
life, someone in my daddy's life she thought, so often headed
to New York, and he doesn't want to tell me about her, he'd
rather lie, what a sneak, as their gazes connected and wove
into one another there in the bright afternoon sun sparkling
on the water, Ari wanted to say you know I have sculptor
friends in New York and my entire professional life, Lou you
know that, and what wouldn't he have said just to divert her
vindictive anger, would he, supposedly a free man, forever be
condemned to confronting his daughter and her mother, you'll
see when it comes time for you to hang around boys, you'll
see how men are and one day you'll understand, oh how Lou

longed to tear out Rosie's hair, every bit of it, one by one from this obedient child's head who still went to bed at eight every evening, same time as her little brother, Lou's rage would not leave a single strand in place, and Ari, the man who no longer spoke true, no longer her friend, whose dreamy faraway look now shamefully, oh so shamefully, looked at her unseeing while seemingly polishing the mahogany flanks of his boat, *The Boat*, hers and his, distracted and unfaithful father that he was, she thought of bringing all those other little girls here just so she could pull their hair out like that Rosie's, this was how much her father's wandering eye tore into her, the parade of young women, mistresses, that didn't matter, but for him to be in love with a real person, no that was not going to happen thought Lou, he already had a home and a wife, Ingrid, and a daughter, Marie-Louise — Lou herself — and there were to be no additions to that, no more of those usurping outsiders to take her father and all that from her, as some had already done right beneath her unsuspecting eye, and then here was Rosie looking in stunned admiration at her and the other *gifted* kids with the fastest computers, and why don't we have those in our school, I mean it hasn't even been fixed up and the walls are cracked, asked Rosie, because they're just for us and no one else was Lou's answer, because the really cool computers are for the important people and you're not one of those, and we're the ones education is meant for, oh Lou knew what she said always bordered on insult, and she really had to nail this Rosie, like everyone who set foot on the boat, and she'd face down her father and bait the trap by offering them fries and hot dogs, then she could pull their hair and make them scream so loud she couldn't describe the all-powerful feeling it gave her over all these tin-pot despots, when the one she really wanted to harm by her words and actions was her father; unfortunately he had the strength to resist and she could never defeat him, just look at those arms, that frame, she, she could do nothing about his loving another, the immunity she thought he had to love, this old grownup, and Robbie, tired of Reverend Stone's oratorical flights, walked back to the Porte du Baiser Saloon with Petites Cendres, thinking how much fun life with Fatalité had been, not like this weepy, prayer-laden evening they'd just had imposed on them with orchids and rose petals cast onto the sea, no, life with Fatalité was quite simply a farce, a comedy, and nothing sinister about it either, not like tonight's performance all wrapped up in prayers, masquerading in sermon, merely Fatalité in all her reality, Robbie's friend, laughing hysterically together, the two of them opening every door in the saloon so passersby and tourists could just drop in and sing and dance with them that night, join in their ramblings and trances, *kiss me, love me*, a very corpulent woman was zeroing straight in on them, oh my darlings listen to the sound of my voice, let me writhe like a snake with you all onstage, so close to the stars and in the divine hysteria of tonight, and listen to this deep voice of mine from deep in my heavy guts, isn't it wonderfully painful, oh God my husband's watching from across the street, I do hope he doesn't come and stop me singing with you my sweet scatterbrains and nutbars, boy this bra is killing me, what a straitjacket for a woman to haul around, hell, just let it fall where it may, anything so I can sing with you my starlings, and here we go headfirst into the earth and its bare breasts after balancing them on the end of our noses, so you see how much I love you my sweet good-for-nothings, *kiss me, love me* sang their bounteous Madonna while her husband urged her with a glower to put her bra back on, now is that any way for a woman to act he thought, so disconcerted that he said nothing, she just went on that way for quite a while, singing as she held our faces and hair against her ample bosom, o blessed domain, at least until her husband roughly ordered her out of the bar, and this was Robbie's true Fatalité, calling love and the generosity of sharing down upon him, a wild woman dancing across the boards between purple velvet curtains, the whole luscious banquet of sex and the senses, my own Fate, a risk to be run without trickery, life, unbridled frenzy, perhaps I loved it too much, Robbie confided to Petites Cendres, and the way we live, it's better not to get too attached, even if we are a family, non-attachment is a law that can't be broken except at great risk, believe me Petites Cendres, a danger that brings you back to life all the better to cut you down again, you see, don't you, the way she is, your desirable Yinn, inaccessible even in our arms, I kiss you and fly away, belonging only to Jason, my round-armed tattooed one with vests even in the cold, maybe a flattened straw hat when he's singing, sharing with Yinn the long Bermudas with cargo pockets, one glimpse of Yinn's coquetry and show-off style is enough to make him spurn the slightest bit of decoration, he lives and breathes Yinn's rich diversity, her batting eyelashes, the shift of her shoulder blades under the orange straps of her evening dress, he says she's my princess or she's like this or like that, he doesn't know what to say anymore, Jason the man is not very talkative, except certain demonstrative words or outrage, and it is all for Yinn, Jason says, Yinn preferring to design outfits she can show off down in the street, a prince flying over the abyss on a silken sail or climbing the wooden stairs to the cabaret every evening and night, no longer parading herself but standing upright and lifting a fold of her dress, wondering if she had to go on with these shows, invited to New York and Los Angeles, if we had to repeat all our gestures endlessly from night to night in a decor that just intensified and can be broken like the set around Fatalité and her voice and laughter, Fatalité, once so vivacious, that flower of mine, but the game with men, whether exercising their charms or not, the voices of Jason and Yinn and their dances onstage, whether Yinn be indifferent or given over, had first and foremost to survive, sordid as the misery of so many bizarre creatures may be, incongruous species Robbie said to Petites Cendres, that's what I think, we have to perpetuate ourselves, fly over the gulf and the abysses end to end, like Yinn, without asking too many questions, touching without touching, running between clouds and earth but not breathless, as eagles fly, gliding in a straight line like Yinn at some ancestral plane unique to the race perhaps, and you have seen her eyes, both fixed and disoriented all at once, a hardened look she must have learned early on, though still tender at times, you've seen how she looks at us, a blue arrow of a look, haven't you Petites Cendres, that impassive oriental gaze, so brother, remember the look disappears as easily as it came, Petites Cendres again saw the refugees on the Thai beach, all of them tied up with Yinn among them, then thrown into the sea, and when the young dealer approaches from the street, the drug gangster asks Yinn if he's got any salt, meaning a quick fix, no, Yinn's definite, a quick little bit of salt the dealer repeats, when a blue-arrow glance from Yinn transfixes him and sends him on his way before Jason does it for him faster and dirtier, and Yinn announces enough of this shit, enough, he imposes his authority, and Petites Cendres once again sees them tied up in the waves, one upon another, Yinn with them and looking at him while the blue of the sky blurs their being sucked down into the shark-infested depths, and Robbie says Yinn's mother told me three guys tore him apart, who were they, do you know, who before Jason could have broken through her obstinate resistance, who, three boys Mama Yinn said, three broken hearts, three lesions, finally it was too much, he married, then when it was done and Jason had a wife and three kids, the other woman, Yinn, shows up in all her celestial androgyny and falls in love with him, and Jason finds himself racing in all directions at once: his first wife, his children, Yinn and Mother, could that be what caused the fourth trauma, my son, heartbreak, no I won't have it, and here she is, playing queen to her prince, stitching his outfits, showing him how to design and sew, she doesn't like him taking on these lowly jobs, cleaning up after all those men and their secretions at the saloon, the sauna, the Jacuzzi, still hot from steam, carrying a bag of other people's laundry on his back to be washed, bent under its dark weight of humiliation, her son shouldn't be subjected to that primitive legacy, no he must not she says again seeing the face of Yinn leaning down, and repeats no that must not be, not you my son, beneath the anger of this filth, why him and not Jason, still he continues bowed, unperturbed and unseeing, toward the street, unrecognizable behind the mask of a child slave said Yinn's mother, yesternight's prince nowhere to be seen in him, nowhere the silks and finery, and she rushes to help him but he says no Mother, no, Yinn says you've been like this too, even heavier loads on your back in the days when we hadn't a thing in the house, and so he went on, bent double, three lesions, three heartbreaks, three boys Robbie said to Petites Cendres, I'd love to know who they were, how they could get through to him like that, three wounds to fell him, Yinn, Robbie said, and Petites Cendres thought of getting that black bag off Yinn's back and onto his own, those rags and whores' underthings from the cabaret, Petites Cendres would get him out from under this servitude with dignity, the sequined mermaid's dress, the most sparkling of all, Yinn had told Petites Cendres, kissing him on the cheek as they paced up and down the streets before the evening show, while Petites Cendres hustled in the passersby and sent them up the wooden stairs to the club, no he told Petites Cendres, this is a job I have to do, I mean there's always underwear to darn and sew, painstaking and thorough as Yinn was with every scrap worn by his girls, Robbie, Cobra, and the others . . . his mother saw to them too, and the night was already enough of a shambles she said, so little sleep poor kids, some of them so young they could almost be growing still, all living together five in a house as if working together at night wasn't enough for them, and she too had a room but still shared the bathroom with them, at her age that was something to be annoyed about, and she tried to ride herd on them odd as that may be, rather touching too in its noisiness, her own brood of children sometimes, dissolute maybe but hers just the same and an open book, it was a rewarding love but when she lost one of them, Fatalité for instance and how many more in the past, it was always a disaster, what a bounty of nightly metamorphosed bodies and yet what a tumult of sadness in this house, she didn't know which one to console or pacify next, God what a mess, oh Fatalité, Fatalité, they sang all through the house, farewell Fatalité and *au revoir*, we'll keep the light burning in your apartment night and day always, *Fatalité, au revoir Fatalité*, and Yinn's evening kiss on Petites Cendres' cheek out there on the sidewalk, sure he did that with everyone, lips red and smiling, but Petites Cendres latched on to him in mid-air, catching a breath of his skin and resting his head on Yinn's arm, considering this to be his transgression against the laws of sadness that had governed his life so far and against the johns who mortified him by day, a kiss that for Petites Cendres meant a redeeming hope in defiance of the mocking nastiness he was bound to undergo from one and all as he walked the streets alone or set off to meet some scummy customer, but here Yinn's offhand kiss buoyed him he thought, especially the way he felt now, but he always felt obliged to amuse Yinn, distract him when he was melancholy, distract him from the images of those trussed up on the Thai beach then sunk to the bottom, distract him from a deep bitterness that only his mother understood from their wanderings, a sudden lassitude as well that distanced him from both the man and the woman, the boy and the girl, whether running in high heels or platform boots with jeans and a white vest tied over his stomach, nothing more, from the Porte du Baiser Saloon to Decadent Fridays, in sudden, panicked flight with his wavy hair flying in the January wind, captive in whichever sex he felt like and freeing himself from the gaze of Petites Cendres, although his catch basin of friends still held him, eagerly awaiting his unfailing presence at the nightly 2:00 a.m. show, the wooden staircase was already filled with bodies of those hungry to see and hear him, teens approaching him in the street begging for a picture taken with him smiling by their side, he held them close by the waist, supplely managing their overwhelming youthfulness, but Petites Cendres knew one needed to look below the surface for the melancholy ennui of one held captive, just then, on a wild impulse, Petites Cendres approached Yinn or let him approach, and the cheek kiss distracted Yinn, liberating him in a flash, it happened, thought Petites Cendres, as he passed (in his conservative boy outfit) on this very bit of sidewalk just in front of the saloon where the steel bars on the open window take the shape of a bird, here no one recognized him smoking cigarettes and wearing sandals, his hair drawn back down his neck and ending in a slip knot, now he looked like a boy struggling with his wayward temptations, maybe even whistling between his teeth or spitting on the ground, so resembling that boy with the black sack over his shoulder that his mother came toward him and said this is how I raised you my Thai prince, like a street urchin, and for god's sake cover your mouth when you yawn my boy, where on earth did you learn such manners, maybe from the kid with the black bag or this kid hanging out in the worst places (though nothing in Yinn was like that), which drew Petites Cendres, when all of a sudden Yinn's trembling lips, his whole body, expressed delight as his masculine and graceful hands described Jason's charms to Robbie, and Petites Cendres, whom no one desired with this kind of passion, listened rapt as though the incarnation of Jason's languid body was offered up to Yinn's lips then and there, just a passerby on the fringes of desire and with the most vulgar of men. Actually I often stroll through this golf course to keep company with Adrien, Daniel told his daughter, just so he's not lonely ever since Suzanne left for Switzerland, so, thought Mai, here he is talking about leaving, visiting, that's what was on his mind as he drove along the foggy road, twisting words to suit himself again, always the same sly tricks that adults use to hedge round the truth, the only trip the ageing writer's wife had taken was one her father couldn't really name, a one-way trip for an assisted suicide, so why not say so Papa, it is what she wanted isn't it, so why not just spit it out she said to him, but all her father did was drive faster and avoid looking at her, boy what a fog he said, and Mai felt darkly that she would never hear Suzanne's voice again, never feel her arms around her, where every earthly traveller she loved went, especially the women: Caroline, Suzanne, her father's frequent companion for breakfast by the sea, little Mai joining them even though she didn't understand a thing they were talking about, now tell me my young friend what you think of this poem said Suzanne, always radiant and beautiful, I don't dare read it to Adrien, I'm afraid as a critic he might diminish it somehow, but with you it's different, actually it's barely anything at all, just a moment of essential solitude, quintessential that's it, just a moment in a woman's life, read it dear friend then forget it right away, they stared at one another for a long time before her teasing laugh sliced through the air, Daniel, not that you aren't someone I take as seriously as my husband the accomplished writer, oh no, still don't you believe, though I'm always afraid his poems turn out a little too four-square, pontificating, I mean he's always right you know, which means, like many women, I'm always in the wrong I suppose, how was it that Mai remembered this perennial expression of Suzanne's courage only now, far too late ever to see her again, could it be because this was exactly what she meant by quintessence, you know Daniel, I've been reading the life story of a young writer who hanged himself at forty-seven, he'd long been a student of philosophy and the medication was no longer helping to relieve his chronic, really chronic distress, and now here you see my own strength, this same body that might fall apart tomorrow, if it were to cause me pain and deep humiliation like that young writer, would I be able to withstand it I wonder, I'm entrusting you with this poem that says as much, you know I've been so spoiled my dear, would I agree to it, perhaps not, and Mai heard these words, treated well by life and love, shouldn't things just be left untouched as they were at their epiphany, now above all say nothing, absolutely nothing to Adrien, this is strictly between you and me, silliness my friend, this young man, as Adrien has written, mastered an infinity of words, but does that matter if their force is diminished, no Mai's father said again, no I don't want our friend Adrien out alone on this golf course, because *she*'s around you know, oh yes here as always, that chauffeur who drives Caroline's black car, oh no if even once Adrien got in it with her — of course Daniel didn't share these thoughts with his daughter — Charly, he mused, with that fake child-like innocence of hers, no Adrien definitely should not be left alone out here, because there she'd be, as glib and seductive as ever, with few words but well chosen ones, saying come on, I'll be your driver, I can see you're not the same since your wife passed away, surely I can be of some help, remember how at dusk like this Caroline couldn't do a thing without me, you remember me don't you, Charly, and from the moment she felt her mature flesh was affected, corruptible, Suzanne's decision was already made, she would write to her daughter and son, remember that drawing on blue letter paper, *Daleth*, it's Hebrew, opening to the light, the blue lotus represents Chinese Buddhism, so she decided her own fate and left you on your own Adrien, and when Daniel and Adrien were out here on the golf course together, Adrien said once isn't there someone driving my car, somebody, a young woman who's waiting for me in my own car, what mirage was Adrien seeing, Charly of course in her chauffeur's uniform coming toward them over that green carpet with hand outstretched to the elderly man, saying come, come, Caroline never had a single complaint, I was always the model employee, I'll just take you home to rest and put a carafe of cool water by your bedside, I'll never leave you, Caroline had no complaints at all, did she, Daniel of course reassured Adrien, saying that was no ghost coming toward them over the sun-brilliant green, really nothing, no one at all he said, though he'd feared it might be true that Charly was nearby and coming closer in the chauffeur uniform she'd been wearing lately for her new employers, Daniel wondered how she'd been able to worm her way into those rich peoples' villas in such a short time, and who exactly were they, rich reclusive ladies no one ever saw in town, no, Mai's dad reiterated, no way our friend Adrien's coming out on this golf course alone now Suzanne's gone, but he couldn't finish his sentence because Mai interrupted him, saying Papa, why don't you just admit she wasn't just taking a trip to Switzerland or anything like that, just say it Papa, she'd written to her daughters on blue lotus paper long ago to say she was weak and faltering and no longer could embrace her life, go on and say it, just say it, Robbie did tell Petites Cendres, I don't know which wig to wear tonight, the blonde or the redhead, Cobra often steals the pink one topped with feathers right out from under me and then tears off down the stairs to be first in the street, and only Yinn gets to wear those boots someone brought him from New York, you know the ones with leather laces that come up around your thighs and high, tapered heels like blades, I don't know how he can walk in those all night without taking a tumble, always his nose in the air somewhere above us, and when he rubs his face against you, you get a brush from those curled eyelashes, then in his raw, guttural voice, he says don't be late Robbie, when I'm in Los Angeles you get to replace me, and not too much playing around with those rubber sex toys, okay Robbie, they're dumping carloads of college kids on us, so use a bit of restraint okay Robbie, yeah he talks to me like that, scolding like, then Yinn works me over with those capable hands of his and those erotic eyes, he adjusts my fake boobs, just air bubbles, that's all they are, I can tell he likes all flesh, and not even women leave him cold, that's why everyone gets that comforting lingering touch, so many lonely lives he seems to think to himself, it's his look, I can't let it go, and whether he's wearing a new dress, say one he designed himself and spent all night making, so it's light and airy with butterfly wings and Japanese motifs that move with his body, his hips, and the skirt is slit up to the thighs on both sides to show off his legs, women's legs, though in a boy's outfit they'd look too thin, still, curved and perfect between the stripes of this winged dress, the legs of a slightly scrawny kid, everything for Yinn being part of the art of illusion, the stuff of dreams, he exults in the knowledge of all this as he walks along the street, outlined and detached with the pale rays of the full moon on his face, deigning to belong to all and sundry without yielding, come on in he says to passersby, the girls are waiting for you, come on in, Robbie, Cobra, we're all here in the cabaret, he despises crowds and the stain on his soul on the verge of blossoming forth, yet here he is, bored and intact, were he that divinely superb woman perched on glass heels, he'd spit on the ground just like when he was small Robbie said, but no he had to stand straight and still, when he went back inside the bar he'd slip in next to Jason for a moment, as though in complete abandonment, he'd hike up the narrow black strip of a slip over his almost hollow stomach, the girls are ready I suppose, he'd ask Jason, this G-string's killing me, Christ will this night never end, why can't we just go and lie down on a beach the two of us, sweetheart, okay if everything's ready, let's start the show, boy what a crowd, what do you think of my dress Jason, I got the idea from my mother's dresses, you ever notice how elegant she always looks, no sulking, she's tough on you but she does love you, it's imprisonment that's all, it's the idea of marriage being a life sentence that bothers her, not you, my father wasn't faithful like you my love, and gently Yinn laid his head on Jason's shoulder, you sang so beautifully tonight my sweet, domestic life with Jason had a calming effect, if he'd just do the dishes Yinn's mother would like him a lot more, but he is a musician and such jobs aren't for him, true though, Yinn's mother would really like her son-in-law to do his share around the house, at least tidy up a bit, it's like living in a submarine and it was true, Robbie agreed, without Yinn's sense of order and cleanliness plus her mother's, this team would have sunk below the waves long ago, and all the girls would have gone down with the ship, the girls and their wigs plumped on the chairs, their pets, Cobra pushing her little dogs in a baby carriage, Yinn's place had a passageway to the cabaret that earned them all a living, well barely, some nights it depended, and Yinn's mother wasn't putting up with any tricks, how on earth are we going to eat she'd ask him, if those students keep sneaking up the emergency stairs in back without paying, son, we have to eat, don't we, all she ever made was oriental food but her kids were always well fed, we never go without she said, yup tonight it'll be the blonde wig Robbie said, there's a frail thirty-year-old little woman I keep my eye on, fragile as a little girl, her and that frizzy little dog she carries, the first time she came here I thought she was eight and we wanted to turn her away, I'm going to sit her on my knee and let her kiss me and play with my hair said Robbie, she often has this giant of a friend with her, the colossus and the tiny kid, I know it takes all kinds to make a world and maybe even understand it too, I mean if life is a horror story I just weave my way through it like a bunch of elves, as though it's all nothing but pleasant and tolerant and peaceful where they are, and it's all just comfy like the blanket that dog's sitting on in the little girl's arms and here I am faced with the innocence of these two guileless creatures, no ostentatiously sexual gesticulation, when it's my turn to dance and sing, it's just me, Robbie, they admire, and Yinn making himself up in the mirror, eyebrows arching and tapering, lashes expanding, I'm a kabuki actor says Yinn, it's the strange visage being drawn little by little in the mirror they admire, no longer concerned themselves about being too huge or too little, no blame for their sizes, tonight or tomorrow you're gonna have to eat says Yinn's mom, and some smart-ass student has already made it across the passageway, so be on your guard, yup the blonde wig is for tonight Robbie says to Petites Cendres, who replies my how virginal you look, no matter how low you've sunk nothing's beaten and bled you like it has me, you keep your fluttering virginity fresh under those back combed curls, you actually are crisp you know Robbie, blessed in that unabashed virginity of yours and still inexperienced in the sadistic ways of humanity, it turns us all off, the disgusting abuse they pour on us, you don't even love yourself Robbie, said Petites Cendres, so tell me where we're going, will you Papa, Mai insisted, all the way to the archipelago he replied, do you want to see Fawn Park and the tiny females we were able to save from the last hurricane, but it's too foggy for that said Mai, we won't be able to see a thing, the mothers and fawns were nearly wiped out said Daniel, whatever damage man starts nature finishes, too much fog on the road Papa, Mai said again and I want to go dancing tonight, my friends are waiting for me, then all of a sudden there they were and her father stopped the car, all of them outside the fence and all over the road, lost fawns staring at them through the curtain of fog which outlined them in snowy white, too visible somehow to be without their mothers she thought, motionless and hypnotized on spindly legs, with cars moving round them yet unafraid, and her father said I promised you a surprise didn't I, there aren't a lot of them in the woods around our place anymore, Mai said they're lost but they're free, but they weren't he pointed out, see they're sheltered, they're too easy to see she answered with spots of light bouncing off their reddish backs like when we're too easy to see, then she fell silent because after all maybe her father was right that there would be a new herd tomorrow, which means that foxes will follow, and he, Daniel, would protect the wildlife, he could assure her of that but her father's faith in the future, she thought, was a bit naïve or else hard-nosed, maybe he was just a gullible intellectual, confirmed ecologist and all that, rocking himself to sleep with theories of this utterly corrupted and exploited earth, this park somehow struggling back to life, we made it ourselves you know, her father went on, look at this, animals running free and drinking from the lagoons, and maybe it was true after all that under his protection it was all beauty and proportion, the reserves, the parks, and he would always have that effect wherever he went, balance and cohesion, whereas in Mai's world all was too much out in the open, vulnerable and unprotected, too easy to spot, right down to the last animal bareness of fawns along a railway track looking for the first shoots of wheat under the frozen puddles of snow-covered fields, nothing there for them but perhaps the candid offering of their bareness to all, ready to be cut down at the instant their hunger left them defenceless, alone or even in a herd it did not matter, go on living or just surrender as Suzanne did, thought Mai, and Petites Cendres saw them once more lined up in the street against the front of the bar whose doors and windows never closed, Yinn, Cobra, Robbie, Santa Fe, all awaiting the last show of the night as if their flowered and feathered selves were for rent for a few hours, decked out for the secret fairy-tale wedding, a melding of sexes and colours, fusing for one memorable moment in the stage glow, soon forgotten like a rented movie, Yinn, Cobra, Robbie, Santa Fe, if these girls lined up in the street were only this one instant of mixed entertainment, thought Petites Cendres, just this and their ephemeral eclectic jumble, so easy to spot with the makeup still fresh under their eyes and so explicitly vulnerable that a contrary old man stumbling in his lofty drunkenness walked across the street toward Robbie saying, huh you're all just treacherous bitches, treacherous, what the hell are you doing there anyway said the old man, always impeccably dressed, you liar Robbie answered him, cynical as ever though still joking thought Petites Cendres, who recognized the man at once, just waiting for my taxi to take me back to the archipelago and my alligators, my dogs, my wife, and my five kids, 'cause underneath those sick padded bras of yours there's nothing but treason, all of you have betrayed me the man said, and as for you Robbie, you want to turn me inside out, but I go to church every Sunday and I'm faithful to my woman, I told you that already, I love her and you ain't gonna change that, so get lost you traitorous bitches, all of you, even Yinn waltzing from the Porte du Baiser to Decadent Fridays, sublime betrayer, yup her too, lucky I only come see you on Sundays, you trash says Robbie, liar with a secret hidden life, your poor wife, I feel sorry for her Robbie said again, you pin those wet eyes of yours on me and just me, don't you, but for her your heart's like ice, oh no the man shot back, I love her as much as anything you've got, that's just the way life is, but when you wear that gypsy scarf round your head and over your forehead I could just nibble you, bitch that you are, the hell with coy prudishness, I choose the betrayer Robbie and his bed of luxury, damn that taxi got away from me, ah life's a string of betrayals, traitors all, that sophisticated drunk can talk all the crap he likes Robbie told Petites Cendres, those are the phantasms he spends his nights with, not with me anyway, at dawn I practically always walk home alone to the house we all share, and the other girls will be hanging out in the kitchen still practically in shock from the night's onstage high, chatting and nibbling cookies, watching Cobra's Yorkies as we laugh at our petals falling out and our faces getting whiter in the dawning day that sends chills right down our spines, I mean how are you supposed to march down the same dark, deathly hallway as Fatalité, we all can't help thinking about her, and I dream that she's still alive, and I think I even know where she is now Robbie says,

I see myself buying her dresses and even houses, and she says to me would you hold on to this white coat for me, I'm just going out for a minute, I'll be right back, so I hold the collar between my fingers and I wait but she never returns, her cigarettes are there in the pocket and she'd never go for long without them I'm thinking, so I wait some more, this is a house with its own inside lake and I figure Fatalité will be back to take a swim with me, the house is sort of on neutral ground, uninhabited and uninhabitable, but here I am waiting on the shore of the lake with her coat on my knees, and I wait so long I wind up smoking all her cigarettes, just a long, blah, desperate day, and I don't know where I am or even where she lives, and when I shake myself out of it, there's Yinn sitting next to me, okay sleep now he says, just sleep, it's all right, you can, and I see the pencilled eyebrows on his bare face staring at me with irritation yet he cares just the same, he's tired, very tired of shows and street parades, tired of the girls, everything, that's what he seems to be saying without actually saying anything at all, I can't do this alone, it's too hard, well get used to it, Fatalité's not coming back he finally does say, you're wearing me out with Fatalité, I don't know where she is any more than you do, just be still now and sleep he says before leaving, I close my eyes as if I'm still holding the coat, a coat for February nights, the last coat Robbie says to Petites Cendres, Fatalité is history now and tonight I'm singing he goes on, a dark, low-cut dress and a cute hat tilted at an angle, that'll be my look, I mean Yinn'll come and fix the folds in it and use one of her jewellery pins for my corsage, the red hibiscus over my left breast, it'll be just great, it'll be our present, yours and mine, the wave will carry us far from the here and now, shores we've shed so many tears on and one of us is never coming back from, Fatalité, the prostitute's girl and a hooker too that Yinn bailed out of prison, got sorted out and transformed into the great Fatalité we all know, no longer a junkie condemned to die with a police record for porn and juvenile prostitution, oh yes Yinn saw that spark in her, a spark of life bursting into the illumination of a princess no one else knew was there, and he dressed her as what she'd become right there in the street and in the cabaret, a sparkling gem too tarnished to notice, and there they were now, all of them, only too visible, a bright, noisy, outrageous splash of them with their men's voices thought Petites Cendres, touching his pimply cheek with his fingertips, the one raked with spots that Yinn would kiss absently, saying my what a day and where are you off to Petites Cendres, why don't you stay and hang out with us tonight, Yinn's penetrating stare crashing into his averted gaze, as Yinn was saying to Fatalité just yesterday, why waste your time with people who don't respect you, you don't really have to live under a cloud do you Petites Cendres, those customers just tear the life out of you more and more every day, though nothing was actually said, Petites Cendres just touched his pimply cheek and Yinn's kiss brushed his cheek, oh this was balm for his night's wandering, a slave to his needs, Petites Cendres figured he had no choice but to follow his customers from one hotel to the next, still secretly hoping that Yinn's kiss would stave off his drop over the edge for just a few hours more, maybe loved, even saved by Yinn's fierce spell just the way Fatalité had been, and as the fog rolled in around them in the remote park, Mai now knew she was under her father's affectionate dominance and he had the hidden intention of reading her secrets, charmer that he was, he made it difficult for her to articulate what was almost an inner quake for her when he harked back to what he shouldn't have, the episode with Manuel and the Mercedes when she was eleven, that whole clandestine world she thought he really wasn't entitled to bring up, and sinking deeper into the morass of words and explanations he suddenly said I really didn't know a thing about your going to the doctor with your mother and grandmother, if your grandmother can know why not me, I mean I am your father aren't I, Mai flashed back to

the fathers riding shotgun on their daughters' virtue at ban-
quets in the abstinence and purity clubs, what a laugh — her
father was acting just like that, reassuring to the point of suffocating her as though he were there in the hall with them,
dancing with their daughters, lulling them into torpor with
their sedative presence and suppressing any and all reaching
out to freedom from this rigid marriage to Daddy, and was it
futureless but for his own egotism, Mai's dad was benign
though, he only wanted to understand her, not counter her,
she thought to herself, her grandmother, Mélanie's mother
were women allies and had perhaps never told Daniel about
her painful visit to the doctor, a day of arbitration and judgement when Mélanie would be consoled to hear her daughter,
herself a child, was not pregnant, what a relief for both of
them that neither would receive a guilty verdict, Grandmother
Esther would no longer be able to walk in a few months and
the trembling in her right hand would spread, sending out
danger signals to her heart, the danger of being consigned to
approaching nothingness, Mère had told Mélanie dear daughter don't let that doctor get you down, he's probably not all
that competent anyway, I feel fine, just great, and anyway
we've all got to live with the thought that anything alive on
this earth is condemned to die, haven't we, Mai nodded her
approval though her grandmother now walked with a cane
as Jean-Mathieu and Caroline had once done, and Mai, often
accompanied by the governess Marie-Sylvie de la Toussaint
who now had less time for her and was gradually being
shunted aside, the Haitian woman didn't really like her anyway, in fact she couldn't stand her compared to Vincent, who
was her favourite, even if he was off studying medicine and
no longer lived at home, Marie-Sylvie could never say his
name without love and deference, Vincent her baby, this Mai
though was no longer any concern of hers, always running
wild and coming home late or not at all, Marie-Sylvie had less
demeaning things to do than watch out for this one, what if

it's true thought Mai, her grandmother in faltering health was still so feisty and brave that Mai could never quite make out what the old lady was really feeling, jollier than she'd been for quite some time, and Mai thought I do love her, she's here by me and she'll stay that way, nothing's changed, and I'm not having a baby as Mama was afraid I would, and now here was her father sitting and waiting for some sort of admission when she didn't want to say a thing, boy this didn't feel right sitting here with him in the car like this or out walking in the foggy park as the reddish-backed fawns retreated to their enclosures, suddenly afraid of the approaching footsteps, Mai and her father were now invaders of the animals' harmonious existence, Mai thinking about the visit to the doctor's with her mother and grandmother and about the moment of judgement so full of imponderables, Mai flashed back to the girls in hand-cuffs with a sort of guardian tugging them toward her till they tripped over one another, Marie-Sylvie was something like that with Mai, and after the medical exam their judgement and trial would come too, bunched up against one another with their long hair tangled together, waiting for the disgrace to end, you may think these are innocent children standing before you the guard seemed to say, but be very careful, for when we caught them they were armed and in possession of drugs too, saying nothing more, Mai in between her mother and grandmother had nothing to say either, irritable and nasty just like Marie-Sylvie thought Mai, and whatever was going to happen to them, the girls in handcuffs and Mai, who was only able to calm down when she felt Mélanie's hand on hers, it's okay honey, everything'll be all right Mélanie had said, really, though it had to be one of the most devastating days of Mélanie's life to learn what was happening to her mother, the one person she loved most in this world thought Mai, still it was nothing, really nothing, and where would the girls in handcuffs spend the night, in what disgusting dining hall would they have breakfast in the morning, always squeezed

in next to their guard, not able to go anywhere, just go, the
summary medical exam would tell all, and they were hemmed
in for good, nowhere to go, nowhere at all to get away from
all this, never, and that was the moment Mai saw the June
bride behind the line of little girls once more, there on the
beach, the tall fiancée with blackened teeth seated at the table
with her men on the wharf, yes Mai remembered full well that
walk along the beach with her dogs when the men laughingly
stroked her, a lingering hand touching her hip, hey sweetheart
where ya going they all yelled amid wild laughter, and the tall
drunk June bride in her white dress and soiled bouquet of
roses did too, saying yes, one day Mai would wind up right
there with them on that same beach, the same docks, just like
her with globs of dirt on her legs, no, no she wouldn't, a child
in her own right just waiting for her father's car, a writer and
speaker, allowing time for her to finish running her dogs
along the beach, so special and so distinguished, ah the old
Mai would be no more, none of those white jeans and tops
washed by a household servant for her to wear at supper with
Grandmother, boy when was he going to honk that horn for
her, Mai saw them, every one of them, seated at the table
under the pine trees pouring wine, filthy every one, dimly
anchored in groups or clans, go tell them all yelled the June
bride, that I'm not marrying the man my parents picked for
me, you go tell them that right now, 'cause you're gonna be
here with no enamel left on your teeth just like me, crazy for
one drug or another and getting raped right here under the
pines day and night, and Mai remembered that when she
drove by these same beaches and docks with her father, the
groupings, families, and clans seemed to have multiplied with
the overflow of those evicted from their homes, now camping
out everywhere, often in cars with their cats and dogs, in tents
by the side of the highway, in public parks, the June bride
had malevolently predicted a succession of these massive
squats while the rare few who were burying them like Mai all

had homes, although there was nothing wrong in being loved by one's father and walking through parks perfumed with pine and acacia, Mai hugged her father in a moment of unexpected gratitude, and though Daniel still frowning looked just as displeased with himself, certainly because he wanted to know all about this visit to the doctor when Mai was accompanied by Mother and Grandmother, sure everything about this child was no longer his child, what had gone on there, dare he even ask, and why this complicit silence from your grandmother Esther, now Mai tell me the truth, but he saw her face as she shut down still more with beads of sweat forming on her brow, better not get home too late with all this fog beginning to show on the road. Come on up to my dressing room said Yinn, the space backstage behind the red curtains, usually closed but now open, Petites Cendres wondered as he followed Robbie how each of them would look, first undressed, then made up with their hair dried and all of them in a small room fixed up backstage, it wasn't just hot and well lit in there, the atmosphere was jumpy too with all those bodies uncomfortably close together and brushing one another, Yinn had already forgotten about Petites Cendres and was thinking about his girls, Cobra, Robbie, Santa Fe, and a few he didn't know emerging from the backstage passageway beneath plumes and pendants, Yinn spoke easily to them and got one of the boys to get some cigarettes from the bar as well as his cocktail, something pink smothered in ice, and in a few steps Robbie had done that by going first down then up the wooden steps again under posters that advertised the show, Cobra said Yinn needs to have the queen knocked out of her, what is it you want now, I thought you said you were quitting he said with mocking laughter, they all loved one another thought Petites Cendres, with a kind of explosive, cacophonous tenderness, often using street-kid words and gestures, and Petites Cendres thought about his customer who turned out to be not only a stranger but brutal too, Yinn's art was to create a love without attachments, that way he seemed to love Robbie, Cobra, and Santa Fe, as well as some new kid making his entrance from stage left, all equally, this is Robert the Martiniquan Cobra said, can he come work here, he was brushing his long black hair down over his shoulders, Yinn said to the newcomer come over here and take off those undershorts so I can see what you're made of, his tone was one of strict competency, not lasciviousness as Petites Cendres thought, and how on earth could he be so thoroughly professional yet indifferent, after all, Robert's athletic beauty was something to contemplate, Yinn's skilled, graceful hands touching the boy's buttocks, yes that's good he said, but for Decadent Fridays you're going to have to get your package out front, so shake it a bit, then I can see how you'll dance naked, yes nice, you're going to make some of them jealous, you can't hide such abundance under some old pair of green shorts just sagging round your thighs like that, you're definitely going to win the Decadent Friday manhood contest starting tonight, no need for false modesty, leave that to the older guys, eh, what do you say Cobra, he's too shy isn't he, no point being timid when you've got that on you, hang around for a while, I'll help you shake off that habit of yours, you're a bit like one of those horses that need stroking, no need to rear up, you'll learn, you're young yet, Petites Cendres watched Yinn and saw his lavish seduction of total strangers like Robert who'd be trained for erotic shows, especially Decadent Fridays where the younger ones discovered the glorious vitality of their organs during the midnight dance, none of that daytime camouflage for them thank you, training Robert's body with his skilled fingers and hands which also knew how to be tender, Yinn had never stopped overflowing with the serene sensuality he'd imbued in Jason, sensuality to appease an indefatigable love, the art of love he felt free to spread over any and all who caught his fancy, a knack for loving that seem inborn in him, perhaps something his mother had noticed when he was still very young, the blossoming and slow voluptuousness of her son's body, a mystery she did not wish to dissipate too soon, the opening of this erotic flower that would grow and fade soon enough, for her existence consisted first and foremost of war against the misery and poverty that threatened her children, why need she dwell too long on the singularity of her son who was also a daughter, yes daughter in every sense, languid at even the most manly of gymnastics in school, and if Yinn was that feminine why then she'd teach him to sew, or perhaps later on get him to join a dance company, after all, they weren't always going to be as poor as all this Yinn often told her, and the thought of Yinn as a child reminded Petites Cendres that he too had once been a street kid, practically a beggar at times, so why was it he had just kept right on free-falling when Yinn had pulled himself up this way he thought, nothing like the meanness of Petites Cendres' life, no, yet he'd so love Yinn's fingers and hands to play over his skin like they did on Robert's hips, though those buns were full and round, way more enticing than his own, which were almost as spotty as his face, those absent yet knowing fingers on his skin, oh what he wouldn't give to be nearer to him, actually belong to him, though he had nothing to offer, not even to the lady in black, Yinn, elbows on the bar and so sought-after evenings and nights, and Petites Cendres marvelled at how she could just suddenly rise and discreetly walk over to the stairs holding her dress and with supreme grace go up each step, even when it was to head for the washroom, the men's or the women's, powder in hand, oh how Petites Cendres would have liked to follow and watch her pose in front of the mirror, laughing, embarrassed, yet still proud of being so indecent, sticking out her tongue at men yet enjoying them, tossing her skirts in the air to reveal the black G-string, teasing, letting them down with a thump or just allowing their unrequited dreams to soar, Petites Cendres marvelled at how she managed to keep them all flocking round her enigmatic purity, he remembered one afternoon with Yinn and friends, chatting at the bar, a white tank top and barefoot in beach sandals hooked by one toe, all of them sitting on their stools with their feet dangling and Yinn, so relaxed now, had just bawled out a young boy at the bar, hey no heroin in this place, yes I know you've started that crap again, stealing meds from your father's psych office, you're welcome back here, but only when you've kicked, so get into rehab first, you ought to be ashamed of the pain you've caused your dad, he hasn't a clue what to do with you, respectable man too, since you were eleven you've been messing up your family with heroin and all, and look at you, wild-eyed and out of control, and it was true too, the boy had no control over his movements, arms and hands all over the place, his sweet curly teen head on Yinn's shoulder, Yinn who in an instant could still lay down the law for the boy, c'mon he said gently, go on home and calm down, but barely was he out the door when two cops grabbed him and flung him against the wall, then with their white gloves they searched him, Yinn appeared in the street with an air of authority and said there's nothing on him, I can assure you, someone should take him home to his parents she said gently, he's vulnerable, the police like everyone else paid attention to Yinn it seemed, deliberately avoiding force as they took him home, siren wailing, we know his father one of them said, and this happens even in the best families, still what desolation it was there in the daylight, Yinn standing straight-backed, his curved forehead showing his concern, Petites Cendres could see his eyes were no longer blue as his lashes made them look at night, it was their length that created the illusion, in this light though they appeared golden brown and his pronounced cheeks were as pale as the rest of his face, more oriental, seeing this kid crippled by heroin he thought of Yinn as he used to be, having seen and tried it all, or so he said, just like the boy he was now trying to shield, and here we go again thought

Petites Cendres, probably a victim of abuse or maybe he'd just done that to his body all by himself from age eleven on, already collapsed and demolished even before reaching his teens, when this brief scene was acted out and the kid was gone, Yinn went back to his friends sitting on their bar stools, once again his happy self, feet dangling gracefully from dropped sandals as he raised a glass with them, Petites Cendres noticed the light scarring on his forehead, shadows barely noticeable, but it was an obsession with Petites Cendres, whose skin in its progressive deterioration seemed mined and pox-ridden, always admiring other people's skin along with the slightest marks or shadows, on Yinn's clear skin they must have been signs of childhood battles, his mother even complained that however delicate he might be, his belligerence brought out an unexpected force, and how different he was now, this dancer's body, gracious and oriental, always armed and ready to fend off blows in its own way, Robert from Martinique had left Yinn's dressing room but not without a complicit wink from him, as Petites Cendres observed, oh how just one such look would have settled Petites Cendres' beating heart and sweetened his loneliness, but this close to showtime Yinn had other things on his mind, and he asked Cobra how his hair looked, then slipped on Cobra's bracelets for him and sipped something pink through a straw, okay girls, let's go we're gonna be late, and he said to Robbie that linoleum floor's all cracked and disgusting, Geisha put your running shoes under the chair will you please, not on my table, you know it's our sweaty feet night after night that have cracked it like that, those high heels put holes in everything, what's that song you sing under your breath Robbie, *I will be your inspiration Daddy, oh Daddy* Robbie answers, *but you have to get the best for me, yes oh Daddy*, do it higher this time ordered Yinn, don't forget it's a woman singing, and a tiara in your hair would be good too he said to Cobra, when oh when am I gonna break you of this queen thing you're carrying

around Cobra replied, I mean this rich black hair isn't enough
for you, you've got to have a tiara too, *Daddy, oh Daddy*
Robbie sang low, okay let's forget the crown just this once
Yinn said, and, sheet music in hand, Robbie paused, wandering back to his dreams from the night before, amid the tor-
rential rain, everything taking place in this weird house, here
I was dancing in front of this crowd of people not knowing
who they were, not knowing how to sing or dance either, I
could think of one thing and only one, I'd forgotten Fatalité's
deerskin coat, I could see it was still on the hanger, the sole
thing in this weird house in the pouring rain, and that meant
Fatalité would be out with no coat on, deerskin and lined with
fine fur, nice and warm, snap out of it said Yinn, enough
about coats Robbie, tonight we've got work on our minds,
death may follow us everywhere like a sister but life goes on
just the same, so just let forgotten coats stay forgotten okay,
anyway Fatalité never wore anything of the kind, lined or not,
never, she loved animals, oh I do like the clink of those bracelets Cobra, boy have you got sex appeal, tonight they'll only
have eyes for you, queen or no queen I'm billing you as the
poster girl for sex appeal, *ladies and gentlemen, here she is
the young, pretty, and slender Cobra, our very own Cobra*,
look really, can't you put those sneakers somewhere else, I'm
trying to get made up here, you've got to admit it's kind of a
sacred ritual when you do your makeup Yinn, said Cobra,
who had no idea what to do with his faded sneakers and wool
socks in such a cramped space, it's my daytime wear, I go for
my run at sun-up and flush all those faces from the night
before out of my system, it stinks of sweat here Yinn, really
it's pathetic you're right about that cracked linoleum, *oh
Daddy* sang Robbie, *I'll do it all for you Daddy oh Daddy*, then
Yinn rocked Petites Cendres and with one swift move took
Robbie's waist, slipped the elastic that smoothed his gut all the
way down to his lower back and said look at the words on
that standout scorpion tattoo — ROBBIE BELONGS TO DADDY — and

I can't get that thing erased said Robbie, I'm telling you Petites Cendres, don't but don't fall in love, Daddy tore me apart, made me his plaything when I moved out on Yinn, Cobra, and the other girls to go live with him, I'm telling you he tore me to shreds body and soul, that's what happened he said, suddenly filled with melancholy, his punk hairdo falling down over his temples, no no, don't do it Petites Cendres, don't fall in love, it's the total depths of horror, any kind of passion just has to be deliberate martyrdom, yeah but that's exactly what you're gonna do all over again said Yinn, I just know it Robbie, that's how you are, impulsive by nature, compulsive too by the way, oh no said Robbie, don't you worry about that, no way I'm getting into it with some man who's gonna own me, make me his plaything, no never he repeated, yeah but I still think you'll do it all over again said Yinn as he applied a black felt-tip to his arched stick-on eyebrows and Robbie hiked up his belt, because you just won't learn Robbie he went on, Petites Cendres could not help thinking that he'd love to have those same words raised across a scorpion tattoo on his own backside, except it would be Yinn and Petites Cendres instead — PETITES CENDRES BELONGS TO YINN — property like Robbie, but his idle daydream evaporated into thin air with a whiff of strong delights, the combined perfume of all these bodies around him, their excited yet gorged senses, like Yinn's or Robbie's some nights, emanations of these healthy bodies, not like his, probably smelling more of something dreary and sad, maybe even sickly, still the passion that had drawn him here to Yinn in this dressing room, this intimate closet the girls shared, this at least was wholesome and satisfying, their wild costumes and frills all so carefully laid out, a backdrop to the tangle of their bodies, all this gave his soul a sense of rebirth, none of headlong Robbie's ragged debris, oh no, Petites Cendres had no time to waste now Yinn was up and covered in queenly diamonds, telling them all it's time people, onstage everyone, and from backstage Petites Cendres could see Robbie, Cobra, Geisha, and all the others join the procession. And Mai told her father it was because he wouldn't let her use the cellphone when they were together, this wasn't going to be more than a few hours out together after all, though of course he hadn't expected the drive along the seashore to be this foggy, cellphones were out, a no-no when Daniel went out with his kids, his rules that's all, he said, as all the red message lights stayed dark pursuant to paternal orders, boy what a tyrant laying waste to all her freedoms thought Mai, cut off from the entire outside world, her world, not her parents' or grandparents', Daniel's pretext was he didn't see her that often, none of them in fact, yet he depended on these gadgets as much as they did, still he didn't want them to get in the way for the few moments of real talk they had together, though maybe he was the only one doing any talking, in any case this despotic device would not always be allowed to come between them like some music box held right up to your ear and that you answered with a narcissistic attitude, yeah it's me, I'm listening, chit-chat with no resonance at all thought Daniel, though he didn't yet know who it was that called her so often, what voices did those waves carry, he just knew that this ball and chain attached to his daughter in her jeans pocket or on her belt knew every secret mystery that he didn't, so sometimes when he was alone with her it had to be silenced to give them some respite from the rapid-fire volley of rings, each one a supreme emergency like some urgent signal whenever she stuck it to her ear, then bowing her head as though to file it away, she briskly strode away from her parents, betraying not a single syllable or sound to them, especially her father the all-divining writer, or so it seemed, it was his job he said to read people's thoughts better than most, alone with her, one true confidant always by her side day and night, stroking her cheek on her pillow with the cats, her one true dominator, not her parent anymore, that's certain, but today, today well Daniel had it silenced and rendered harmless, the tiny, dark thing with its dull screen humbly hanging from the belt on her jeans, but sometimes she just couldn't resist brushing her fingers across it to awaken the languishing sounds, and from the bridge of her very own boat Lou called Rosie, who was standing just feet away while she watched her father polishing the mahogany hull, knowing he'd be totally absorbed in thoughts of the woman he loved, knew it because of that particular smile men get when they feel sure of a conquest, they'd talked several times on the phone already today, nothing, no nothing could keep him from his mistress, even when his daughter was around thought Lou, and that so offended her that she grabbed up her cellphone and called Rosie who was right next to her, as if to defy him by imitation, Hi Rosie she said, you know one of the girls at school lent me her snake and coiled it around my shoulders, it was a long one with cold skin, but Rosie, dumbfounded, replied you're not supposed to have snakes in school, oh well it was right in the bottom of her bag and no one saw it, she takes it everywhere said Lou, you'd never be brave enough to walk around with one around your neck would you, I know you wouldn't she went on, you're afraid of everything and you go to bed at eight o'clock, same time as your little brother, when I go to my mother's place I can go to bed at midnight if I feel like it, what does it feel like asked a terrified Rosie, I mean having a snake wrapped around your neck, I wouldn't like it, I know I wouldn't, it feels like one bite could be the death of you said Lou, so you try not to disturb it, you get some courage that's all, nope I'm not afraid at all, that's for little kids that go to bed at the same time as their little brothers like you Rosie, but a snake is beautiful and very dangerous she continued, I could feel its cold, scaly skin all around my neck, but snakes are not allowed in school Rosie repeated, my mom would really punish me if I had one, that's why I don't, my mom would tell me so, but sharks, you're allowed to go see those, she added, sharks and dolphins when you go to the aquarium on Sundays, only you can't swim with them because they're behind some glass, well, Lou cut in, in our class, the gifted class, we can do whatever we feel like, when we go diving, if the water's calm we can see the sharks come in close to shore, Lou went on as she continued watching her father out of the corner of her eye, his art had caused him to be absent and cruel, his success with that retrospective in New York, of those spirals *Corridor 1* and *Corridor 2* spreading their metallic wings against the green background, giant sculptures dipping and weaving in the wind night and day, weightless and bodiless he proclaimed, that's what drew them all to him, all these women, female artists and critics, all partners in his adventure he announced, so exasperating and pretentious, totally incapable of living without a woman won over by the force of his ideas Lou thought, and sure enough here she was, a young sculptor and critic for an art review, Noémie, that was her name, Noémie, a charming young woman, her forehead beaming with willpower, that's how he put it, and here she was at the feet of his aggressive, phallic *Hanging Mural*, a heavy, overbearing shape Lou disliked so much, no matter if her father kidded himself with all sorts of Buddhist thoughts on the subject, to hear him tell it the encounter with Noémie was mystical, and though she was every bit as athletic as Lou herself — big for her age and looking ever more like her mother and hardly any taller — she was also meditative, which is what brought her to the foot of Ari's suspended wall, barefoot in the grassy park she was actually meditating, her perfect proportions contrasting with Lou's overgrown youth, and they were bound to get on just fine together Ari said to assuage his daughter's anguish at not being Daddy's Only Girl, you'll get on like a house on fire, and if you study hard you can come visit us at Noémie's apartment in New York, we'll take you to museums, oh he had his conditions all right, bargaining with Lou, dropping her off at her mother's or at Rosie's whenever he had to go off to

Noémie's, the basest fleshly pleasure it was, and her father was only a mystic as far as common ordinary love would take him, a slave to instinct, basic primal needs, no longer the farsighted, attentive man that Lou had once loved, he'd betrayed her and he'd do it again, the same as her mother Ingrid, and she began to doubt he meant it when he said they'd sail to Panama together with her sitting on his lap as she learned to sail, such a long way to go, it had to be just one of those comforting lies he told, just one of those useless promises she thought, because from here on, from here on his real companion was going to be Noémie, yes *her*, she weighed all the pain in that one word, wasn't she. And this fog kept on burying the hood of the car in its black smoke thought Daniel, not a heat fog or a sea fog, maybe it was some toxic stuff he couldn't protect his daughter from, but Mai didn't seem to need him now, locked in her rebellious silence, yes if this carbon cloud kept enveloping them in its bitter shadow, from Los Angeles all the way to the slums of Mumbai, melting glaciers in the Himalayas, industrial smoke had started to cover the oceans from the Arctic downward, and even the paradise Mai and her friends inhabited was being draped in a funeral pall that caused millions of premature deaths every year on and off the island from sheer suffocation, and what to tell Mai, that it was too late, that this carbon cloud might be coming for her tomorrow just as it might for the polar bears or fish, the melt and burn no measurement could comprehend, an unredeemable tragedy his daughter was too young to imagine Daniel thought, no more than the deer herds or the foxes that he and his ecologist friends had saved from entrapment and certain death, the carbon veil drawn over all of them alike, its invisible pellets blackening all before them, pond water, rivers, the leaves of fruit-bearing trees, but he steered clear of these troubling matters with his daughter, frustrated that his efforts were so often in vain, and simply said I don't know when this sea fog's going to lift, but don't you worry, we'll soon be home, his way of telling Mai she wouldn't be late for her evening out and that now she could even use her cellphone, he could see her hand getting fidgety, though he hadn't yet touched on the real reason for their little outing together, which was to tell her they'd decided to take her out of the public school where she'd been subject to such bad influences and would soon be sending her to a private institution, no, not just yet though, being highly intuitive like him she had an inkling something serious had been determined without her knowledge, being as hard to manage as she was she wondered what words he would choose to back them up, that the school was close to home, no, then she'd say the distance didn't matter, she was soon going to learn to drive, they were wrong to see her as the same turbulent child she'd once been, still who knows where she'd be tonight or tomorrow, camping on the beach like the tall June bride maybe, hanging out with the filthy men under the pines, feet shredded by glass shards, no roof over her head like thousands of other so-called *new homeless*, women and men out of work and living in the crop of tent cities that was springing up along railroad tracks and under bridges, feeling the cold through their nylon tents as far as Fresno, California, and she'd soon be looking as haggard as the June bride, staring fixedly at the great white clouds, still better a nylon shelter on the beach than nothing, that's what the tall girl or one of her friends said, garbage is better than nothing at all, each one after his own shelter, the Pacific coast railroads or bridges, entire families in fact, an exodus of the rich turned poor in a single day or simply overnight, just like that, leaving behind their beautiful houses with swings on the lawn and two or three pups at the window barking with no one to feed them tonight or tomorrow, then to the pound where they'd be put down, leaving behind their crimes, their rejections, their surrenders, harassed and in flight like criminals, that too in a single night, charged with the crime of abandonment, pursued and guilty, lying down for a few hours in her tiny cottage on the lawn, Mère rested her cane on a chair by the bed and contemplated the reproduction of the Albrecht Dürer engraving she had long kept over her bedside table, how long would she hold out as its untiring devotee, struggling for life while others looked on, expecting her to wane or fall from the saddle, she'd noticed these annoying attentions of theirs, the Sonata for Cello and Piano, Opus 40 by Shostakovitch put her in mind of Augustino's turbulent existence, in a still legible hand she had noted the music she listened to this day as she did every day in the isolation of her little room out on the lawn, and the attentions of her daughter Mélanie and of Mai's governess Marie-Sylvie de la Toussaint irritating her now she and she alone in this house received all the attention, though she could stand and walk perfectly well on her own, admittedly she did tire quickly and she'd asked Mélanie to leave the blinds half-open so the brilliant midday sun could reach her, then later in the afternoon before her nap she remembered listening to Schubert's sonatas for piano and violin, yes she'd been taking these afternoon naps for quite a while now, and in the garden the sometimes strident music of the birds accompanied her writing, setting it all down, sometimes using her left hand so as not to overtire her right, at night you can hear the toad-song, she thought to herself, thus closing her eyes she thought of Caroline in her summer robe who once appeared to her coming for a visit in the garden cottage, so happy and quiet, she bumped into the tall wardrobe when Mère said wait, I know what you're looking for, I'll help, no don't get up Caroline said, there's no point since I can't see, I'll never find what I'm looking for, I knock into furniture and all sorts of things, I can't see anymore, sleep Esther my dear, I'll wait till my sight returns and I can see you, perhaps tomorrow, then Caroline wandered around the room complaining that the wardrobe was so high she couldn't reach a thing but, she explained to Mère, her sight was gone and she couldn't see a thing anyway and if Mère touched her, brushed her arm or her hand, she didn't feel a thing, such a pity it is she said to Mère, this void of contact, Mère could no longer stand seeing the shadow of blind Caroline continually bumping into all sorts of things in the room, her fleshless arms no longer able to embrace the one she so longed to confide in, oh the end of all physical touch is the worst privation of all, isn't it, Caroline said tonelessly, so Mère thought I'll get up, and when she feels the weight of my hand on her shoulder, the movement from somewhere else will brush her summer nightdress and awaken her, but Mère noticed she was still in her bed, that feet and legs were heavy as stones, preventing her from greeting Caroline, a sound ran through her mind, a piece from Schubert's sonatas, what would become of her if ever she could no longer hear this music that was her lifeline, I shall come back later Caroline said from her vaporous nightdress, and already she was on her way soundlessly, not even a footstep, oh how Mère wished Marie-Sylvie were here to pour a glass of ice water from the jug, but she'd asked to be alone, imperiously in fact, not politely, poor servants, always putting up with the bad temper of their masters and mistresses, Marie-Sylvie de la Toussaint, though, was neither poor nor really at Mère's service, she was just a fixture in the house now, like Julio or any of the other refugees they'd always sheltered here in this kingdom where Mère was crumbling a little at a time, this kingdom of the heart not long for this world she thought, not tonight though, oh no, and not tomorrow either, Mère was that indefatigable, the stalwart knight in the Dürer engraving, through all of this Franz was away rehearsing, forever leading his orchestra, and wasn't this about the time when Samuel always used to jump from the high veranda straight into the pool, Mère replayed in her head the Schubert sonatas she'd listened to and duly noted since morning, also the memory of Samuel and his swim, of Franz and his orchestra, in decline perhaps but still a solid man, Mère wanted never to let one of these scenes escape from her yet her mind seemed to be giving way, more and more, to indolence, and so it was with the symphony Franz had written in his younger days when he was inspired by the Psalms, how was a man so carnal and celebratory of life inspired by religion, still that was Franz through and through, revelling in all his contradictions, it was precisely his celebration of life that kept him on earth for so long Mère reflected, wondering would the old miscreant be coming to see her today, always in a rush, bustling up to the door with his scores under his arm, would he be shaking his wayward hair among the African lilies that formed a bower overhead and drooped their heavy corollas over the garden path, and shouting it's me, Franz, I can only stop for a minute my dear Esther, just long enough to embrace you, would he now talk about his women, so many of them, and his copious offspring or perhaps his latest opera, still not finished what with all the biographies coming out recently on him and his work as a conductor, one of them illustrating his career with photos of a time gone by, such as Franz stretched out on the deck of a transatlantic liner next to one of his first wives only to be divorced a few months later, the sun-framed picture was part of his European tour not long before he met Renata at a university in Chicago, Mère thought with the brilliance of his success and sporadic moments of wealth he seemed happy, darkly beautiful, and attractive, though it was a mirage, the woman beside him shared that comforting radiance and they did seem so very much a couple bonded in this Mediterranean landscape, their tanned and barely clothed bodies, even a black-and-white photo made evident the pleasure that welded their two bodies wildly together, Franz would have torn that one up, saying what was past was past, that's what they always do, try and make us things of the past, but I, Esther dear, live only in the present, and I can't look at that picture without suffering for the hurt I caused that woman, yet still you can see how much happiness melted us into one another with a perfection that could only be of the present, before instinct led me to destroy everything, but that's the way we're made, always we must have more, more, more, taking more than life could offer freely, you are a woman of duty Esther, who can't comprehend this headlong destructive impulse that drives us, but then perhaps he would simply look at the picture with inexpressible, silent nostalgia at the sight of these bodies in their transatlantic abandon and surrounded by an azure sea, oh adieu, adieu youth, he'd surely remember the colour of the water that day, the smells of that day, the happy exhaustion of the senses by this woman's side, then a long shudder right down his body at the memory of it, would Franz be coming for a visit today Mère wondered, elbows on the bar at the cabaret in the soft lighting on stage where it was Robbie's turn to sing, emerging like a sprite from behind the purple curtains as Yinn introduced him: *our splendid fairy thug, our adorable Robbie, be generous as she strolls among you with her tip bucket,* Robbie, don't forget the bucket Yinn murmured in his ear before his entrance, dragging him by the sleeve because he was so eager to sing that he'd forgotten it again, we can't live on air you know, Petites Cendres thought he was hearing the voice of Reverend Ézéchielle through the thunderclaps outside, asking him what have you done with your friend Timo, my son, why on earth was the Reverend hassling him about Timo, couldn't he even have bit of fun, Timo, I don't have a clue thought Petites Cendres, honest, Reverend, I really don't, to each his own in this world of men, there's nothing I can do about it, what have you done with your friend Timo, replied the Reverend once more in the thunder over the cabaret roof, and it was seriously getting in the way of Robbie's sentimental melody, ah geez all this thunder has to happen just when I'm singing, sure we're all used to it, but with all this going on his voice just might waver, I don't know anything about this Timo, besides, ratting out is the ugliest sin of all Reverend, I'd never turn him in Reverend

Ézéchielle, no never, but the sight of Timo maybe killed by the police would not go away, first they lay you flat on the ground, three of them most times, often shoving your head into the sand, or the mud if it was a swamp, if not, into the asphalt or cement that burns your face, or the steel door of a car, like the stolen Sonata maybe, they give your back a total pistol-whipping before they slap on the handcuffs, I haven't done anything, and Petites Cendres just kept repeating why would I turn in my brother, they grabbed that splendid hair of his and in his fall Timo had struck his head against the steel door like a whiplash, then the hair, once so clean, was drenched in blood, Timo my friend, Petites Cendres thought, but none of this is true, Timo's still driving that Sonata, he'd get away again through the swampy brush trails or scrambling on foot where alligators crouch with pale green eyes, nobody would be able to get around Timo, and for a few grams of cocaine he'd always win, and Robbie's melodious voice rang across the stage, complete in black velvet décolleté, long white gloves all the way to the shoulder, and scuffed and worn leopard-skin boots, of course everything Petites Cendres saw was a staged illusion, interchangeable on Robbie's enticing body, only to become someone else again in a few hours, singing differently, dancing differently, as though he'd switched bodies as well as costumes, and winding almost serpent-like with such supreme ease that no one would ever suspect, and that voice with its *I am your dream* which beckoned to Petites Cendres, luring him far from whatever torment Timo was in, dead or alive, why did he insist on persecuting Petites Cendres with his unending drama, why, well because *I'm your dream*, that's why, Robbie sang but then remembered he had to pass the bucket through the audience, oh how reality stood out in such painful contrast against his enticing words, for each and every one of you, ladies and gentlemen, I am the dream, your very own dream, yes, *I am your dream*, and the money flowed into the bucket when Robbie and the red hibiscus Yinn had strategically pinned on him bent low and suggestively toward the unknown choir that had come to see him dance and sing, men, women, all reaching out to touch him, licking him with their eyes all of a sudden, *a sinner or a saint I am your dream*, as that suave voice sang, enchantress, but now a very masculine hand grabbed the money bucket as he walked up to the customers at the bar, begging and bold, you liked the show did you, for adults only you know, thank you ladies and gentlemen, would you like to see what I have on underneath, want me to lift my dress just like Yinn, later Robbie would confide to Petites Cendres that the whole time he danced and sang that night he couldn't think of anything but Fatalité, slowly fading away all by herself in her room, a tiny candle in a stiff northerly wind, barely glimmering, not a breath in the emaciated body stretched out in the dress she wore for late-night shows, as though left lying regally in state on a shore, oh Fatalité he thought, Fatalité, and recalled the moment in Yinn's dressing room when Robert from Martinique came in and he felt dark jealousy eating away at him, Robbie didn't like seeing Yinn get so familiar with the new boy like that, sure, he'd soon be dancing nude on Decadent Friday, maybe around midnight in the display window, that's what he told Petites Cendres, so that passersby could see him from the street as he danced away on one of the tables slipping his underwear down over his buttocks, making the voyeurs drool before revealing the ripening fruit, sure this was how he said it and sure this kind of jealousy was mean-spirited, but what can you do if Robbie felt it too, though he had noticed Yinn's approach to the boy hadn't been lascivious, barely even tender at the sight of his round buns, touching without seeing, detached in that terrible way Yinn had, and thinking Fatalité was no longer with them, this family of girls, he wept backstage, forgetting the tip bucket and the evening routine, because routine is all it was he said to Petites Cendres, and of course Yinn had to remind him, the tip bucket Robbie, the bucket, we don't live on air now do we Robbie, it's for Fatalité you know, the funeral costs, of course Yinn had paid for all of it without a moment's hesitation, if we all lived and died depending on God's fatherly mercy, and we all know what a crushing weight that is if he even exists Robbie said, it's always a good idea to have a mother like Yinn's to make up for it, anyway Reverend Stone says he does and he's a father to Fatalité, and Fatalité was needed in the House of the Father as much as down here with the rest of us, so that's why he's gone, what a pile of crap said Robbie, a real father doesn't kill his own kids one after another, but then of course Reverend Stone and his prayers needed to be there explaining the unexplainable, so he had no choice except to say there was a place for Fatalité in the house of her almighty father, so you see friends, that's why she was snatched from us, taken hostage, 'cause it's just too miserable down here with the rest of us, a princess, isn't that what Reverend Stone said, no wait, he said your friend, honoured and worthy but so afflicted, for now the candle's snuffed out, though we do keep a light burning in her apartment of course Robbie said, yes, that night Fatalité was all he could think about, this could have been avoided said Dr. Dieudonné, declaring him dead, it didn't need to happen, Fatalité's sacrifice, with prevention and medication, still what's the point now, utterly useless, once it was tuberculosis that tore through the population like this and it too was preventable, all those shawl-covered infectious faces in India, China, or Russia, but no, we didn't want to hear about it, neither did Fatalité, him and so many others, wave upon wave of them, remember those photos by James Nachtwey declaring it a crisis, the crisis of forgetting epidemics that are still with us, buried and forgotten but more and more destructive, poor peasants in places like Cambodia or India — Chennai for instance — twisted in suffering, thought of only by international health organizations, men, women, and children often in their last agony and battling meningitis, just another one we don't know about, an emaciated child in its mother's arms, Asian Madonna and Child on a small metal bed frame, was anyone talking about their crucifixion there on that bed frame, sure it was preventable Dieudonné said, yes it could be stopped, of course why not, but who was interested, throwaway people that's all they were, them and their infected mouths, their shawls, their wide dark eyes and the fever being fed, sure said Dieudonné it could have been stopped or avoided, Fatalité too certainly, I mean we aren't in Cambodia or China are we, and yet look at what happens every single day, what the hell thought Petites Cendres as he listened to the doctor, angry and shaken, why bother going through all that today, nothing was done, the medication wasn't there for Fatalité either, might as well be Cambodia or India, no way to pay thought Petites Cendres, he'd never had any money either, and if he left just as he'd come he should at least have been told, but here we are too late for that, so why bother, why, that candle had flickered out in a well-lit apartment, too late to prevent, too late for meds, same as for that other human wreckage in India and China, too late he thought, too late for all of them, so why bother repeating it over and over, why does the doctor have to talk this way like some prophet of doom saying again and again what everyone knows already, forgetfulness covers everything over, burying the atrophied conscience of the world, this, this is what Dr. Dieudonné was saying to Petites Cendres, who somehow hoped his body was invincible, well he very nearly was he thought, nothing could touch him when he was near Yinn and Robbie and those luminous, bubbling nights, oh for God's sake shut up Dieudonné and let Petites Cendres finally experience the joy of life, dazzled, stunned, and bouncing back unharmed from all his trials, a drunken string of days and nights, feverish hours and moments alive, yes this life, this short life which was all he had. Petites Cendres recalled one of Yinn's shows, something that shook him, a performance of such excess he did not fully grasp it, whether overdone in freedom or in provocation he did not know, but surely it was because he himself could never be that free or provocative, only Yinn could get away with that, besides Petites Cendres' day-to-day life was one constant state of infraction in one way or another, but Yinn broke all the taboos and rules, even the ones that might have flattered his beauty, not that he really needed to, so it came about that Petites Cendres saw him jump with legs intertwined into an onstage transfiguration that lasted only seconds, from the loveliness he was to a thing of such insane, hysterical, and wild ugliness, with monstrous teeth and rolled-back eyes, abusive and wholly unappetizing poses, he had to wonder if the magic link between spectator and performer had been broken, there had been murmurings that crazed moves like this had taken Yinn and his bodily narrative too far off course and left the diva stranded in a whirlwind delirium like Nijinsky's, who, more than jumping, seemed to levitate heavenward amid thunderstruck peals of laughter, unabashed sylph that he was on the stage, and instantly shameless as if by design, Yinn overturned any notion one might have of him, somehow reduced by some disagreeable pleasantry, this outlandish yet impenetrable disguise so blended with other images that per- haps it wasn't one after all, and yet none of this was true thought Petites Cendres, in those few seconds Yinn insinuated his own laughter into that of the audience, natural now, not exaggerated, cooing deeply, then a rapid about-face from ugliness back into beauty with a single wave of his fan and all was as before, disorder and madness, tigress teeth unclenched into an affable smile, bravos cascading around her, ah yes, Yinn was back, the plunge into nightmare mad- ness and disconcerting ugliness over, as though having used the masks of beauty and ugliness to express his disgust at opprobrium and oppression, inviting the most radical of revolt against the hidden face of intolerance, calling on the

imagination to outstrip every last limit and dive straight into
everyone's conscience by any means, whether in excess or in
moderation, but always to outrage and shock, this was his
aim, to oxygenate every remaining bit of fetid life with the
breath of creative revolt, leaving no part of consciousness
unawakened as if the divine word had come down to the
modest cabaret stage to change all that surrounded it, then as
the applause faded, Yinn stepped elegantly from the stage,
money bucket in hand, asking for nothing, approached Petites
Cendres as though not seeing him at all, shone his red-lipped
smile on them and gave the indifferent kiss on the cheek that
Petites Cendres had longed for all day; Mère was amazed to
see all the shutters and blinds on the street closed, not a ray
of that brilliant sunlit day allowed in, some street procession
had caught her attention, a black band marching to the
Cemetery of Roses, so maybe this curtaining off along the
street was a sign of mourning she thought, her heart beating
to fill the silence, then the band struck up its slow, deathly
slow beat, the timbre of their brass instruments, the plaintive
trombone and sax, and Mère shuddered at the thought of such
slow music in the silent afternoon, or had she overslept her
siesta straight into the evening, Justin must have played in one
of those processions wearing his white suit and canvas hat,
all their faces were hidden beneath them so that even with
the blinds raised you still couldn't make out any features, yes,
Justin dressed in white must have been part of those funeral
processions they write about in books, right up to the day
they played and sang for him too, the terrible slowness of the
music, the same plaintive trombone and sax, too bad the
writer-philosopher in him attracted so little attention compared to this, so few accolades for his denunciations of
Hiroshima and Nagasaki by this vicar's son from China, so
scrupulous, so delicate, prey to the indifference of his peers
thought Mère, when he wrote that burnt flesh is my flesh and
your flesh, burned on the metal of armaments, and while

Charles and Frédéric understood with the same compassion, Caroline had clashed with him in patriotic phrases so arrogant they were injurious thought Mère, wanting to side with her friend, she had shared and defended them, now Justin was no more and Mère was too late to apologize for an insolence that suddenly seemed cruel and perhaps irresponsible, and the plaintive trombone and sax in the silence of this afternoon, actually what time was it anyway, recalling this wrong called up other lapses of hers, how often, she wondered, was she right about Mai for instance, had her instincts played her false when she caught Mai in the Mercedes with that fellow and the smell of smoke in the air, did she do the right thing in speaking to Mélanie about it later or had she betrayed the loving trust of a young child, the ugliest sin of all, especially with someone so young, imperfect and scarcely mobile as she was, needing a cane even to get out of bed, Mère hoped Justin would pardon her for the things she said or didn't say, she'd bolstered his confidence about his books before he so delicately slipped out of this life in a bare few months, taken by a raging cancer, oh the brass sounds were a painful reminder of him who she missed and whose soul had surely returned to his childhood rivers and mountains of northern China, all of them, she missed them all, Charles, Frédéric, Jean-Mathieu, and still more Suzanne, though Mère did not yet know for certain if she was already gone, she could almost hear the laughter still, and how many times Mère had run up against Mai, her face, her inquiring eyes asking everyone where is Suzanne, Papa, Mama, Grandmother, where is she, why aren't you telling me the truth, I'll never see her again will I, her trip to Switzerland with Adrien, she won't be coming home with him will she, assisted suicide, that's what it is, isn't it, Suzanne, where's Suzanne, you're all lying, why, at other times Mai simply said nothing, asked no questions, the severity of her gaze cast its own judgement, and the worst thing of all thought Mère, but Mélanie would reply, oh there's no point in troubling

the poor girl any further, she knows everything anyway, all
our weaknesses, our lack of courage to talk truthfully about
life and death, something none of us is capable of, yet here
was Suzanne's laughter ringing in Mère's ear, an invitation to
pure joy, she might as well be right there in the room, getting
ready to go out to a party with Adrien, teasing him because
he didn't like that sort of thing, nights of silliness, and now
blended with her laughter was Franz's voice as he came into
the shelter, shouting dear friend, do please forget about that
cane and come on out into the garden on my arm will you,
I'm afraid I might be a bit wobbly Mère said, do be careful
and don't jostle me, but Franz laughed and said oh but I will,
that's exactly why I came here, to jostle you, and he offered
his arm, Esther dear you're looking wonderful, maybe a little
pale, but you need to get out more, you spend too much time
here listening to music all day long, even the sweetest music
leads one to melancholy, come along, come along, and in
Daniel and Mélanie's garden they encountered the gentle
warmth of the air, the perfumes of orange and lemon trees,
Mère showing him the fruit tree she had planted a long time
ago, it came from faraway islands she said, Lady of the Night
it's called, its blooms open only at nighttime, I planted it for
Samuel she said, clinging to Franz's arm but feeling less frail,
then suddenly she stared at her exuberant friend, grateful yet
intimidated in his presence, feeling it awful that her gait was
so unsure and the trembling in her right hand more pronounced and bothersome than ever, this morning I listened
to Schubert's sonatas for piano and violin, such grace, such
beauty, she told her old musician friend, but tell me what
you're working on, do please, her words seem clumsy too, as
though spending so much time bedridden she had lost the
ability simply to converse with her family and friends, whereas
Franz was so voluble, perhaps he even sensed she was having
trouble expressing herself comfortably, and the treacherous
malady had deprived her of the ability she could not

somehow define, everything was so different lately or perhaps it was just the tiredness after all, she worried so about them all: Mai, Mélanie, the activist daughter who gave her so much pride, visiting women in prison, still, what actually became of them, they also defended women's rights in Russian prisons, or women kidnapped from their homes and killed, destined for barbarous repression as in so many other countries, executions of young rebels reported by these same women in their writing, and these would be their own death warrants, killers already at their doors when they thought they were safe with their kids in Grozny, then suddenly down come the walls, for they were highly organized and trained, these men, for just this form of assassination and these targets, and all of them disappeared without exception, Mère's attention snapped back to the enthusiastic Franz next to her, his conductor's hand waving in the air, oh my dear Esther, plans and more plans he was saying, one must always spill over you see, now let me give you a sneak peek at my next season, to begin with there's Mozart's K. 595 with my sister soloing on piano, I won't be conducting though, that will be someone else, oh I've been dreaming of this moment for so long, and I also want to revisit Shostakovitch's Fifteenth Symphony, and so Mère listened to him thinking oh how his energy depresses me as I feel myself growing increasingly numb, is it really fair for things to be so different for each of us, or is it precisely this artistic fervour that allows him to be reborn, to live and be reborn yet again, such youthfulness, oh and what vigour he displays, she actually felt ashamed of a recurring dream that now haunted her every night, where have we been shunted to, what a world of debasement in these defiling dreams, barely wearing a nightdress, she was being carried on a stretcher in plain sight of all her children and grandchildren, and in it her caregiver Marie-Sylvie de la Toussaint appeared as a forbidding nurse dressed in an intimidating uniform, this sister to He-Who-Never-Sleeps declared now it is my turn to give orders, her sarcastic laughter beginning to resemble that of her unhinged brother, yes my time has come round, and Mère knew that in this woman's power every last shred of her dignity was now gone, dignity trodden underfoot, her powerless body exposed for all to flagellate yet again, then suddenly it was Mai who came toward her with her arms full of flowers, dispelling the shadowy presence of Marie-Sylvie de la Toussaint and saying here, Grandmother, are the flowers that opened during the night, flowers from the Lady of the Night you planted for Samuel, your tree, the one you planted long ago, I told you how nasty Marie-Sylvie was didn't I, but you didn't believe me, Mère wasn't at all sure if Mai was on her side in this dream or not, being as pouty as she was in real life, I warned you to beware of her didn't I Grandmother, but you wouldn't listen, and Mère told Franz there's this dream that keeps coming back every night, but that was all she said, thinking however threatening our dreams they're nothing really are they, we're the ones who worry so much about our children when our health runs down like this she told him, but here you are walking and taking my arm, now what could possibly trouble you my dear Esther said Franz, you who've given so much, what can you possibly have to blame yourself for, remember that Mass I once composed for Christmas night in some small church in Finisterre, a child soprano singing I am your guide and your shepherd, it's as though I'm hearing it again here in the fog of this winter night, it was so cold in that church, I've never been one for piety as you well know, now Esther how would it be if I were your guide and your shepherd, how would that be, suddenly after so long, these words have an effect on me, you see we're always somebody's shepherd whether we like it or not, what do you say to that, kind of funny isn't it, that I who am always the first to stray from the straight and narrow, never persisting in a single unalterable direction, that I, in these times we're living in, you and me dear Esther, that I am now your carefree shepherd, Mère still wondered if it was day or evening, for the sunlight on the flowering trees seemed spare and diminished though their perfumes were still every bit as vivifying, and she went on thinking of Mélanie, Mère recalled her depression after Vincent was born, postpartum depression they called it, the healthiest of mothers sometimes died from it, one of the saddest subjects Mélanie spoke publicly on, studies of guilt in mothers who stopped eating altogether, who no longer slept after the birth of their children, now why was it Mère hadn't been more help to her daughter in those moments of psychotic pain when she described all the symptoms and her anxiety at failing as a mother, when he's asleep beside me in the large bed Mélanie said, I'm afraid to look at his face when he wakes up too hot under those long lashes, as though we were still a part of one another in the flesh, will he have something to hold against me when he's three or six months old, will I be able to bear it, who's there to help the mothers of newborns, why is it such a natural act, as they're fond of saying, is it because no one wants to know about what happens after the birth, the drugs that helped Mélanie through it all, and what if she hadn't been able to help Vincent get through it when his breathing was so irregular, what if she'd been responsible for that anomaly even before he was born, where were our husbands, the men, where were they all in those insane suicidal postpartum days when newborns suffocated on their own vomit, it was a mother's original sin from their birth Mélanie said, a depressed young mother's regret much debated, how does one alleviate it, Vincent's overheated face weighing on her, forcing its way back into her guilty flesh, for guilty she would always be, the life and survival of Vincent, the most appealing of her children and so very much loved later in life, her joy and contentment after saying no to him at birth, no, go away, I don't love you, that moist look of his, the riveting stare from beneath those lashes never to let you rest, no sleep, no appetite, Mélanie well understood the distress that claimed the lives of young mothers after two months, and it was then she asked her own mother why did you bear me, because I wanted you, longed for you, so wanted to know you came the answer, and wasn't it she wondered — weighing on Franz's arm when he walked too fast for her instead of letting her take a break and sit on a garden bench and listen to the birdsong — wasn't it something of a fraud, a half-truth, for she'd hesitated a long time before having children, filled with doubt, even fear, fuelled by her husband's infidelities which left her indecisive, and she knew a mother consumed by the burning desire to have children could somehow be swallowed up by it, it was then she felt herself backing away from it, though she would never tell Mélanie this, and she said nothing of this refusal by a woman trained to motherhood by men of all civilizations and societies, no never said anything about it to Mélanie, yet suddenly realizing she had lied to her daughter when she recalled the dream in which an earlier, lighter, slimmer version of herself allowed her daughter to lead her by the hand as though flying away together toward a very simple old and austere Victorian house up on a hill, and looking through the windows one could see nothing had been moved, and as she guided Mère toward it Mélanie said Mama, do you remember that French governess you liked so much, well she never left, she's still here waiting for you, just open the door and you'll be home, your exercise books are all there ready for you to study, your childhood chair is waiting for you too, nothing ever changes here, all you have to do is open the door Mama, oh how it bespoke the closeness of death, and Mère trembled despite the very real joy of meeting her governess again, in dreams of course, now speaking out loud to Franz she said oh my friend, were it not better to forget those dreams, those traitorous dreams that serve only to hide what we don't want to know, what lies ahead of us, eternity she said very softly, dreams that take us so far, so very far and force us to visit a

world which is not ours, she sensed Franz stiffening at the
sound of that word *eternity,* my dear friend the old fellow
said, still skeptical and in possession of his youthful gifts, this
eternity of yours doesn't exist, what on earth are you talking
about Esther, that's just something the priests made up and
you know how I dislike them, I never complain about dreams
that have a whiff of pleasure about them, maybe even lasciviousness, so much the better he said, holding her arm which
seemed to be detaching itself from his, you really must relax
my dear, and Franz hummed a piece from one of his sympho-
nies, which he would soon conduct, but Mère, listening tiredly
beside him, wondered what she was doing here in Daniel and
Mélanie's garden on this man's arm, come now Franz was
saying, here they come, it must be time for a drink by the
pool, happy hour, but it seemed to Mère the light was fading
too fast, no longer knowing if it was still day or early night,
and once again the smell of acacia and mimosa did her so
much good. When Yinn stepped down off the stage, bucket
in hand but asking for nothing and surrounded by a crowd of
spectators, she appeared not to notice, her faraway gaze
meeting Petites Cendres' then escaping elsewhere, cut off
from it all, Petites Cendres remarked that Yinn had so many
different faces while staying true to every aspect of himself,
like Petites Cendres he could navigate a clandestine other-
world no one knew anything about, not even Jason, and in
this way they were closer, Petites Cendres and Yinn, hiding in
the toilet the way Petites Cendres did to sniff his forbidden
powder, their nostrils flared in the same delight that would
jump-start their nerves into the apotheosis of risk and fear, but
although Petites Cendres let himself be taken into bar toilets
all over town, Yinn never did, no you'd more likely see him
there making himself pretty, alone and getting ready for the
nighttime, seeming to think and meditate as if in a temple, his
face illuminated little by little in all its features for the stoic
celebrations, and if he went with anyone it would be Robbie,

perhaps to demonstrate some part of the act or a dance step, a better, more seductive move, a tone of voice when he sang, or how to purse his lips if he forgot the words, although solitary, Yinn had so many friends and how could you tell thought Petites Cendres, then there was the handsome jack he called My Captain, one of the night-show dancers as well as a terrific navigator, of course he climbed aboard his boat from time to time, maybe just one of the many who were dazzled by Yinn, another of her subjects, but Petites Cendres didn't see them together that much without Jason, alone together in the washroom at the cabaret and coming out laughing with My Captain's arm on Yinn's shoulder, more like casual acquaintances or buddies, ah it was all too much for a jealous man like Petites Cendres, and if My Captain, so very seductive out on the water, nested among the coiled ropes, such a good swimmer too when he dived into the middle of the ocean, yes if My Captain was the provider or if it was Yinn in secret, these gorgeous young men that Jason's intense stare never managed to catch at it, no, so frank and open himself, Jason never made it through the veil of clandestinity to the inner hell that was in Yinn's nature though not his own, its turbulence and slippery slopes were nothing to him, thus the one he loved was immune to them, he, in his scanty vests, never even considered them, Jason climbed the wooden stairway to the cabaret, tattoos shining on his rounded arms and bestowing on all a wave, a bright smile, and a direct gaze that would last all evening and all night, then again he began climbing, only this time it was the wooden ladder fixed to the cabaret ceiling, and inside a gable above the stage he set about his lighting, he it was that combined purples and mauves, a bit like the velvet curtains that hid the backstage area, ready to open any and all horizons for Yinn, this was the job he carried out so meticulously, a model of serene adoration, no thought Petites Cendres, Jason could never have perceived the dark and unfathomable designs Yinn and My Captain had on one another but Petites Cendres could, the sly understanding between them, in the toilet and out, oh yes no one knew better than he the power of the white powder to draw people in, as Robbie said nope I don't touch the stuff just then Petites Cendres sensed the presence of Timo's ghost, Timo whom he'd left to his fate, all these little cocaine peddlers left in a helicopter Robbie surmised, and they never come back, did you ever think about them Petites Cendres, all the way from British Columbia in the cold wearing their winter parkas, the glacial froth of their breath in the frigid air before the departure into one of February's nights, then in darkness throughout the flight, nothing but blackness all around as they carried a package of Mexican cocaine to Los Angeles, what fevered excitement in those moments of taking off when the entire cockpit trembles and the smells of fuel and oil fill the lungs, was this one going to be their very last, now the helicopter taking off in the snow amid smells of pine and cold, when you're twenty this sort of thing sets your heart to beating wildly for one last race, three years they've been smuggling or maybe two, and why not one more, fooling them at the border crossings, as much cheaters, frauds, and liars proclaiming themselves innocent as ever, so why not one more try at straddling the bounds of innocence, adventure, and conquest, but this night clouds were piling up over the Selkirk Mountains, a peak they knew very well, over how many rivers and bridges had they cycled on their legendary sport bikes then suddenly switched routes right there in the February night, total, unbridled risk, this time no one would recognize them like in the videos of the bridge exploits, no tonight snow and fog blanketed the sky, and they sent a text message that they would be there tomorrow and tonight I'm working but I'll be there tomorrow, or so they thought, but in fact they wouldn't be at their destination, and their bodies would be found in the snow a few days later, adventure, that's what it was about, adventure as they say, merchants, providers of no great means,

Robbie thought about them and said to himself he'd never touch the stuff again, no more coke, although this seemed pretty late as conversions go thought Petites Cendres, he could remember sniffing it for hours with Fatalité only a few nights ago, well I mean I was just along to keep him company Robbie protested, Fatalité my brother could see damn well what was coming for him, poor babe, I kept on saying over and over I'm here with you Fatalité, whether it was some morbid excitement or fever and a bunch of sleepless nights I don't know, maybe I was fighting off sleep or maybe I was daydreaming, anyway I felt my body rip open like an envelope and out I came and danced all over it, but what scared me was the thought that I might not get back inside if my body forgot me or fell asleep or cooled off, I mean I liked the performance I was putting on but there was nothing real about my feet or legs, and I thought I've got to get back inside that thing of mine right away which seemed to have fallen asleep, refrigerating itself without a single memory of me, so I quickly got back in the envelope, every muscle and bone, still terrified that open space and the night would seize hold of me forever, and that's when I said nope, never again, no more coke ever, of course I didn't say a word of this to Fatalité, and who knows maybe she too was already gone from us, after all her earthly envelope was long gone too, remember how he was always so cold, like the chute-less pilot in the Selkirk Mountains in one last dash through the lightning, so I said to myself no Robbie, no more, not with Fatalité, not with Daddy, no way Robbie, then Petites Cendres, smelling Yinn on him — the night and the jasmine that perfumed the town, the red of her lips imitating frangipani that splashed their colour on the sidewalks and wooden houses — impudently blurted out oh yeah and what about Yinn and you, that special thing you have going, is that just professional, so tell me Robbie what are you up to late at night in the washroom eh, Yinn just helps me get dressed, that's all, those short summer dresses, Yinn keeps an eye on everything, the least pink thread hanging down your thighs, just like his mother he wants everything perfect you know, refined, and with those words Robbie buoyed Petites Cendres and removed all doubt, though maybe doubt would have been a good thing if in the depraved shadows of Petites Cendres' own excesses he could catch Yinn out with a secret partner, a partnership sealed in secret debauch that Petites Cendres could use to hold him hostage, kept only for his own private dreams, Robbie had pitiless words for Petites Cendres, reminding him how he had been put down at the bar by Yinn and Luis too, the kid who stole meds from his father's office, and how he'd put down another young black prostitute who sold drugs in the street, this one not yet twenty though and wearing black shorts with a white top and bloodshot eyes, out there right now waiting for a client to give him cigarettes and then light them, just like Petites Cendres at that age, how could Yinn manage to be so hard when he gave no sign of judging Petites Cendres, so much like this kid, look he's not an adult yet said Robbie, how do you know said Yinn, how do you know, without harshness he simply said to her better not hang out here, go home, just go home, he looked at him with sadness and said better if you don't come back here girl, but how could you tell what he was feeling said Robbie, it just got worse when she said she had no family, no home, no job, so what're you going to do, he shrugged and disappeared to answer Jason's call from the stairs, are you coming, we have to filter these lights, what do you think Yinn, yeah, yeah I'm coming Yinn answered, someone was always asking for him, waiting for him, a few feet away in the street a hooker was begging cigarettes from two male tourists she'd leave with, but Yinn, already on the staircase with Jason, didn't see any of this, he would have been furious said Robbie, but if there's nothing you can do there's nothing you can do, what about you Petites Cendres Robbie suddenly shot back, where do you wind up at night, where do you go to sleep at dawn after the show's over, oh on the red sofa under the bar sometimes he replied with feigned detachment, if Jason lets me, or else the hotel with a customer from the sauna at the Porte du Baiser, that's not a life Robbie would say, you need a man, a real husband, but Petites Cendres he could never get attached to just one person, all the men who picked him up were so nasty or ugly he couldn't stand them, that's what Petites Cendres would say, nope, no one, and anyway the husbands of younger prostitutes often fought with them, Petites Cendres didn't like fights either, either that or he's been mistreated, of course he'd undergone a lot of that without ever doing it himself or even consenting to it, what you want is a husband like my Daddy said Robbie, I had my own apartment and God knows how many credit cards and now look at me, no Daddy, no nothing to pay for Fatalité's funeral, just my salary, and Yinn won't even give me that when I'm back on the powder, oh sure she pays it all up to date when I'm straight again, as he listened to Robbie Petites Cendres gradually became convinced that Yinn belonged neither to his hell nor his vulnerability to addiction, removing him still further from the one he loved, Yinn continued his enigmatic rise just as Petites Cendres sank lower and lower to the inevitable darkness that would one day swallow him completely just as it had Fatalité, Petites Cendres never telling Robbie of the hope that kept him awake till dawn on the red velvet sofa in the bar, through his magnificent nails which were his special vanity he observed Yinn suddenly resembling some weary lady drinking with the bedraggled denizens of the night, a pink drink with ice and a straw, while Jason replaced his ladder so it wedged tight against the ceiling and turned off the spotlights one by one, and Yinn getting ready to leave with him but readily engaging in the camaraderie of the others in the phosphorescent glow of the set, her lips still red and barely brushing against the drink she would never finish, what exactly was that weary voluptuousness that lit up her face wondered Petites Cendres, the pleasure of singing and dancing till she dropped perhaps, or anticipation of the pleasure she would have with Jason, perhaps some languid unwinding that would not last, her dress pleated at the throat, black hair spilling over her shoulders as she brought the cigarette to her lips, Yinn was suddenly a woman, a lover tormented by adulterous love, an indolent and fading Eurasian princess and the object of Petites Cendres' love, of course she realized none of this, the colour of her eyes becoming that of the smoky room, oh this was no time for Jason to come up to him and say shouldn't you be getting on home Petites Cendres, we'll see each other again tomorrow, oh how long, right up till dawn and beyond, the full sunlight of day on the front of the bar outside and Petites Cendres felt nothing but bursts of ecstasy, if only they would leave him these moments of idleness when he could make a fan with his fingers and nails and contemplate the goddess of obscurest temples, his, his own prince, Jason's that is, languidly withering behind her cigarette smoke, then suddenly by Yinn's side appeared an Asian boy with a brush cut and a very short pair of briefs in blues and yellows, with a slight movement of the upper body Yinn bowed to him as he did to his own mother, a ritual that came from deep within, here is the Next One declared Yinn with irony, see all of you, with talent, merit, and inspiration he is going to take my place here one day, this is the generation I'm grooming to take up our craft all across the country, Petites Cendres was astonished to hear Yinn speak so lucidly at the drop of a hat, not even drunk after the nouba of that night, ours is a noble craft after all, and you the Next One, don't you feel proud, you say you have a role as a transvestite actor, and I know just how to dress you o prince of the Orient, but what have you been up to all night to be undressed like that, dancing said the boy, I have no choice, act by day and dance by night, even so I'm not making it these days, Petites Cendres was sure Yinn knew perfectly well the awkward clay he was to start modelling in this one, out of this clumsy boy he'd draw the most exquisitely feminine lines, always to be lightened and perfected, one day this hair the Next One didn't know quite what to do with, head bowed into his blonde locks like an angular doll, another he'd be lost inside one of Yinn's evening gowns, floating adrift on the cabaret stage, where Yinn's shoulders were too wide, his were too narrow, the folds of the dress rolling back over his tiny frame, but Yinn was guided by his vision alone and would listen to no one else, and one day they'd all be confounded when perhaps the Next One became the magnificent creature born of Yinn and his flair, at this Petites Cendres was inconsolable, for Yinn announced to everyone at the bar that one day, who knows when, he would no longer be among them, like Jesus saying farewell to his disciples, everyone around him was having fun of course and paying no attention to what he said, so what was he leading up to, was he expecting to be so different in his multiple careers that he would have to be far away from those he loved the most, or was he just being provocative to make Jason desire him still more, to make My Captain run to kiss her with his arm on her shoulder, how on earth could Petites Cendres, still stretched out on his sofa, be deprived of this passing embrace between Yinn and My Captain, as though rocking on the deck of his sailboat, nights of flowing champagne without wind, what did Yinn say to that boy wondered Petites Cendres, you Next One will be my progeny, my race and posterity, yes you, gawky and clumsy, gracelessly androgynous for now, will become irresistible, hard to believe as that may be, Petites Cendres turned toward Jason who was enthusiastically skipping steps down the wooden stairway to turn off the TV monitors and chimney-sweep out the leavings of night to make way for the raw light of day, then his round arms gently encircled Yinn, what a day and what a night, time for sleep sweetheart he said, brushing her neck with his lips, with eyes for her and her alone and breathing only her sweet perfumes while Petites Cendres, stretched out on the red sofa for the night, was forgotten, this was the upside of being on the wrong end of a sublime and unrequited passion he thought, often, spending the night here waiting for day, before they put out the lights no one even noticed him folded into the shadows of the alcove, stretching out his legs, not Herman of the sharpened oratorical skills, master of ceremonies for the evening in his knee-length dress and beige boots, now oh so virile as he climbed onto his motorcycle in jeans, curls flying in the wind with classical Greek majesty, always hidden under outrageous wigs until now, either at night or out on the sidewalk in front of the bar haranguing passersby that the show was starting in five minutes, and why are you just walking around aimlessly instead of stepping inside and giving us a hand, oh well that's your loss, our bar's got the best send-ups around, okay so just a smidge vulgar I'll grant you, but under it all you get the point, what kind of world are you living in that you can pretend we don't exist, and hey if vulgarity's what it takes to get to you, that's just what we'll do and with a laugh too, you and your sad phobias, come have a laugh with us at your own expense, and this is what worried Yinn a bit, that Herman, after his years as an actor in New York, might be just a little over the top in his street touting, maybe not quite wary enough about his rage at society's tut-tutting on this island which already made a splashy enough setting and where it might easily and suddenly attract violence, okay so I don't have as much class as you he'd reply, some nights not a soul would even notice Petites Cendres, not Herman or Andrés, who'd once had a troupe of his own in Brazil and who sometimes filled in for Yinn's mother on weekends, closing up the ticket counter, Andrés of such exceptional elegance in costumes that changed every single night, quick to anger like Herman, as Robbie said these men who've struggled to liberate us all with such courage and suffering, well you could understand how they felt

downtrodden and oversensitive like Andrés, for Herman
though it was different, this was a rebel who was disgusted
with the world we live in and refused to consider anyone on
earth as undesirable, he had his work cut out for him didn't
he, so Yinn was constantly afraid Herman would be attacked
in the street one night or when he crossed town in his boots
and those crazy wigs to advertise the show, standing upright
on the back of his multicoloured motorized tricycle like some
racing jockey, he might overdo the harangues, yelling and
daring the crowd up and down every street where he could
find them champing at the bit, and not giving a damn about
their hatred or contempt for what we are, Yinn said don't
overdo it in those redneck parts of town, but sacrilegious
Herman the outsider wasn't having any of it, so Yinn said look
I'm afraid for you Herman, but Herman just got angry: you
know what, Yinn, I've had just about enough of your nobility
and your patience, humanity is dead of gutlessness and I'm
going to revive it, how about that eh, so let me alone okay,
aren't you bummed out about how few customers we get on
weeknights, and if I want to be out in the street for hours with
this bottle of water, I mean eventually it comes down to drinking that and nothing else, that's for me to decide, especially
if I don't want to go crazy and explode with anger, so leave
me alone Yinn, what the hell does my life matter to you anyway, actually your life means everything to me, just like
Cobra's or Geisha's, all of you girls, your lives mean everything to me was Yinn's reply though she bristled in her own
pique and tossed her little black evening purse onto the floor,
when oh when are you going to listen to me Herman, don't
you realize that very same stinking humanity you're telling me
about, you know it's everywhere in everyone you meet, that
you're putting your life in danger, they'd often had collisions
like this without actually fighting, I don't want to upset you
Yinn, you're like a mother and we're your little chicks, in fact
I've never known a girl as maternal as you even though you're

a guy, you're a samurai momma, still I really think your life's more dangerous than mine is, 'cause your provocation's a subtler kind and the vengeance might eventually be more treacherous, I'm more afraid for you than you are for me Yinn, and so it went on, always quarrelling though they loved one another, that's how Robbie put it to Petites Cendres while Andrés was having a set-to with his lovers over at the ticket counter, if they acted up he had no hesitation in throwing their stuff out into the street, of course he took them back in again next day, often after Yinn's mother accused him of being intolerant, look they're much younger than you, Andrés, why not just forgive them, that's what I do with my son, pardon everything, I even accept his husband though he never helps me around the house, too bad for me they're married she lamented, married you understand, and Andrés, in a Persian tunic and wearing a black ribbon round his head, listened to Yinn's mother that night, yes I have to admit I'm intolerant he said, but if you knew how much it costs me to have those kids living with me when I'd really rather be rereading all my books in solitude, I mean what's the point in being cultivated if you've got that bunch overrunning the place, but don't you see that's exactly what they want from you said Yinn's mom, they want you to educate them, teach them about yourself, your travels, the troupe you worked with once, standing lost in thought counting the night's receipts at the counter, Andrés changed his mind, he was last to leave the bar and didn't even notice Petites Cendres on the red sofa and asleep by now as if in the arms of Yinn, so close to that impenetrable heart and soul and still surrounded by the damp smell of smoke from Yinn's cigarette that found its way to his nostrils. In his new choreography, as Samuel wrote to Mélanie, this one to be called *Venice in a Night*, Venice, once grandiose, a marriage of art and sea, all those mythical centuries, and all we saw of it now was an invasion of water, floods and high tides, destructive winter winds, underground galleries already eroded, it was common knowledge that the water level had risen overnight, submerging cathedrals, streets, the city of a thousand bridges awash in sullied waters, and the casual denizens of cafés, like those praying in the churches, would be swallowed up in their chairs and armchairs, coffee cups or missals in hand, and everywhere the deluge, women's and men's hair leaving upward-spiralling traces modelled in the water like salt or ice sculptures, how could he capture that erosion by water from a creeping climatic devastation that no one expected to set in so rapidly, now, today, in a single night, this is what Samuel wrote to Mélanie, and oh how he loved these dawning hours and slightly before, when he could spread out his pages of notations and choreographic directions while his wife Veronica and their son Rudolf slept in the bed where he would join them, the green lampshade hanging over him adding its tinge to the hesitant light from outside, already the sounds of New York, never fully asleep or silent, echoing voices, the ever-blazing furnace beneath his feet, then soon breakfast and an end to peace and relative quiet, Rudy's toy planes buzzing overhead and all around the kitchen, his passion for planes and his sturdy legs that distracted the others in his beginning ballet lessons, overactive, too much so, not a thought for his steps, the barre, or anything but running about, playing, and throwing open the window to watch those other planes in the sky, solitary, anarchic, impersonal, on their way to who knows what target as in the painting by Hiraki Sawa, both motion picture and motion painting, Samuel would be that artist depicted in the portrait or video in black and white, the choreographer of notes and directions, while the planes streaked across the sky and in through their kitchen window, then landed on the table, alone, anarchic, impersonal, and pilotless, would they land here or in the bedroom and on the bed where his wife and son slept, impersonal as images on their plasma flat-screen, Samuel could only follow their path helplessly, waiting for one of them to sow its mushroom cloud, would the bomb land on him or on the captivating face of Veronica, fast asleep with her little boy held tight to her breast, on them or on Samuel in the abandon of all his sheets and pencils lying on the table, or perhaps on his computer, and would this be a dawning of cataclysm or of creation, the sleepers knew none of this, still anchored by the cornerstones of buildings and by steel bars, all there during this sky traffic, always there, were they ready to see their own legs, arms and hands waving white flags, the inhabitants of this city, and the late Tanjou with them, Tanjou, Pakistani student and family friend, and in *Venice in a Night* every canal spilling its water over palaces, cathedrals, houses, a man reading the paper in a café, first seeing the sinister sky-coloured Adriatic as it ebbed, then seeing the hand that held his cup shaken, the coffee still boiling hot, then his hand, his entire body sliding beneath the waves, this is the mirage dancers will create, the illusion of dancing beneath the corrupted waters Samuel wrote to Mélanie, oh how I love this hour of rich solitude when I experience complete serenity and I can write to you Mama, and here I am, Mama, a father myself, surely the best role of my entire life, and would the planes land on the bed where Veronica and Rudy slept or on this table turned to mute debris he thought, the mushroom cloud abolishing them all, Rudy who still sucked his thumb at four, Veronica near him and deep in sleep, would today be the day those legs fell, those arms, round and desperate, floating with the planes in the blue, you know, Mama, I worry when I hear so little about Grandmother, when she writes she never mentions her health, I want to know, I'm so far away from all of you, Augustino in Calcutta, Mai, you, and Papa, do be careful Mama, I know how committed you are to what you're doing, visiting prisoners, attending conferences, and all that, do be careful Mama, you are all we have, me and incorrigible Mai and all those others you care so much about, I told Rudy I named him in tribute to

Nureyev, the great Soviet choreographer and dancer of such incomparable beauty, he gets bored when I tell him stories and asks his mother more, more planes and tanks, I liked that last one, and I tell him the story of the dancer Rudolf, the story of a virtuoso, first a miserable child beaten by his father, then overcoming that and all the other dangers that lay in his path, and this is how we must live, Rudy, overcoming all obstacles in our way, fleeing the beatings, Rudolf exiled himself and became one of the greatest dancer-choreographers of all time, more planes and more tanks Rudy says, running all over the apartment on those stocky legs, sometimes he comes over and sits on my lap and asks me what it is I do when he hears me shifting notes and drawings around on the table, it's my work for a piece of choreography I tell him, *Venice in a Night*, we were always on Papa's lap when he wrote, remember, he said he couldn't do it without us, I'm like that with Rudy, I like having him near me always, but he's not getting any tanks, you and Papa wouldn't let us have any in the house and neither will I, this piece has to be weightless and delicate like Arnie Graal's work, we want to see the dissolved city, the living city of poets and writers who lived and worked there, there it was, clear as a scene or an outline, yes he thought, a film unwinding in a stream that sliced open the surrounding space with its ghosts as if they still walked the earth, souls of poets and artists, supernatural in their resilience and benevolence, the spirit that survives always, no matter if they were impotent witnesses to disaster, back to a time of serene arrogance when they knew nothing of the threats that face us nowadays, buried underwater and the earth corroded, the palaces and regal homes they inhabited, Lord Byron in his palazzo writing *Don Juan*, miserable in marriage and soon to gondola away to his mistress, less tyrannical than his wife or perhaps not, writing while buried in the commands, the words of one's wife, in chaos, consoled by the company of caged birds, monkeys and dogs, writing as did they all, or Henry

James in his Gothic palace, honourable guest in this mythic city, his own stone-vaulted gateway, mysterious visitor leading a monastic life, writing among the portraits of doges, searching in his books for sovereign links between Europe and America and not knowing if he will find them, tracing the imperishable portraits, or the poet Ruskin, living twenty-two years in the Pensione La Calcina, which would later bear his name, and rejoicing in being there, dazed and obsessed by the city as he wrote about its features, its stone, and its mystery, knowing them all the way back to its origins, all these shades drifting through the luxurious restaurant terraces now crumbling to the depths, where their lives had been so very fine and their nerved skin tanned by the summer sun, through the grand hotels about to melt into the lagoon, still writing before the seascape, whether shining or grey with its beaches and a sky filled with birds and the deep melancholy that was its gift to them, some fragile in health or hypochondriac as Thomas Mann in his prescience, for he had seen the oncoming plague, not quite ours though, the cholera that ate away at the city will be replaced in my choreography by the plague of water, vitiated and poisonous, causing cramps in its own way, killing after its own fashion as surely as the cholera once did, such ruination, human and natural, ruins drifting in the grip of the howling tides, yes the set will rotate and howl too, and music as though we are locked in a soundproof room, we will need that young Japanese composer with some cello parts, it will have the heavy rhythm of the waters, of the rushing flood which overturns bodies, while he wrote all this to Mélanie, blinded by the words on his screen even as he added to the notes on the table, still multi-tasking and enrapt, knowing his son would soon be by his side waiting for his breakfast in whining impatience, and Samuel felt he'd given his mother an over-idealized family picture, the couple, the sentimental image of mother and child in bed, his all-exclusive love for Veronica and the boy even as he sat all night at the table working till dawn, still this was a result of problems he had to face during the day, precisely with them and Molly the babysitter, because Rudy couldn't always be at daycare, so Samuel the good father was nevertheless an egotist, more so than Daniel had been with him and his siblings he thought, was he really ready to give up his career as his own father would have done if called upon, was he really that devoted and concerned when sometimes nothing seemed less natural than fatherhood, especially while the child was still young, loud, and aggressive, not yet the charmer his parents dreamed he would be, his parents going out to dinner and paying the sitter, so many monotonous annoyances of life as a threesome couple these days, but here at his table he could see the planes taking off and criss-crossing the sky over the city, anarchic, impersonal, would there ever be a target for them tonight or tomorrow or whenever, more sleep and less work would surely have made Samuel a more loving husband and father he thought, poor sleepers are unstable, out of sync, but just a few more nights and *Venice in a Night* would be done, yet still, lately Veronica had seriously criticized his absence of female characters, who sometimes thought very differently, yes that's it, he'd simply forgotten about them, he'd go over it again tomorrow, no point talking about it the minute they woke up, he had to be in class by eleven, *Venice in a Night*, oh and he had to see the musician at three this afternoon, light sleepers get so they just don't understand the lives of ordinary people, unstable, out of sync, between worlds, he mused, no such thing as an ordinary life of course, these days anything and everything is out of the ordinary, especially if you're a choreographer and dancer, what could be more amazing he wrote to his mother, what could be more amazing, though he was besieged by doubts now, just at this, the breaking of a new day, was this a dream or was Petites Cendres awakening to a kind of intimate nocturnal stage play, no music, soundless, only Yinn dancing nearby, his arms keeping waltz time, his long bare legs beneath a pink tutu so short his black G-string could be seen, a black bra strap dangling from his shoulder while he moved forward, black hair in a bun on top, repeating what he said at the bar to his friends a few hours ago, dancing then too, that at thirty-three he'd be leaving them, not just for a few days in New York with Jason for a film, Herman of course had laughed, saying our star Yinn's going to be in a super-production, they'll be no talking to her from now on, our indestructible queen, nossir we'll never break her of that, will we, our sleek and muscular queen, consort to King Jason, Geisha put in whatever's gonna happen to me when my sneakers get on your nerves, whatever will you do then Yinn, will I be subject to my sovereign's commands to get those sacrilegious things out of here, and so they railed and mocked on, Robbie wondering if he'd get a part beside Queen Yinn, who answered, maybe a little drunk on rum, why they were all her stars and queens all, oh but we aren't all wardrobe mistresses, makeup girls, dancers, and singers like you, Yinn, Robbie picked up again, they'd all be in the film Yinn said, we'll see exactly how it turns out later, but at thirty-three he'd be leaving them all, that was exactly what he'd said, and Petites Cendres heard it just that way, but now it was still nighttime and the red night light under the cabaret's poster haloed Yinn as she danced, soon the street noises would be welling up but now Yinn must be waltzing to the sound of the girls' voices Petites Cendres thought, Geisha, Cobra, Robbie, Defeated Heart, Herman, every one of the girls, during the seaside procession for Fatalité's sea burial, voices like those at Mass, pure, Reverend Stone cut in sometimes with his prayers and saying that Fatalité had accomplished what she had to do on this earth and now it was up to her father in heaven, but Robbie stopped singing and started yelling, more of this stuff about the father, I've had enough, and the singing of the girls in the choir in the January wind from the sea, amid the sound of happy students putting their boats into the water beneath the quay, irreverent, but then how could they know what ceremony was unfolding over the water, and it rose in the wind, Yinn holding the ashes under an armful of orchids, modestly dressed in his red vest and shorts, sober and boyish, so sober on that day that not a soul would have taken him for the queen and star, though all the other girls were dressed for the night, coats hastily thrown over their outfits to ward off the cold, and Robbie asked him, asked Yinn so what happens to all his actions, his deeds or the things she didn't do, like mentioning the sad heroism Fatalité had showed under a life of blows and insults beginning in childhood when his mother sold him to buy heroin, right up to the age of thirteen, when he was in court for child pornography after having sex with a girl of thirteen like himself and other kids too in a friend's house while the parents were away, why was it forbidden to want to know about sex at thirteen anyway, even with friends, so Robbie said to Yinn why did they have to prosecute him, spy on him, and there he thought his performance had been so good they wanted the video, what else was stored up in Fatalité's mind, profiting from sex, why his own mother fed him that way, all the kids, every one a suspect identified by detectives in the video, and this pervert Fatalité arrested, no family to come to his defence, his mother busy debauching herself in some other town, not even the same county, who would tell his story, this time Robbie said it to Petites Cendres, and still he had the guts to live life to the hilt, so where now would his mistakes land him, deeds no one understood or else judged without understanding, sold by his mother for some heroin, a junkie himself from childhood, shot through and through with the stuff, uh-huh, so where exactly were Fatalité and his courageous heroism headed with all this living on the edge, that's what Robbie asked Yinn, and everyone was surprised by the answer, nothing is lost, it's exactly his mistakes that proclaim his innocence and it will all be made up for in the next incarnation, though this did not seem entirely convincing despite repetition, no, nothing could be done for Fatalité except to love him or at least admire him as he fully deserved, this was to be Fatalité's coda, and whether dozing or fully asleep, Petites Cendres still felt the hollow need in his belly and on his sweating temples, no clients tonight it seemed, he was bound for a long dive into the empty depths of this vertigo he thought, yet why on earth would he need it with Yinn dancing right there in front of him, what was it, why yes, dancing without a partner, Yinn occasionally turning in his direction with a smug smile on his lips, red lips, breathe in the jasmine perfume on my body Yinn said from his slow waltz, and most of all don't listen to those bells tolling their angelus for Fatalité in the night, no don't listen, then maybe there really was music playing Petites Cendres thought, was he hallucinating or asleep anyway, from the street below came the plaintive sound of a violin played by his old father, oh my old, mixed-blood parents, are they already sitting out there on their portable benches on Esmeralda Street and selling Bibles to passersby while they preach to anyone who will listen those unbearable sounds they bow out from the pained strings, have you not read what is written in the Bible my son, thou wilt not lie down with a man as with a woman, yeah so what's the difference, the son wanted to ask, were they really there in the streets already, his dishevelled parents, father playing his sharp and bitter music, get you hence evil son, may we never see you again, Bible held high in Petites Cendres' face, oh he had run all right, these same sins will win back your innocence, that's what Yinn had said as he danced, don't listen to that bell tolling in the night, just breathe in the jasmine that's on me, rose and jasmine petals all over the city, don't listen to the funereal tolling in the night, my voice, listen only to that, my provocative smile, see only that, Reverend Ézéchielle would welcome him to her Community Church, come lost lambs, my little chicks, whatever your condition, Petites Cendres would find refuge in the white folds of her surplice, there really would be chickens at the church door, cocks too, pecking at the lawn with the pigeons and mourning doves on the church gables, come and eat at my table the Reverend would say, drink at my fountains, then Petites Cendres could forget about his scruffy old parents selling their Bibles in the streets, and those screechy violin noises on Esmeralda, could it be a good thing that Petites Cendres heard them with Yinn now dancing so sensuously right in front of him, the sharp sounds of bigots who had never loved him, don't listen to the bell Yinn had said, just don't listen, if it tolls today for Fatalité it isn't tolling those macabre sounds for you, but tomorrow, tomorrow it will be thought Petites Cendres, in the shark-infested water rushing beneath the boats and rafts with hands, hands of Haitians, holding on for dear life in the never-ending migration of the desperate and landless, hands on, Petites Cendres, hold on to your own little boat for dear life, for it is the hour of horses stolen from the fields, taken out to be killed, oh their misery will be long and hungry, legs smashed by garden hoes and dying in ignominy as though eaten alive in the hour of madness, the hour of the tolling bell thought Petites Cendres while Reverend Ézéchielle was saying come, come one and all just as you are and tell me, what is that Petites Cendres, how can your father raise a hand against his son, what is this you're telling me, creature of God, it is written love one another, and I do love you my son, it is written that you are loved and protected in this life, it is also written that you must pray for your soul my son, and that you must steer clear of saunas and dives if you can and that love is not hatred, Petites Cendres repeated all this to himself in his sleep or when he dozed, love is not hatred, and all the while Yinn danced for him under the reddish night light, a waltz just for him, Petites Cendres, and in the garden of Daniel and Mélanie, on the patio by the pool, Mère, recollecting the bitter taste of a martini and the feelings of joy at cocktail hour with those she felt close to, had come back to her own private place with Franz and Mélanie, leaning on both their arms, wrapped in tenderness and caring, remembering, yes, but what an odd detour of memory weaving its way in from the past, a memory of these trees she'd had brought in before any of the kids themselves had started to grow, Augustino had learned every single name, *Jacobinia carnea* which grew best in the shade, the African tulip that closed up against the cold, the jacaranda from Brazil, orchids from the Philippines, a Texas olive tree, amaryllis, these were trees and flowers that would not bow to storms or even to the island's hurricanes and would last until long after Mère was gone, always, always they would be there she thought, how incomprehensible that a human life should be so short, burnt out and consumed, so very short, while others found it endlessly long, they told her it was time to rest when she really wanted to go on talking to Franz, and they wondered why Daniel and Mai weren't back yet though he had phoned to tell them about the fog on the roads out where they'd gone, far into the archipelago to see the does and fauns, deer and foxes, oh well perhaps they were right, it might be better to get some rest even though it was still early, she was not quite sure whether it was evening but it couldn't be night yet with its shadowy hues and silence, soon they'd be hearing the sound of toads, the cracking of branches under the weight of Mai's cats by the open window, her dogs barking too, amid the silence any sounds were dispersed in echos, and in the brownish shadows Mère feared the return of the nightmare in which she walked through a station seeing nothing at all, picking her way through a crowd of people she didn't know, a flurry of bodies whose faces she couldn't see, walking in the midst of a thick fog with her cane, afraid of hurting someone as she went, touching the shadowed heads with one hand and saying to herself who are all these people, are we all headed for the same train, all of us shrouded from the others, faceless in the deepest of shades that nevertheless

presses us all together, I'd so like to be alone, especially when
they're strangers, what are we all walking toward anyhow and
why am I following along, a noise in the room brought an end
to the nightmare, a presence in the shadows, but since she
didn't have the strength to light the lamp she remained mired
in her sighs and uneasiness, unable to see who was there,
whoever it was opened a cupboard and held out a secure box
to her, it seemed to be the one where she kept her jewellery
case with all the gifts Mélanie had given her over the years,
medallions, chains, rings . . . all of it, all she had to do was
simply light the lamp and she'd see the person, wouldn't she,
and if she did who would she catch off-guard, perhaps Mai's
old governess, now her own nursemaid, Marie-Sylvie de la
Toussaint, better to pretend she was still dozing, out of it, then
Marie-Sylvie de la Toussaint would just leave with her takings
if it was really her robbing an old invalid in her room, and if
it was, better to forget the whole thing Mère thought, no point
in worrying the whole family, especially Mélanie, besides,
with Mère one never knew if things were true or not, such
were the byways of an overactive memory sometimes, and
what if it was real after all and Mélanie never knew, she was
calmer now and actually did half doze off, remembering how
much she'd enjoyed hearing the Schubert this afternoon, what
delight she thought, what was it that Fatalité sang just the day
before the funeral, *kiss me, love me*, debauched and aloof
under her plumage, that's what she was singing, *kiss me, love
me*, and though it was still night there was no one in the
streets yet, and Herman had rearranged the prayer fixed to
the back of his electric tricycle in lights of every colour and
rode all over town singing of her who transgressed every law
there was, *kiss me now before it's too late, kiss, let's kiss*, and
these were the words that galvanized Yinn's dance and all
who heard it through their sleep, as though written in fire in
the night air, *love me, kiss me* thought Petites Cendres, also on
the back of Herman's cheeky tricycle was the racehorse

Robbie had spoken about to Petites Cendres, Victoire it was called, or that other filly Neuvième Beauté, and Victoire running, running even with an injured leg, operated on and then bandaged, running, running with the white dressing on her right leg, nasty little mafia jockeys pulling on her reins almost to suffocation, Victoire or Neuvième Beauté, and run they did like haywire locomotives on the very track where they'd be put down, unable to stand again, oh for a rest somewhere in the country or in their stable with the other horses, rivals, when, when would a kind master rub their ears, they understood all, saw all with those oblique eyes, the crooks, the jockeys, they saw it all, never to get up from the track again after winning and wounding, no never get up again with the gleam of a dream in their eyes of rest and pasture in a field and the rain, impertinent Herman now, he was that horse, Neuvième Beauté or Victoire, whichever, that fell as he danced on Yinn's set the night before, Herman couldn't care less about the roadblocks in his way, maybe not a real injury, just a sprain in his left leg, forget about it he'd say, yeah forget about it, and standing on the back of his tricycle he sang *kiss me, love me*, too bad if you don't get it, this is what galvanized Yinn's dance in the glow of the red night light, but just as he held out his hand to Petites Cendres, Petites Cendres realized he was alone, where had Yinn got to after this private dance, where were Herman and Robbie, *kiss me, love me,* parched with thirst Petites Cendres ran into the bar to douse himself with water, his hair streaming with sweat and water, he all at once saw Timo in the reddish glow, hey friend what are you doing here wearing only boxers and a hat, you can't go around like that with nothing else on, you've got to put some pants on Petites Cendres said to him, Timo showed him the white suitcase he was carrying, in here I've got everything we need, it's full of money, his voice was chilly as though reciting a dictation, you thought I was gone or lying dead from a gunshot wound in the mud somewhere, actually I was in Mexico,

Culiacán, down there it's hard to tell who kills the most, druggies like me or the guys who try to catch us, it's an equal-opportunity fraternity, sheriffs are always after us but anything they can do we can do, even decapitate or throw a grenade at them, yep fifty-fifty, I'm telling you Petites Cendres, it's just a matter of strategy, I mean our guys in the forests are commandos right, Culiacán, yeah I was in Culiacán and I'm going back there, no need to do without down there, nah, the paradise of coke, the bandit capital, they've got their posters and cemeteries, their due, graves people pray before, I'm going to be a lord like them, you'll see, Petites Cendres, a local saint, that's me, I'll be one of them, Felix is one too, they're not going to gun me down out behind my truck, I'll be the one doing it to them, like we say down there, better to be a millionaire for a few days than broke all your life, I want one of those diamonds the women wear on their little fingers in the Culiacán casinos and nightclubs, that's what I want Timo said, bye Petites Cendres, I'm headed back to the pleasure capital of the world, you can't go like that without a decent pair of pants Petites Cendres said again, hey have you got a bit of coke for me, just a little, bye said Timo, you thought I was gone, run over or shot down in the mud, you did, didn't you, then Petites Cendres felt the water dripping down his chest and the back of his neck, *kiss me, love me*, that Timo was something else, I mean he'd got away from the sheriffs four times already, once they arrested him in a bar while he was on probation with a white suitcase full to bursting with illicit substances, when they caught him he said okay let's not get excited, let's just all chill out for a second, it'll do us all good, I just wanted to see the sun on the bay, that's all, so let's just stay calm, that's all it was, the sun on the bay, okay you can put the cuffs on now gentlemen, I won't try to escape, who knows, maybe he really was down there in Culiacán, not gunned down, not yet anyway, maybe it is true after all Petites Cendres thought to himself, a price on his head but still alive or maybe running through sandstorms with men behind him carrying machine guns, running, running like Herman on his multicoloured tricycle, like Victoire and Neuvième Beauté along a track where they'd be surrounded, put down, running but with no strength left and thirsty like Petites Cendres, so maybe Timo really was down there in Culiacán, no need for Petites Cendres to worry about him anymore, sure, what was he so worked up about, what for eh, the little girls were all exhausted from playing and fast asleep on a foldaway bed in the cabin, Rosie's parents had said she could sleep over on the boat and Lou wrapped a possessive arm round her shoulders, this proprietorship didn't sit well with her father considering how mean and dominant Lou had been with her friend all day, even making her cry at times, yet here they were like two angels on the folding bed, really only one though Ari thought, this daughter of his was turning out to be a little devil, what had happened to the sweet Lou from before, Ari flashed back to the bus ride through the mountains of Guatemala with his friend Asoka on their way to the poor people's clinic in Champerico, I don't know when I'm going to get to see my goddaughter Lou, Asoka said to him, when you get back, tell her she's my one and only child, the only one I can ever have, being a monk, bless you Ari for having a joy I'll never know each and every day, there was an unmistakeable tone of regret in this confidence and it must have hurt him to know what was forever forbidden him as long as he remained in the order, ah but you are the purest of Buddhist ascetics Ari replied, and your charity makes you the father of every underprivileged child in the world, feeling a pain of his own for the distant little girl, imagining her at that very moment in her mother's house while he was out here wandering the byways with Asoka, and the man with AIDS and a towel round his neck sitting in the bus not far away, pain and suffering all around maybe but he, Ari, had a little girl, still what did this kind of posterity really mean if his painting and sculpture declined as time went by, if all his life were reduced to just this one child Lou, she was all he ever seemed to think about since her birth, the order bestowed on Ari must surely be his art then, Asoka's stern profile enclosed his meditation and prayers but Ari couldn't discuss it any further with his friend, it seemed that the young man with AIDS was smiling at him as he sat in his seat wiping his lips with the towel, unhappy no doubt yet smiling at Ari in all his faults as assuredly as his daughter would have hers, whatever could make him worthy of a friend like Asoka, a father, a father was just someone who would atrophy without a child, a child who was doing what now, doing well in school, being good for her mother, her manners really needed some work, yes definitely, starting when they got back, she had it all, a throne room of computers, canvases, pencils, brushes, dresses, toys, oh yes she had it all, anything she might want and she always wanted more, like dinners out in seaside restaurants and he never should have let it happen, he'd caught her cutting off flower petals with scissors and made her stop, no when he got back he was going to have to be tougher, he'd tell her your godfather Asoka, Asoka never sees a child who owns anything at all and often they die very young of colic, Lou, how could he get her to think of them, the young, the very young in Guatemala and India, how to get her to understand, both the girls Lou and Rosie in pyjamas on the folding bed in the boat cabin, the usual disorder that also reigned in Lou's room in her father's house, damp towels, scattered underwear, he really should be picking this up for the laundry, as if he'd never needed to clean up here on the boat, books scattered around too, colouring books, a barely nibbled sandwich, candies, but there they were sleeping like angels, what could be more charming, Rosie and his Lou in their pyjamas on board under a foggy sky, fog that he hoped would lift by morning so they could go and see the herons and egrets on a tiny isle nearby, that would be perfect, now he recognized the daughter he longed to see when he was on the road with Asoka, how were they to know about the earth's most abandoned children, about their wretched clay huts, their insides eaten by polluted water, the debilitating emptiness, how could they know anything but the things their parents smothered and spoiled them with, what had happened to his elf-ballerina-butterfly-chrysalis, what had emerged after all, a fully formed girl, a swimmer, who might seem angelic and harmless at times of course but never missing a chance to contradict him, hey let's go to New York, Noémie so wants to meet my little girl, and what a fuss Lou set up, oh yeah, well you can go on your own Papa, no way I'm meeting that woman, how can I love anyone else, and you can love only Mama and me and no one else Lou replied, but we're divorced and I need a woman to live with, and why, Lou would answer implacably, shouldn't I be that woman, no no you're still a little girl though you were easier to get along with when you were smaller, I always had you in my arms, remember, we went everywhere together, we were inseparable, even when you got bigger, so you see it could be even, one week at Mom's place and one week plus holidays with me in New York, what do you say, oh yeah and what about my gifted classes and Italian and Spanish, you're a real nasty dad and all you ever think about is that woman and yourself, she was intractable, you're supposed to spend your life with me Ari and you know that, don't you, you know you're doing a really bad thing, look I'm a man who's in love, that's just the way it is, was Ari's reply, well you just should have thought of that and not be in love, she's too young for you anyway, it's nuts to be in love at your age, that's what Mama says, I didn't invent that, I'm just passing it on, any dart or arrow she could lay her hands on was aimed straight at him, she disapproved of her father, even repudiated him, innocent as he was of anything but loving and desiring a woman, Noémie, and worst of all Lou treated him like her personal maid he thought as he

gathered up beach towels and clothes for the laundry, he'd
waited on her hand and foot ever since she was born, hadn't
he, so why all this trouble between them now, his karmic
comeuppance, is that what she was, just another test, good
thing he had Noémie then, the freshness of new love late in
life, you can't live without it, or was it just him that his daughter was upset about, him and his renewed passion and desire
that caused her to be shunted aside just now when she was
so attractive, but she was still only a young girl just growing
up, could she impress him with her height the way Rosie was
impressed, soon she'd be overtaking him, then suddenly bear-
able compared to Ingrid, in all Ingrid's beauty back when she
had said out of the blue I don't want to live with you anymore
Ari, all that matters for you is your art, not your wife and child,
so that's it, goodbye Ari, Ingrid in Lou's body or vice versa,
how could he resist one any more than the other woman,
Noémie, Noémie he thought as he climbed the spiral metal
steps to the fog-bound bridge, talking to Noémie would help,
here was the cellphone in his hand and Noémie's voice on
the other end saying she loved him as the boat rocked on the
evening breeze, there at least, out under the stars, his daughter couldn't hear he thought, she was fast asleep with the
other little angel in the cabin below, he was saying to Noémie,
he had to lie just a little and say Lou was dying to meet her,
Lou, don't worry about her Ari the enthusiastic voice at the
other end said, I can help her grow into someone fine, all I
need is to meet her, the will and the proprietorship in her
voice made Ari shiver as though it were his daughter speaking, women, these women he was to tell Asoka, surely they
were his karmic incarnation on this earthly voyage, Petites
Cendres saw the man climb out from under the bench where
he'd slept by the bar, and it turned out to be the elderly
sophisticate, Robbie's friend, who said that's right, I bought a
round, okay fine then another and a third, and so, well here
I was under the seat, I live out in the country and I don't make

it in here more than once a month, then I head back out to that jungle and the family and my animals, hey where is Robbie anyway, he was s'posed to call me a taxi, where the hell is that boy-whore, yep that's what he is, always on display like that every night, now do they really have to look like they're for sale, 'course they don't, so tell me how are they gonna get people inside so they don't play to empty houses answered Petites Cendres, 'specially on weeknights, I'm an old sea dog the man replied, navy, and I travelled all over Asia and I know all there is to know about men and boys and brothels, yes I do, and what I want to know is why does Robbie have to put himself on show like that eh, traitors all of them, that's what you are, traitors, that's why I want to have Robbie all to myself, but she's one too, a bit of cash on the line and she'll trot off with any couple, then you know what happens next don't you, an orgy, betrayer I said, I wonder if I took three rounds or was it four to slap me under that bench, where's Robbie and that taxi he was going to get me, Robbie's got no morals you know, listen to me Petites Cendres, and off he was again calling them all traitors, still he couldn't tear himself away from this place, always well dressed and freshly barbered, this was his monthly night out with the betrayers, and a man's got to spill his seed so he doesn't end up killing someone, though this time he hadn't got lucky, no traitresses available tonight he told Petites Cendres, hey you're soaking wet, you're trembling, oh I'm hurting 'cause I need some Petites Cendres said, too weak to help out the talkative old sophisticate, besides this was a fashionable bar and prostitution wasn't allowed, maybe sometimes in the Porte du Baiser sauna, that's where the old man would sometimes trot off with someone who was willing but not that often, turncoats every one of them the old guy went on till Petites Cendres said I'll find you a taxi, but he had trouble standing too and he didn't like hearing Robbie called a boy-whore, I've got to get rid of this one, I don't want to listen to any more of his garbage, a girl-whore maybe, the old guy was droning on, Robbie, your Puerto Rican friend, says he doesn't want any more of those daddies, he's had his fill, hey does he really come from an old family of musicians and showbiz people in Puerto Rico, who knows, all lying bitches, mythomaniacs, talkers, mind you that's what the customers like don't they, 'specially this Robbie of yours, she was always partying with Fatalité, cannabis, hash, coke non-stop, do you really think just 'cause you're young you won't get what's coming to you for all this evil eh, living for the moment, tangoing on the edge of a cliff, you think there's no bill coming in for all this don't you, that Yinn and My Captain too, no consequences no sir, Petites Cendres finally yelled at him that Yinn was beyond reproach, brave and blameless, sure he arranged with Andrés to withdraw money to pay for things in the house, mostly before Robbie could snort it all up in powder the old man admitted, Petites Cendres could see by his allure of a gentleman farmer all slicked up to come into the bar that the old guy was fragile like Petites Cendres' old man, just a hand on those hunched shoulders and his fingers would have felt every single bone, I'll go out and get you a taxi he said, thinking about his father and the stack of Bibles he had for sale, scattering bread crumbs for the hens and chicks out on the sidewalk along Esmeralda, they both seemed pitiable to him, maybe even a little touching, Reverend Ézéchielle had pardoned Petites Cendres so many times maybe he ought to do the same, forgive those who have trespassed against us my friend, still it is not for a father to raise his hand against his son, it remains to be seen if God in his charity will forgive a father for hating and cursing his son and raising his hand against him, this we will see when the time comes she said, I'm getting you a taxi Petites Cendres said again, listen to me just a bit more said the old man, they're all mythomaniacs, yarn-spinning, bullshitting girls, fakers, and that actor Herman, the one that played Beckett in New York, says he got hurt tripping on one of

Yinn's sets, not even true, worse even, still he doesn't say a word 'cause he doesn't want to get fired and how's he gonna get another job eh, dreams and make-believe all of it, but that's gonna come around too, your immune systems are so shot you guys could catch anything, yeah listen to me, malaria, the killer fever, a fly or any insect can do you in, maybe that's how Herman'll go if he doesn't stop going around yelling on that tricycle of his at night, he knows he's going to get hammered so he gets a thick skin, had a heartbreak they said, well who hasn't eh, Petites Cendres, liars and cheats all of them I'm telling you, here, your taxi Petites Cendres announced, but the old guy fell back on his seat and disappeared from sight and Petites Cendres was alone in the silence of the bar again, then the street racket started up and a shaft of light lit up the red sofa, thirsty and shivering, Petites Cendres once more held out his hand to the memory of Yinn dancing oh so close to him, the vestibule was aglow in the reddish tinge of the night light and a hermaphrodite mannequin held out its hand to Petites Cendres, the silky wig made it look a bit like Robbie or the Adonis called Vanquished Heart, half-boy, half-girl, mourning his mother who had recently died of alcoholism at fifty, tears still pouring out from under his long lashes through the whole performance, this much sorrow on earth and yet a father has to hate his son, why, that night though the mannequin wasn't wearing a thing, not even its wig, bare naked under a flag and looking as defeated as little Vanquished Heart was, sobbing backstage and saying I've got no mother, no one, it's all over, like in a coma, yet this was the mannequin that held out its plaster hand to Petites Cendres and said come to me and I will console you, at least that's what the lifeless lips seemed to say with no small irony, look Petites Cendres, this place in all its smokiness has not known only tears, there's been laughter as well, alcohol sliding itself into glasses, cascades of laughter, night and day, listen to me, as the Old Man would say, we've all had our heartbreaks in love, a person undefeated is a person who hasn't lived, that's just the way the heart is, the skin at least can keep healing itself all the way to death, Vanquished Heart had to change into Triumphant Heart, one night when he wended his sad way through the crowd, bucket in hand, he found himself face to face with a boy in a cap who said every night I've come and admired you Vanquished Heart, and that brought him right back, from now on the boy in the cap, sometimes backwards, sometimes not, would be there by his side for good, Vanquished Heart said it was my mother who sent you wasn't it, she's always loved me so very much, after that they were never apart, yes he said, but I don't have anyone like that thought Petites Cendres as he looked out the window at the sunrise and imagined he still heard the old guy saying over and over traitresses all of them, plotters and liars and fakers, I'm telling you Petites Cendres, well okay Yinn's still in the arms of Jason and they're living together, right, but you, Petites Cendres, you're alone, it was then he saw the huge white horse onstage where Jason sang soprano as he always did on dance night when they were all in the chorus, led by that calming and beautiful voice of his, newcomers and regulars alike amidst the smokiness and alcohol, the cascading laughter and whistles Petites Cendres heard from the voices on those nights, Jason's voice rising and floating above them all, enchanting Yinn standing but discreet in his red vest, hair untied and falling over his shoulders, not distracting at all from Jason singing so beautifully, Yinn no longer standing out for a change, just one of the crowd, transformed into an ordinary boy keeping time with his sandalled feet, at that instant Petites Cendres looked at him and thought just a little boy all of a sudden, the huge papier-mâché horse, something Yinn and Herman had thrown together without too much artifice, was up there as silent as the mannequin under its flag in the red glow of the night light that never went out and the yellow blinking lights on the stairs leading to the cabaret, motionless on its rollers, the white horse seemed to be waiting to be hauled out for the spring and summer parties with its bridle dragging on the ground, the same one Herman would use to yank it through the streets yelling last show is at midnight, only five minutes to go, five minutes, adults only, explicit language, and on the horse's rump would sit Herman and Robbie entangled in an embrace and laughing, back when Herman's smile was a little less sad thought Petites Cendres, his words a little less brusque, his voice a little less hoarse, what was it in him so toxic and all-devouring, suddenly there he was astride the horse, bridle in hand, in his costume for the second show, a sort of white fringed culottes over beige boots, hair curled amid the smoky air like drooping, ragged wings, and he was telling Petites Cendres you absolutely must not miss my most stunning, rip-roaring number where I appear as a woman and bit by bit I disrobe into manhood, showing the power that we all have to be in harmony, so what do you say Petites Cendres, you coming to see it, his eyelashes, like Yinn's at times, seemed misty and flat, which gave him an exquisite air, my parents are intellectuals and they get what it is I do, they let me be just what I always wanted to be, not everyone's that lucky Herman said, you going to come see my routine Petites Cendres, I wasted enough days and nights drinking in this place because the boy I wanted turned me down and he didn't want me contaminated, and I cried, hugging the emptiness for nothing, just like you hold on to that ethereal Yinn, my friend, now don't you think it's about time to get out our horse and have some fun on him with Robbie, surely we've had enough of weeping over Fatalité, parading down to the quay, enough parades and processions of all kinds, isn't that so Petites Cendres, and Petites Cendres pictured his parents getting out their Bibles down in the alleyways of the port, trotting around the streets declaring the word of God as they called it, and when the owners of shops and restaurants chased them away, yelling after them we don't want peddlers and loafers hanging around here so get lost, and if you don't we'll get the mounted police to chase you off, horses, *horses*, that was the word that terrified them as if they had found themselves bent beneath the unholy masters' whips like in the olden days, laid low in shame and slavery, so no soliciting and no hanging around was what they yelled at them, trotting, always trotting down the alleys by the sea, alleyways for whites, this is the way they got to their steamers and yachts, there was this man, who was he, selling iced tea from a little electric car, he took pity on them in this dry heat, here this is for your dad and mom, they must be thirsty Petites Cendres, go on, give it to them, it's cruel times, and tell them not all men are alike and steeped in evil, the cool of the drink on their cracked lips, yes Petites Cendres remembered it, the consoling, comforting drink spreading through them, horses, horses they muttered as they trotted, trotted all the way to Esmeralda, maybe it was time to pardon his old, mixed-blood parents pathetically trying in vain to spread the word of God and being chased off by merchants and restaurant owners with shouts of peddlers, loafers, what enchantment in these Schubert sonatas marvelled Mère, just then she saw her daughter approaching with a tray and she said to Mélanie, you really mustn't be getting up in the middle of the night for me, but Mama it isn't nighttime yet Mélanie answered, you are always saying your feet are burning at the end of the day, she held out a bowl filled with ice cubes, here let me cool off your feet slowly, and she wrapped some of the ice in her scarf to chill her mother's feet, remember when I was small and I did this, oh sweetheart said Mère, what a delight it was on those burning hot days, do you remember that, then suddenly changing tack she asked where's Julio, couldn't he come back home so Marie-Sylvie can get a break, I know what a burden I must be to all of you, yes yes I know, oh Mama doesn't this feel better Mélanie asked as she rubbed her mother's numbed feet, Julio's busy with his political refugees, he'll come though, I promise

you Mama, you know Julio, Marie-Sylvie, and Jenny are also
my children Mère mused, still she could not repress a shiver
at the mention of Marie-Sylvie, now tell me asked Mélanie,
why oh why don't you just come live with us, that way Daniel
and I can be nearby day and night, all you have to do is agree
to sleep in Samuel's room, but Mère replied oh the time will
come for that soon enough but not just yet, I do so love the
joy of listening to Schubert's sonatas, there will come a time
when I'm no longer with you, my child you know I've always
been a free spirit, been running my own life ever since your
father left us, yes Mélanie, do ask Julio to try to visit me, you
how I've loved every single one of them, each one my own
child, ah how beautiful this music is she said again, Mélanie
replied there now, doesn't the ice help a bit, see you're moving your feet, now Mama you'd better rest and I'll look in on
you in an hour, and no it isn't nighttime yet Mama, the fire in
her feet now extinguished, she dozed off, was this true sleep
or, if not, what else could this tumultuous torpor of a life be
that drowned out the music and made it irritating to her, the
birth of her composer, the story that Franz had told about him
over evening cocktails in the garden, son of a servant, born
into a family of thirteen of whom only five survived, Schubert,
fierce, star-led child, wasn't long for poverty and privation,
that music, where did it come from Mère had asked Franz,
one of his works says it so well came the answer, Schubert
was the song of the water sprites, though the sprites of the
great German poets he set to music were the songs of disgrace
from syphilis, the waters were the physical and mental torment out of which the composer's spirit emerged to serenity
but only reached that ineffable joy at death's door, indeed that
must be what Franz had said, the ineffable gift of joy, that's
where the music comes from, the depths of desolation my
dear, and in this bustling torpor of life that was neither sleep
nor rest, Mère saw Caroline calling to her, come Esther she
said, all dressed up for the evening, come my dear I must

show you where I am, and where was it, this hermetic world that was now her home, follow me said Caroline to Mère, just follow me Esther, that's all, and they went into a darkened house with unlit corridors, God thought Mère, not these frightening dark-coloured walls and halls again, and here's the room I share with strangers Caroline said as a diffuse light dawned in the room and Mère saw a fairly young man and a motionless woman of some distinction, both of them seated in armchairs and appearing to notice no one but themselves, I don't know why I have to be assailed by these people Caroline, they can neither see nor hear me, they are pathetically absorbed in one another, obviously well off and never having done without, bound up in their sterile passion for money, look at the luxury they surround themselves with, oddly now it was Mère who was explaining things to Caroline, things she noticed in this couple, I know what they've always venerated and idolized, they are not flesh and bone, only the money they always wanted, look Caroline they are all malleable white metal, barely able to move and breathe, held in its vise-grip, Caroline wondered why am I condemned to be with them, they can neither see nor hear me, Esther tell me why, but Mère didn't know what to say, no this is not sleep, no it's an overwhelming bustle of life amid torpor, whether with Caroline or by herself, in which she no longer heard Schubert's music and seemed to have forgotten everything Franz had said about him except that only five out of thirteen in the family survived, he was a predestined offering to the gods, a sacrifice Franz said, that was what he said wasn't it, as he turned toward the sign over the entrance to the cabaret, Petites Cendres read under the yellow light bulbs leading to the stairs: COME SEE WORLD-RENOWNED YINN DANCE FOR YOUR DELIGHT, and a drawing of his eyes stared out at him, lashes black and lush, not unlike Herman's, who also straddled the white papier-mâché horse saying it's time, yes it's time to drop all the processions and parades by the sea and let Fatalité rest in peace, yes rest under the waters that welled over and dissolved the most charming features of his body, nothing, no there was nothing to be done about that said Herman, that was the saddest part, dissolution, and as Herman spoke Petites Cendres thought of all the arguments and quarrels Herman had had with Yinn right there in front of their comically conceived horse, the Spring-Break Horse as Herman called it, soon to be trotted out onto the sidewalk and into the street, and it was right next to this rather clunky-looking pseudo-equine that Herman told Yinn I'll love whoever I please and even if Fabian is plague-infested, isn't that just one more reason to love him, this world's riddled with plagues and no one seems to care, seen any worldwide campaigns against hunger lately, no, 'course you haven't, not a word right, thirst, how about thirst in all those dried-out countries pockmarked with war, nothing, nope, and as for the serious cases under a doctor's care like Fatalité and Fabian, Fabian, brown-skinned and handsomer than Robbie with that virile hip action he's got, Fatalité didn't go see Dr. Dieudonné till it was too late anyway, too bad, they might as well truly get some splashy sex 'cause God knows it's all they've got left isn't it, that's right Yinn, I'll love whoever I feel like and not you or anyone else is going to stop me, so, Yinn said, take Fabian to Dieudonné's clinic then, he needs help and a place to live more than anything, and especially Dieudonné, more than all your wild desires he said with a firm voice, besides Fabian's right, he could infect you and I'm not letting that happen, look that's just the way it is said Herman, what can you do, it's just our time, you have to love whatever conditions you're in, take the risks or just stop living for real, believe me Yinn, I'm going to love him and not chicken out and I don't need your permission to live out my splashy life, you want to put Fabian in quarantine with all those others exiled to some remote part of the island, are you really that inhuman Yinn that you'd forbid loving a young man in a time of pestilence, and who's going to forbid it, not you, heartless Mother Yinn, no not you, no said Yinn, I mean no you're not having Fabian, or him you, he'd be up in flames like straw, I know you Herman and I'm not letting you die in unspeakable agony like Fatalité for a stray embrace, no I'm not Yinn repeated, his eyes rimmed with tears, too much Herman, it would be too much, Yinn at that moment felt the overwhelming precariousness of all their lives, every one of those close to him, are we just going to take this yelled Herman, this earth that one day soon will have no one left on it to love, millions detained at border crossings and held in quarantine, shipped off out of sheer hatred and mistrust, are we going to let them ban love, though even now Herman was realizing he really would give up Fabian, yet his words shook Yinn, who was already in tears, Yinn, wanting to save him, loving him, with Herman always so on edge and despairing, constitutionally indomitable, he thought this himself, Herman would have liked to take Fabian to Dieudonné's clinic the very next day, one more sick kid to work on is how he'd put it to the doctor, touching his fingers to Fabian's eyelids and round cheeks as if saying farewell to a precious friend forever, I'll be back and I know you're going to get better Fabian, see, you've stopped coughing now, I'll come see you tomorrow, Herman went off somewhere to contain his rage, drinking non-stop in the bar for seven days, avoiding Yinn, the alcohol gradually drawing the toxins out of his wretchedness, and asking himself do we really have to accept that it's now forbidden to love, then back to work, only this time creating a truly astonishing number of a lady with an eye for the men and vice versa, a real hit with the customers though Herman never really had much use for that lot, thinking them stupid, insatiably vulgar, and drowning in prejudice instead of laughing it out of their systems, the brutal superiority of the public was what caused so many fights with Yinn, who said you have to respect the people who pay to see us dance and sing, they deserve a little consideration and deference Yinn said, I know they have us eating out of their hands Herman said, and without them we'd be out of a job, but don't forget, Yinn, it's just crumbs, we're onstage all night long every night and not one of us is ever going to get rich, you think they can still be reached I know, and one day they'll realize we're true artists, but they just see us as sort of homosexuals in disguise, oddballs, oddities that shock and excite them when we stretch their inhibitions to the limit, finally they get to the point where they come up on the stage undressed and realize wow, they have a body too, then make some dumb-ass lewd move to get over their prudishness, I tell them to turn left, then turn right and they do it, they get off on my hands groping them all over, but it's an illusion, the only touching that goes on is in their heads, my hands just disappear for a second, if it's a woman I tell her she's got nice breasts or I tease a man about his manhood, a man and any other damn thing, same as you Yinn, I make 'em feel better by getting down in the dirt with them, I share it all right down to their rotten taste, hey I say, look here I can make a coin materialize out of your puritan ass, gold nuggets why not, and they love it, it's their favourite number, I am the embodiment of vulgarity, now that's something you can never do Yinn, an artist who vicariously brings out the lowest thing inside you, that's what I am, and I only get on my high horse when it's over and I get to sing or dance with Cobra, Geisha, or you Yinn, in all your night-bird glory, inaccessible princehood, and you Yinn, you tell me to respect them and show some consideration, but Yinn's answer was still yes, you owe them everything, it shows on you Herman, you had a golden childhood, overindulged, then Herman's tenderness for Yinn and his art suddenly showed, for the inner strength that seemed to guide his entire life in flawless purity, yet showing none of the feelings, this was his way, as Herman said with irritation and annoyance, no Yinn, no, you're not going to stop me being who I am, that, Yinn, is one thing you're not going to do, and the steel heels of his boots clicked across the wooden floor all the way out into the street, you could hear them as well as his hoarse laughter for a long way, and he yelled five minutes to midnight showtime, five minutes you indifferent, aimless pedestrians, come, don't come, you all just piss me off, seriously, come or don't come, five minutes to the midnight show. Mère watched as Julio opened every window in the room so she could hear the night sounds and, not far from Daniel and Mélanie's house and hidden by the fog of several days, the barely audible sound of the sea, thanks Julio for coming so far Mère said, but why are your eyes bandaged, have you been attacked by thugs on the beach again, he undid it and said but this time I've learned to defend myself Esther, it's been a while, I was younger then, still vulnerable and grieving for my family, it didn't take much to get my goat, I gave as well as got, and without you bringing me into your home Esther, I might not even be alive today, let alone setting up and running a bunch of houses of refuge for Cubans, Jamaicans, and Haitians in the big cities, would I, when my mom was begging God she forgot to ask for life jackets, and if I hadn't taken one off a drowned man I wouldn't have survived long enough for the helicopter to pick me up, can you hear the sea now Esther, I hear my mother Edna's voice and my brother Oreste, my sister Nina too, that helicopter was so close we could hear the roar of its engines just overhead, so close, but the swell took them anyway, they all swam for the lights onshore, Ramon too, but Edna's prayers weren't answered and none of them made it to the land of milk and honey as she called it, not one, no new country for them, just the shores of the beyond, a long, slow death out on the water, and here I am saved by a dead man's life jacket while they're on a raft going down to a long sleep on the dark ocean floor, Edna, Nina, Oreste, Ramon, you know what we found, one of Oreste's white shoes, Edna's shawl, and Nina's doll intact, can you hear them in the night Esther, their sad lament at being betrayed, that's what I feel so violently, fooled and betrayed by my mother's prayers and her dreams of a land of milk and honey, they were lied to you know, the owners of those rafts and boats to whom my mother sold her soul, knowing all the same that the wood was rotted and they'd all drown, listen to their voices, can you hear them Esther, the betrayed and tricked and lied-to, land of milk and honey, right, no such thing, can you hear them calling out for justice, for truth, for their own bodies and lives back again, no blue glow of the shoreline for them, Mère said all I hear are the murmurs in the trees, come closer Julio, a bit closer, Mélanie told me you'll be in New York in a few days, so Julio, would you hug Samuel for me, Augustino doesn't seem to have time to write me and I miss them all so much in this monastic homebody life I'm leading here, listen to their voices, my mother, Ramon, Oreste, Nina, listen Esther said Julio, come closer Julio, come closer was all Mère said from where she sat on the edge of the bed, but when he did she realized it wasn't Julio but Marie-Sylvie de la Toussaint, you called me, and she placed a carafe of cool water on the bedside table, when Mère saw this large form suddenly looming over her, and despite the sombre colour of the room, further deepened by shadows, she noticed stains rather like ashes on Marie-Sylvie's face, her voice took on a particular sharpness, and the ashen marks on her dark face, oh no I was reading, resting and reading said Mère, I'm sure I didn't call you, it's just that people keep coming and going here said Marie-Sylvie, sounding irritated, all your friends keep bothering me with their knocking she went on, but I'm not expecting anyone said Mère, as though apologizing for all the chaos around her, see, here comes another one, Adrien, God he looks so priggish in that blue blazer and white pants of his, says he just finished playing tennis, there said Marie-Sylvie, slamming the door behind her, my dearest Esther hailed Adrien, sweet friend, your old pal the poet and blasé literary critic is here once again, Daniel said you'd like me to drop in, I must admit I'm not the best of company now

I'm alone without indispensable Suzanne by my side, oh the love of a lifetime, Suzanne he whispered hoarsely, hiding his tears with his hands, do come closer Mère said, here, come sit on the bed, oh we've been friends for such a long time, you will read me some of your poems won't you, I think "Humility" is my favourite or perhaps "Settling Accounts," oh I can do that by heart but its real title is "Day of Justice" he corrected her, one morning after a night of drunkenness, too much wine and whisky, a man sees in a flash every single thing he's ever done in his life and decides not one day of it has any value whatsoever, just a series of gaping holes in the tapestry of his days, he feels guilty and, looking at himself in the mirror, he realizes he's even red with embarrassment although he's alone, artifice, that's all he is, artifice, you should be ashamed of yourself, of course this self-condemnation doesn't last long, the sun has simply moved on and shifted its gaze elsewhere Adrien said, I beg Suzanne to come back to me, at least in my dreams, I don't know why she hardly ever comes into them, when she does, she always seems put out about something, no longer the woman I loved, I can never reach her no matter how hard I try, every door is firmly shut, oh Suzanne we loved one another so very much, our bright golden youth, our books, our work, do you know what she holds against me the most in my nightmares, my wife, my beloved regrets having written so little when she was with me, she doesn't blame the children, just me, I wish, I wish I had written more when we were together Adrien, what are you going to do with my posthumous work, have you found my notebooks, all my poetry, you my poet, world-renowned critic, what do you have to say to me, but these are only dreams said Mère, you mustn't let such things upset you Adrien, the truth is you were both splendid and always sup-ported one another, didn't you Adrien, that's the truth, isn't it, day of justice, day of justice repeated Adrien, humility was never my strong suit Esther, if pride can be considered a quality, well I had plenty of that didn't I, even to the detriment of my wife, plenty of it no doubt, and it didn't get any better over the years either, remember how tight-lipped I was about Daniel's *Strange Years*, my style was pretty bloodthirsty and I can't fully bring myself to regret it, Daniel has matured though and the youthful failings of his first books are no longer so evident, tighten up your sentences, the entire content, that's what I always said to him, if he'd listened to me I bet his writing would be covered in university courses by now, I really believed I was doing the right thing by critiquing him the way I did, okay, critics like me just can't resist being a bit acerbic, it's a temperamental thing I admit, but that was before, when Daniel was still a beginner and new to the game and I too had to sharpen my claws on somebody, so why not him, what do you say Esther, I did do the right thing didn't I, oh that's between you and your conscience my friend said Mère, that poem of yours, "Settling Accounts," is one of the most moving precisely because you admit your failings, Augustino now, in his book *Letter to Young People Without a Future*, didn't escape your scourge either, remember, Adrien, my grandson was most upset, whatever claw marks I may have left on him replied Adrien, a young writer absolutely must be pushed to the wall by criticism, it can only give him a push along his way and force him to shake things up, after all he hasn't stopped writing has he, no of course not, his success isn't any the less for it either is it, again no, he's still writing constantly and travelling abroad, so much so even his father is a bit jealous of him, still I have an article coming up showing that the pessimism and human sympathy between father and son allow Daniel and his own son to share a morbid fascination for the dramas of the past, they share a common belief that the errors of the past are handed down from generation to generation, that we are not born innocent and stain-free, that the curse of error is imprinted in every one of us, born guilty, that's what we are truly Esther, I can't agree with such a thing, it would mean the abolition of all joy in life, I am an earthly creature too fond of life to subscribe to such a disconsolate doctrine, still with my sweet, my beloved Suzanne gone the old joie de vivre seems to have abandoned me, you know I see her on the tennis court from time to time, Daniel says it's just a mirage of course, it's Charly, Caroline's chauffeur, she hounds me everywhere, offering her services, look how alone you are without your wife to drive you around, perhaps I can be of use to you she says, Caroline, indeed yes Caroline had no complaints whatsoever, and she comes on every bit as enticing as she must have been to poor Caroline, must be the vanity of an old man anxious to please and feel on par with young people, she can be dangerously fascinating as a matter of fact, and I think to myself what have I got to lose without the love of my life beside me, everything else bores me, what I read, what I write, what I translate, everything without Suzanne, she was my observation post, nothing reaches me anymore without her, her amused and penetrating stare, I see things through her eyes or not at all, she was celebration itself and without her nothing amuses me as it used to, beware of Charly, my friend, don't trust her said Mère, remember how she drove Caroline mad with her drugs, do look out for yourself my friend, for that way the trap of madness may well close on you, oh my dear how can I protect you from that woman, oh perhaps she's not quite the monster they make her out to be said Adrien, the young woman's attractive in her own way, hard to pin down perhaps but she might be a pleasant change, oh no don't start spending time with her Mère said, now do promise me you won't, then she saw him get up to leave, still handsome in his blue blazer and white pants, oh how she wished she could get him to stay just a bit longer, I'm dining with Isaac tonight he told her, more than ninety years old and still making plans, such a man, if only it weren't so foggy, then we could go off to the Island No One Owns, Isaac says from the towers he's built onto the house you can see not only the ocean but infinity, oh better for me to stay away then, I'm not in the mood to see anything limitless right now, I'd lose myself completely, better for me to stay on terra firma even though I do miss my dear wife so, the companion of a lifetime, can it really be that we've been together so long, dear sweet wife he repeated, through the window of the bar and the metal grille in the shape of a bird Petites Cendres saw Louisa, a young black prostitute, whistling a song through her teeth, her tulle hat was almost a green umbrella held close over her head, hopping from foot to foot she seemed to be expecting a client at sunset over the turquoise and green water just at the end of the street, hey you got a few grams for me Petites Cendres asked her, Timo always had some on him and I bet you do too, but Louisa said she'd seen his old man sawing away on the old violin over on Esmeralda and when he saw Louisa he said beat it, I don't want your filthy money, that's no kind of father for you she said from under the wavy green hat, it's really a shame, really it is to see him wearing that scratchy old tweed suit, now Louisa's parents were living well and Louisa had a lot of customers, so they were all going to get rich and live in the Bahamas, yes we are, what you've got to do she said, is make it out before you wind up rotting in prison like all those pimps, what the hell's happened to that Timo of yours anyway, eh she asked Petites Cendres, they put him up against a wall and shot him quietly, well almost quietly, one revolver shot that echoes round the countryside for just a moment, oh he's fine came the answer, he's in Mexico you know and he doesn't want for a thing, no, no way, no way he's squirming for a fix, nasty little habit, nope he gets his half-gram of coke a day, maybe four joints, meth, really, even his fifty-milligram spoonful of heroin, he told me it's perfectly legal, hey it's manna from heaven, yeah well he's still going to wind up against the wall with a revolver to his head Louisa said, least he hasn't run into those killers wearing hoods, let's face it we all know a whole bunch of us are going to buy it in the end, look you'd better get out of here, find somewhere else Petites Cendres said, Yinn and Jason don't want you coming into the bar, oh yeah well they don't own the sidewalk and that's mine she shot back at him, I can do whatever I want out here, c'mon ain'tcha got just a small hit for me Petites Cendres asked her again, and she shook with laughter under the hat which flapped its green wings, nah not a thing Petites Cendres, you can't pay and I don't give credit, what you gonna use for money huh, then Petites Cendres heard a voice calling Louisa, hey Louisa c'mon over here, I wanna talk to you, hey, and there under the street lamp leaned the familiar silhouette of Herman, come on over here Louisa, I don't want anyone listening in, and with one bound svelte Louisa ran over to him as he spun slowly round the lamppost the way Yinn so often did when she was displeased or annoyed, or so it seemed to Petites Cendres, rotating with one hand gripping the base till he got dizzy, so what's up Herman Louisa demanded, your brother Marcus, that's who I want, he needs to give me some of that pain medication, I'm dancing tomorrow night and I don't want it to show, he's a nurse so it should be easy, nope, uh-uh was her reply, my brother's already got a record, once more and he goes to jail, tell me, tell me where I can find him Herman said, he was standing next to her now and whispering in her ear, he still had all his fringes dripping off him, the outfit he wore for the second show Petites Cendres had seen moments ago, the one where he sat on the papier-mâché horse, I hurt my leg, a few more days and I'll be right as rain, I just want to get rid of this stabbing sensation so I can go on dancing at night, c'mon where is Marcus, it's really urgent I talk to him Louisa, liar she said, it's malaria and you know it, you're lying Herman, no honest I fell over the set onstage he protested, it's that stuff you dissolve in bottled water, all I have to do is take some before I go on and I can pull it off fine, but Yinn mustn't find out, no way, it's just between Marcus and me, hey it wouldn't be the first time we've made a deal, yeah well you and your deals are going to land him in jail, he's the one who'll get caught taking them without a doctor's order, not you Herman, hell no not a rich white man, even if your old man the lawyer helps us, no, uh-unh it'll be my brother Marcus who gets sent away for a second offence, not you, but Louisa was really dug in now, aw come on it's not like I'm asking you for some sort of illegal dope or anything said Herman, just an anesthetic to ease the pain, that's all, Marcus can do that for me can't he, where is he anyway, why isn't he at the hospital, what's he got himself into now, look all I know is it's bubbly and it really works, that's all he ploughed on, he's the only one that can get it for me, where is he, where's Marcus anyway, by now he was distraught and ragged-looking, curly hair standing up, Petites Cendres wondered what mysterious tragedy Herman would dig himself into this time, yesterday it was his wild ride through town on his multicoloured tricycle, now this quest for a cure, but who or what was it really for, he was always rushing headlong into disaster one way or another, had he been seeing Fabian again, nobody could absolutely prove it but he was always alone or with his cabaret friends, Geisha, Cobra, Robbie, Vanquished Heart, and he stayed inside the bar till dawn, when his noisy boot-heels clacked across the floor, hey that was quite some night, wasn't it he said energetically, eh girls, so cool, and Robbie you really made us laugh, one more to your health ladies and then I'll hit the road and get some sleep, you could see him side by side with Yinn, a little more easygoing with his friend, declaring once more boy our queen Yinn sure knows how to have them eating out of her hand, either that or just plain blow them away with something new, way to go Yinn, brilliant, but I mean these people that we entertain, who come to see us dance every night and get away from all their worries, do they ever give a thought to the guys that get themselves shot, hanged, or whatever, say in Iran every day, the ones who model themselves on us, our replicas but really just men like you and me, yeah hanged and shot every day, do they even think about that, otherwise Herman at times would keep all this to himself and share it later with Yinn or Robbie, maybe get their throats cut out behind some dump of a place, yeah men like you and me Yinn, and those countries are never gonna get past it, they simply follow up some war against human dignity with another one just like it to take away whatever freedom they've got, the first human right is to have a totally ambivalent sexual identity, and Yinn even listened to him on those languid late nights by the bar, her black bra showing through her pink transparent bodice, all the feminine attributes about to be taken off and replaced by a pair of jeans, a brilliant gold-patterned belt at his waist, white-flowered shirt knotted at the navel, you're right it was a good night he'd say, and tomorrow please try not to get hung up in the scenery okay Herman, those boots of yours made such a racket I thought the whole set would come down, do you really have to dance in those knee-high things, why do you hide yourself like that eh Herman, then again Yinn might say nothing at all so Herman wouldn't take offence, you never knew what was going on in his head, he measured his words carefully, you can't really dance free when your body's covered up that way Herman, that's how come you scared yourself taking a tumble, for Petites Cendres realized Yinn knew there was no way he could keep tabs without Herman turning nasty, no, no way at all without him snorting like a horse, and Petites Cendres knew there was no chance of safeguarding any of them while they were still growing pell-mell like wild grass in every direction, Marcus, Herman, no two of them alike, and who could I try to reassure or pro-tect now, not Adrien in his grief, not Julio in his exile, not even her own children and grandchildren, what really hap-pens when a tree is uprooted under the full force of a cyclone or a tornado and propelled from its earthly home, the spirit alone remaining, yet in Daniel and Mélanie's garden the Texas olive tree or amaryllis or silver palm, the prince of palms, so very few of them remaining, perhaps fifty species, no more than that, rose higher and higher toward the sky like giant hands with fingers spread wide, their roots at home wherever they found themselves, whether sand or salt air, as luxuriant as they were fertile, life, this is how it is shaped and articulated thought Mère, her mind's eye seeing Mélanie and Daniel there once again, Samuel diving into the pool on a summer night, the house so bright and lively night or day, how much time had simply dissolved for her to see Samuel become a father with a child on his shoulders saying Grandmother how will we get through all this water, how Grandmother, you be our beacon, how else will we guide our boat, and she answered, as if all this were real, yes I too am skeptical of all this, of marriage, Samuel, Samuel I've always thought we were so much alike you and I, did you finally learn how to write properly in school, you were so unruly and you brought home exercise books filled with mistakes, that's because I couldn't think about anything but dancing Samuel replied, that was my purpose in life Grandmother, not learning how to write but wrapping myself in the ecstasy of dance Grandmother, that's what you were all scolding me about, then your parents and I were very unfair to you said Mère, it was unfair of us to think you were being troublesome and distracting Samuel, and now it's too late to repair the damage we did, the apparition of Samuel with Rudolf on his shoulders dissipated and Mère was once more unable to hold on to someone she loved, she always met Caroline in the hallway of that same darkened station, Caroline, dressed all in white, was luminous in the half-dark and she made Mère choose one of the platforms, arrivals or departures, just follow me, it may have seemed simple but it was not thought Mère, who found it difficult to walk and thus to follow Caroline to one or the other, limited in this way she kept on saying Caroline, Caroline it takes me a little while, you seem to be in such good shape, would you at least guide me so we can both visit those unknown continents, I know this will be long, even with my reading and music to accompany me, here's where we go in to get the night train said Caroline, but Mère had already lost sight of her, it would have been better thought Petites Cendres, for Timo to be nothing more than a ghost, not that pile of remains scattered on a beach by the side of some village road in Mexico, the sailor who found him had no way of identifying the corpse of a young man lying in the wrecked hull washed up by the wharf, who was he and what brought him to this, Timo, was it Timo, if it was him the patrol boat must have collided with his before the sharks took him apart, and now the twenty-two-foot boat was washed up here against the dock and the remains looked deteriorated, nibbled, sure of course it would have been better for Timo to be nothing more than a ghost floating out over the water, no longer having to contemplate himself as one of the living, Herman wanted something from Marcus but what was it and why was he being so insistent, Marcus's sister Louisa didn't seem to want to give in to Herman at all, how long would it take for Yinn to step in wondered Petites Cendres, when was he going to step in for Herman under the candelabra fitted with electric bulbs over the stairway leading to the cabaret, Yinn had stopped dancing now anyway so was he about due to come down drunk from the night's sensual heat with Jason and head toward his sewing room on the ground floor of the house, or he was still fast asleep while on the huge TV screen, just like Geisha's and Robbie's, a film or video was playing to no one but itself in the tropical shade cooled by the breeze from a fan, bet you could also hear the rough sighs of Yinn's very, very old dog on the bed or in his laundry basket near the TV, bet Jason has forgotten to turn off the computer too unless of course he was planning to get back to it sometime during the night, maybe add a few decorative touches to the poster of Yinn welcoming the hordes of bikers in the streets to their cabaret, gotta make them feel welcome said Jason, they really like us and, don't forget Yinn, they're not as rough as they seem when they're straddling their bikes, lots of them are professional people, well off, we need to respect them, so Jason touched up the drawing of Yinn that seemed just a shade too erotic for him, they're bikers not strippers but you're right Yinn, the bike is what gets eroticized, like in the poster, then possibly they might even have got up early, at least Jason and Yinn thought Petites Cendres, and were sitting side by side on the sofa watching the film unwind on the computer screen as it showed the drawing and lettering for the poster, would they still be side by side, hands and faces brushing one another in the excitement of their shared labour, so close to one another while Petites Cendres was alone under the electrified candelabra in the coarse light of early morning, or while preparing to welcome the bikers would Yinn's fear of crowds and groups be dispelled by Jason's clear-eyed gaze, white smile, candour, and irrepressible faith in humanity, but there in the midst of the crowd Yinn, seeing a fanatic's picket sign that read GOD HATES YOU ALL, with an instinct for anything hostile or threatening to his brood but still saying nothing to Jason, merely commented ah that'll do the trick, it's wonderful, so expressive, and Petites Cendres remembered his visits to Robbie, and in one room under a steep slope of the roof called the cornice room, you could get in via the corridor, Robbie endlessly replayed his videos of Fatalité for Petites Cendres and all his friends, the TV spitting out noise day and night, in a dishevelled T-shirt and his huge hairdo squashed under a wig like Geisha from his morning run down by the sea and his yoga on the beach, Cobra rarely came out of his room in the daytime, so rarely in fact that Yinn thought that his tenants only came out to dump their bad tempers on him, for daylight constraints fell apart after exuberant evenings in the cabaret, so it was the TV in Robbie's room that blared Fatalité's life day and night as though she herself were there in the room despite having had her own apartment just steps from the nightclub, though in reality she had died alone and in the deepest silence, not even Robbie being there because at that very moment he was up onstage singing, yet here she seemed to have moved into Robbie's tiny room which had no other furniture but the TV and the sofa Robbie was asleep on while Fatalité took up all the space in her repeated passes before the camera, big in real life but even bigger now on the screen, moving her bulk endlessly whereas Robbie gave the appearance of shrinking right down to his hair, and if he could he would have slept all day long in his rumpled T-shirt, Fatalité singing and dancing while the eternal Fatalité wrapped Robbie in sleep even while his eyelids flickered, you girls are crazy to sleep all day Yinn would say, no really I mean on a beautiful day like this it's crazy, right, oh why complain, at least it's quiet in the house and I can sew in peace, except of course Yinn's mother, up and at it and demanding, all the while rubbing it in about his marriage to Jason at least once a day, and although he didn't like it Yinn always went easy on her, and on the landing halfway up the stairs that led to the club he'd placed a stool so she could rest on her way back to the sewing room, from there she could observe Yinn at work and make the occasional comment if she wanted, for she had taught him everything he knew at a very early age he reflected, and that made her happy most of all she used to tell Yinn, now Yinn had all four machines at his disposal instead of the one he used to have, boy you sew fast, thirteen outfits in a week, watch out for your fingers son, she wished she could sit closer to him but knew he wouldn't put up with it when he was this busy, and although he thought of her as bossy suddenly she was no longer just quietly seated on the landing, even grudgingly wearing her glasses to see better, well son your design classes will always come in handy even though you hated them at the time, being in charge of costumes in the theatre will help you out too she said, perched

on her stool, but independence son, now there's a true gift
for a life like yours, why on earth are people so young fast
asleep up there, at their age it's not normal don't you think,
that Robbie for instance, first he's gone and then he's back a
month later with that Daddy of his, then he just sleeps all day
with the TV blaring away the whole time, and that Cobra, I
just went to the trouble of taking him his morning coffee and
there he is coiled up like a snake in the covers and grumbling
to be left alone so he can sleep some more, right into the
evening, these insomniac queens of yours are really quite a
nuisance son she complained, now you, you're so different,
how can you stand them, ah that's because I've got Jason the
best man of them all Yinn replied from amongst a pile of
fabrics and Shanghai silks, Robbie's getting a mandarin collar
tonight, oh and thanks for finding that in your catalogues
Mama, these Chinese silks are going to look so sexy on him,
what about me, they'd look good on me too she said, personally Mama Yinn replied, I like the printed cottons on you
better, really that's what looks best on you, next came the
fittings when the boys would parade into the sewing room
and Yinn's mother would retreat to her room, being as modest
as she was generous thought Yinn as he watched her comfortably climb the steps to get away from the scenes of boys getting undressed, stuffing blue balls into their bras so Yinn
could measure them properly with his tape, he did this with
affection but also with a certain distance, as when he tested
the fleshiness of the Martiniquan Robert's buttocks remembered Petites Cendres, wasn't that always the way with an
artist and his model, trying not to tease or seize or invite anything other than his attention, telling him to stand up straight
while nimble fingers traced lines over a body he already knew
so well, appetizing contours and all, what wouldn't Petites
Cendres give to fulfill his dream of having one of those bodies
to be measured, say Cobra's or Robbie's or Vanquished Heart's,
the best he could do was scrape by with his favourite

comfort-dresses that had holes in them, no Robbie or Cobra or Vanquished Heart here, Vanquished Heart now turned into Triumphant Heart ever since he'd fallen in love, but Petites Cendres was just the loving voyeur of an unrequited love, lover but no lover, living vicarious passion through Robbie and the others, not that the role was a totally unhappy one, in fact he even found a sort of everyday poetry in it, if only he weren't so in need, cruel need he thought, and if only it didn't eat at him even more than his hunger for Yinn, well my friends Yinn said, everyone's set for tonight, don't forget a thing, and Petites Cendres through Robbie's dark eyes saw Yinn measuring at the sewing machine beneath the hanging mannequin in a silky velvet dress, arms raised angelically and hovering over him, that whole costume room full of his wonderful creations, all his own, Yinn's workplace inhabited by as many dissimilar projects as his contradictory states of mind thought Petites Cendres, not just the red paper roses, Chinese roses, Japanese prints on the walls but a wood sculpture of a giraffe under a rubber palm tree by the window, potted plants, and of course those sewing machines beneath the mannequin dressed for a multitude of cultures, layers upon layers of silks and fabrics, and in one of the Japanese lithographs two men, pilgrims walking alone in the desert, his own solitary march through life thought Petites Cendres, surrounded by them all yet still alone, so near yet so far from a world that was closed to him, every bit as long and thirsting as those pilgrims', all their desires suppressed and left behind like their thirst, just detached and prayerful, suspended in a void made of sand and stone, perhaps this was his lesson for the long, thirsting march through withdrawal that Petites Cendres needed to learn from Yinn, detachment, detachment devoid of all hope, arid or not it could benefit him, as if Yinn had been pushing Petites Cendres just a little further every day, pushing back the frontiers where life ends. Mère heard music in the garden, it was a string quartet but one she didn't recognize, then, leaning toward the window, she realized Mélanie had invited the musicians especially for her, music students and friends of Mai, so serene yet exultant as she heard them in the night like this, what a pity she couldn't pin down the name of the composer whose music so soothed her nerves, the singing violins and cellos, now where were we again, was it summer and were we sheltered by the red roof of frangipani flowers or protected from the February cold by the little cottage, the smells and perfumes seemed to declare it summer, but whose music could this be, when was this, what vague season are we in, oh the musicians fled under a hailstorm, and Mère was left wondering where Augustino and Samuel could be under this onslaught, where yes where, in days gone by she'd shelter them beneath her raincoat the way Mai was doing now with her cats, they must be fending for themselves by now, Mère no longer saw them, now Mama it was just a bad dream Mélanie was saying as she took her mother's hands in her own, the doctor's coming to see you tomorrow, would you like to come up to the house for dinner, Daniel and Mai are back, they were held up by all that fog on the road, Mai had somewhere to go, she always had somewhere to go in the evenings, but she promised to be back by midnight, lost in the fog Mère said, they're all lost in the fog, and there under the frost-covered trees mother and daughter spoke tenderly, Mère reminding Mélanie again and again that she was quite capable of being alone for a few hours yet, but where was Mai, she's got a party Mama Mélanie replied, you can't keep a fifteen-year-old girl at home for long you know Mama, I heard that quartet out in the garden, yes Mama it was especially for you, I thought you'd enjoy hearing them Mélanie said, still enfolding her mother's hands in her own, Mère was falling asleep now and the sound of the quartet rose again from the garden, the song of the violins and cellos, exultant yet serene though she couldn't quite recall the composer's name, for it blended with the blues group out in the street a

way off, when somewhere the shutters were closed in a sign
of mourning, the call of a trumpet was sure to be heard, what
else was it about this that reminded her of Justin and brought
her comfort, Justin with his hat and his white suit among the
players, all black. There they were, Petites Cendres saw them
under the street lamp and in the first red glints of day, Yinn
reining in Herman's rage with a grip on the dangling fringes,
his costume from the second show of the night, now you
listen to me Yinn was saying, I couldn't sleep for worrying
about you, that's enough of your games and your little dramas
Herman, you didn't stumble into the set by accident, a dancer
like you has better control than that, the whole thing was fake,
you were just trying to throw me off weren't you Herman, that
thing on your leg, that sort of black flower goes all the way
to the bone doesn't it, you've got one hell of a tumour and
it's getting operated on this week, Jamie the owner's got every
thing arranged, and me, artistic director, I'm responsible for
the lot of you aren't I, and you're the most careless of all of
us, yes you, why'd you lie to us for so long when you knew
for certain I'd find out sooner or later, hey I'm the one that
gets to see you naked every night in the dressing room and
I've been watching you for a while now, Herman you're not
getting away this time, listen to me, Herman, unable to loosen
Yinn's hold on him, shook himself violently, leave me alone
Yinn, just leave me alone, go ahead, go on with your dancing
each night, so what if this black flower thing spreads its poison all over this body you're looking at, living, alive and furious, it'll be over quicker that's all, that's all I want, to dance
and sing, it never occurred to you this just might be incurable
did it, whichever it is dancing and singing is what I've got to
do, don't you get it, yeah well I had a long talk with your
surgeon and he says an operation and a month of rest and
you'll be back on top again Herman shot back Yinn as he
gradually loosened his hold, you can dance, sure you can,
pretty soon, but first you've got to listen to Jamie and me, as

he watched this almost virulent scene between two friends Petites Cendres wondered if Herman was going to lose it again, his hand still holding on, Yinn said, the blue of his eyes darkening, listen to what I'm saying, stop lying to the bunch of us, that's it, I've had enough, who the hell do you think is going to condemn a man who's down, me maybe, is that what you think, Yinn was beside himself with Herman's lying, and seeing these two passionate but different beings confront one another, Petites Cendres felt himself grow even more desolate, who on the face of the earth would defend him with such passion, Petites Cendres who silently nurtured inside himself something far worse than a little black blossom of cancer on his leg, no, something greater, an entire undergrowth of infection that had already erupted to the surface in the form of spots and meandering marks on the skin, he still relished his magnificent nails and bushy hair along with his unshakable longing to seduce, his desire to be beloved by Yinn, if only a fleeting stroke of his hair or a hasty meaningless kiss, obsessed with saving Herman, Yinn had left Jason lying in their bed or maybe touching up the poster on the computer, and of course the ancient dying dog, there he was in the street in his cargo-pocket Bermudas, hastily pulled on and not quite covering his red underpants, waistband untied and fly wide open, tussling with Herman, both equally intractable, stubborn as that pony Neuvième Beauté against the jockey's bridle out on the track thought Petites Cendres, all the way up to the second Herman finally said well okay, if I got no choice I'll listen to you and Jamie, now don't you think it's time we got our horse out into the street, the sidewalk I mean, and don't you think we've done enough parading what with Fatalité's funeral, orchids tossed into the sea and all, enough is enough right, and I know just how you're going to dress me and the others up when the bikers roll in, a straight-up Versace imitation with a nice little round opening in the back to show off our butts, yeah yeah I know you lean just as much to Versace as

Confucius, that's just the way you're made Yinn, but would
you please make me a cape, a really long cape, a lace one,
come on think of something, you know just what I want, and
I'll head way across town on my tricycle, bobbing and weaving through the bikers and their machines on both sides of
the street, just us and them, traffic grinding to a halt, and those
boots of yours, you know the red leather ones laced right up
to the knee, it'll be my last outing before I go under the knife,
forever taking chances aren't you said Yinn, you can't do
anything like other people can you, the whole collection's put
together and you're all going to knock 'em dead, black pants,
and for you a black hat with a black plume, great, great said
Herman, but I want the cape too and I want it so it'll drag
along behind me in the street, how's a cape going to make it
any better Herman, aren't you proud just the way you are,
without some over-the-top cape, I mean you're meeting bikers now, I was thinking more of the seriousness of black, that
always impresses, grabs 'em said Yinn, and even as he spoke
he could see them all forming a train, Geisha, Cobra, Robbie,
Vanquished Heart, right down the street past the bikers leaning on their black choppers, friendly and graceful in their
imitation leather, all the way to the shore, and he'd be in the
middle wearing a red dress, his black hair falling down over
his shoulders, they'd be photographed, applauded like some
fashion parade, then Herman's voice snapped him back to
earth, Pasolini didn't need a cape to meet his end he was saying, and Versace either, Herman seemed to be talking to no
one except himself, all of them, your Pasolinis, your Versaces
couldn't provoke those bikers like I will, see they're never
ever going to forget me speeding across town trailing my lacy
cape on my trike Herman went on, it wasn't going to turn out
the way Yinn planned at all, the slow, languid walk of the
girls across town in their high heels and black outfits, the
exquisite processional, the photos, the overwhelming deafening applause, everything under perfect control under Maestro

Yinn's baton, except of course for the sudden eruption of Herman's stuttering multicoloured motor-tricycle and a cry, it was Herman yelling someone stuck a knife in my coat, who eh who, c'mon and step forward, someone had thrown a small penknife into the lacework of his cape, sort of a Boy Scout knife, the crowd hushed, standing untouched beneath his cape Herman just went on yelling come on out here, come on and face me, I'm ready for you, not even a scratch, you aren't getting me that way he defied them, standing tall and proud on the back step of his trike, see Jason, Yinn, what did I tell you, good folks, right, yeah well there's no such thing, just goose them with a something a little fanciful and they wanna kill ya, but you didn't believe it, no you can't do anything with 'em, Yinn and Jason managed to put a lid on his rage right there on his tricycle and Yinn really felt desperate that Herman's brashness and rebellious impudence would bring someone's wrath down on him though they had to admire his incorruptibility, Yinn was even more worried at the thought of Herman after a few days' recuperation from his operation, at the bar and looking pale as he said I only wanted to greet you my friend, and Yinn yelled back yeah well here you are standing around when they just pulled a tumour the size of a tennis ball out of your leg, go home and get to bed Herman or I'll take you there myself, Yinn took out his red cellphone and warned everyone Herman's on the loose, stop him, he's either in a bar or out on the streets, and who'd have thought tossing a silly penknife during the procession would have cut him to the heart more than surgery on his leg, as if some kid's knife had opened my veins, that's how he'd put it to Yinn, just saying it seemed to weaken him, but he was cured, nothing I can do Yinn, you and Jamie seem to want me alive at all costs, well okay then here I am, so when do I dance, tonight, tomorrow, come on Yinn, I can't wait much longer, not tonight and not tomorrow said Yinn, now get back to bed and don't let me catch you here for a few more weeks, always headstrong eh, look I'm going to tell you just one more time get back to bed and you'd better listen, if not to me at least listen to your surgeon, so cowed by Yinn Herman thought twice before coming in, then in controlled rebellious mode he watched Yinn explaining to a musician how he would wear the black briefs he'd made for the boy in an upcoming show, see it's elastic but electrifying, you'll feel great in it Yinn said, examining the stretch of the shorts with expert fingers, seeing Yinn still busy Herman couldn't admit he was afraid this musician would replace him onstage tonight or tomorrow, who else would wear this thing and why else had it been made to order, he thought he should also get Yinn to fix his cape, the one some evildoer had made a hole in, along with the hole in his heart. The fog was still thick on Atlantic Boulevard thought Mai skating along the shoreline to Tammy's place, well that's where she'd told her parents she was going, for an evening at Tammy's, she skated in-line through the fog this way with a flashlight for a long time, firm legs moving in rhythm, regular, pendulum-like, even melodious as though she were dancing to music, she had a head-band over her swept-back hair, she'd need to be skating for a very long time if she wanted to forget her father and the day they'd spent together in the car, not quite knowing what he expected she hadn't said much, did he want her to confide in him, talk to him, or did he just want to be heard, to have her listen for what he wasn't saying about Suzanne's trip to Switzerland perhaps and her assisted suicide, ah no not that, he wasn't going to talk about that, he wasn't going to affront his daughter with such talk, hard and raw, out-there with no subtlety at all, and none of this talk that Suzanne herself thought of it as a peaceful departure, peaceful for all of them, really the best thing, we all of us have a right to some dignity, our private silence was how she put it, or maybe he'd decided she was going to a private school, something she'd never ever go along with, then walking in a park and reaching out to a group of does and fauns, suddenly revealed then hidden again in a wet cloak of fog, like her father's words behind her own breath, are you going out without kissing your grandmother Mélanie had said, when I get back, I'll kiss her when I come back Mama, she'll be asleep by then and I'll just wake her up if I go now, besides I'm already late for Tammy's, Tammy was today's new lie, every day there had to be a fresh one, Daniel and Mélanie were friends of her parents, writers themselves, though they didn't get together much, all she had to do was get in before midnight, besides did it really matter all that much to them where she was, Mai could handle herself just fine and she knew it, whatever she was up to, hey what on earth was he doing there just now, Manuel, dancing barefoot on the fenced beach with some other boys and girls having their very own banquet, Manuel, no longer a boy but a man, co-owner with his father of a deluxe apartment block with patios and terraces overlooking the ocean, all of them drinking alcohol out of cardboard cups, taking drugs no one was supposed to know about, Manuel had posted the beach as private, everyone warned off, including this unattractive kid in his khaki outfit and head shaved to a youthful redness plus his vulgar mud-coloured boots, so Manuel asked his father can I let him onto our beach, yes you have to make allowances for someone who's returned from hell came the answer, come on kid and share our meal, have a game with us, so it's true you were there fourteen months, so how come he's back here all suddenly, khaki vest and crude boots crunching the sand, fourteen months he said, fourteen months, this fish I caught out in the boat yesterday with Manuel, we've smoked it on the grill, come, eat Manuel's father said, and the unappetizing kid red with shaving rash all the way to his temples, same size as me without my skates on thought Mai, same size as me, had a sort of mad attack, yeah I was there right, fourteen months, now here I am, just got here he said, you got chili and spices, I gotta have chili, and he went over to the well-stocked table and stuffed himself with bread and fish and chili sauce non-stop, got it all over his face and chin and khaki vest, saying more, more fire on my lips and on my neck, 'cause fire's what I know up close and personal, Manuel, repelled, just stared at him, okay gotta be tolerant said his father, just think of what he lived through over there, Mesopotamia, I was on the banks of this river in Mesopotamia the boy went on, then tomorrow they send me somewheres else, conflicts, battles, that's what you gotta have, one after another, no being out of work for me, hell after hell I'll be there ready to dive into the flames, always got a job, not you rich kids though, not your place, it's mine, c'mon let's have something to drink, boy am I thirsty, really I'm dyin' of thirst, the sauce had darkened the red in his face like some sort of mask, nice cities there all of 'em, just knocked 'em down one after another the boy bragged, bang, bang, then nothing but ruins and zoo animals staring at us looking lost, wondering are we gonna wipe 'em out or just let 'em die alone in them bloody streets, sure enough fourteen whole months there, no way you'll ever be there, just not for you is all, my fate not your fate, the brass said I needed a rest, yeah rest that's what they said, so here I am, hey gimme something to drink, an ice-cold beer, whoa chili's eaten right through my throat, yep so let's have that beer, hey two three iced beers, hell I'm thirsty, you got any idea how much I dreamed of these, hey you could drown in this stuff when your bed's on fire, when you're so afraid you . . . he stifled the rest with a fierce swig then went on stuffing himself, so Manuel's father just said again got to be patient with him kids, go easy, you can't even imagine what he went through over there, you'll never know, so they all just went on dancing and laughing on the beach, Tammy was there with them, no telling what her writer parents would have thought about her smoking up, getting drunk and hostile like this, as Mai just stared at the kid, and at the end of the night when it was all over this passing stranger from who-knows-where would just wander off drunk and so very alone through streets he'd never even seen before, he said he'd come to see a friend, a vet like him but didn't seem to have found him, dead maybe, Mai had to tell herself they'll forget about him the second he's gone, none of the kids left dancing on the beach will give a thought to that chili-slathered face of his nor even want to, nope they'd forget about the man-boy and his fourteen months in hell real quick, was it just delirium or hallucination when he said to Mai I'm just an asshole, a sewer, that's all I am, that's how you toss your life away, ambushes everywhere, women shut away though you could feel their hate so far off, maybe it was just suspicion 'cause of all the killings and kidnaps and torture, and everywhere women behind closed doors, you'd think they were blind behind those veils, staring, burning a hole right through me, marching in single file through sewers and rotting corpses, a human sewer, you got no idea you rich girls, hey from our camp named after some city I could see it all, high walls that didn't protect us at all anyway, the Triangle of Death, walls high enough to cut us off from the horizon though, I was eighteen and heading out fully equipped, helmet and all, with the roar of the helicopters, yeah a human sewer that's me, hey ice-cold beer, I wanna cold beer, so back from patrol I look at this heavy-duty watch I got and still can't see right and they're saying advance, advance, hey kid watcha waitin' for, then I hear this country music coming from the base or the sky, I can't tell which 'cause we're gettin' bombed out on the road they call Temple, anyway that's when I hear them yell come on kid, forward, hey you got any T-bones, back there in the mess tent we had to swallow everything down quick, real quick, hey iced beer said the kid so uninviting and unlikeable to Mai, good thing he's standing right there in front of her, not in some flag-draped coffin or something, hungry and so thirsty, non-existent to anyone but Mai, thirsty and all but invisible, might as well be one of the dead they carry through the streets, almost was anyway thought Mai, totally anonymous and forgotten, her pacifist parents would surely understand how this child-warrior moved her, picking out his shapeless, incoherent yell of distress through the hiccups and jumbled words, an ordinary boy they'd reduced to the state of barbarism, the chili sauce suddenly looking more like blood on that wretched face, snatching up the dripping plates to lick, that's how they did it back there, fast in then fast out again, so fast he almost threw up all over his rifle once, as he ordered up more beer from Manuel's father Mai remembered she hadn't gone in to kiss her grandmother as Mélanie told her, what a pain, she'd probably have woken the old lady from her nap anyhow, these light snoozes got longer every day, so at least this way Mai wouldn't be disturbing her, Tammy's parents had dinner outside every evening and when they went back inside they'd probably ask Mai's parents where their daughter was, is she with yours, then of course her own parents would start wondering about Mai too, where was she, isn't she with Tammy, but what bothered her more was not taking time to kiss and hug her grandmother, more even than the sort of tenderness and reaching out she felt for this reject kid who'd never make it as anything but a soldier, a life of weapons, crimes and murders he could never take back from the recesses of his juvenile half-formed consciousness thought Mai, could her parents even conceive properly of a life moulded purposely for the killing of others, this one, this life that had turned eighteen in the Triangle of Death, as he liked to boast though no one was listening to him, dancing to the throbbing of seismic music and having fun on the beach was all they were about, country as well, and the boy said to Mai so your brothers, where they at, Vincent was the one that popped into her mind, up there in his neat, tidy university and its lush green campus, Vincent on his way to becoming a doctor, Vincent studying and trying to tame his irregular breath and heartbeat, Vincent destined to a short life they'd always said, what if he'd been like this chili-smeared kid and destined to war instead, no way he'd ever make it thought Mai, one safely shielded by his class, the other not, no way of knowing, maybe inexplicably redeemed somehow, lying with arms crossed on a pile of dead comrades under the scorching desert sun, say tomorrow, would they find him yelling I want to live, I wanna live, I wanna live, then right there the air-conditioned bus bringing him back to her after all, not in some flag-draped coffin like the others, oh Jesus Christ have mercy I still got my legs and arms, I can make it out of here, then poking his unharmed flesh he'd yell oh Jesus I'm here, still here, thus ran Mai's thoughts as she looked at the boy, he'd be saved too, saved like Vincent, she wasn't one for prayers but she offered one up for him, please let the boy with chili and worse stuff on his face be spared too, T-bones son said Manuel's father clapping him on the shoulder, eat up, it's for young soldiers just like you I opened up my discotheques I call Shelter in bombed-out cities, everywhere so you guys can have some fun, so you kids can forget for a short while, dancing and all the fun of my illicit operations just for you, really, hey we had this same country music over there, I remember now said the boy, my latest one is in Beirut Manuel's dad went on, oh yeah DJs and rock 'n' roll, gotta know how to unwind sometimes, hats off to you guys, besides war business pays good all over, everybody knows but no one wants to say it, discotheques, nightclubs in Lebanon so you can get away from it all, sure he said, tapping the kid on the shoulder, then out of his jeans pocket came the handkerchief to wipe chili off the boy's forehead, hey come on and dance and have some fun, you know they're gonna call you back for another tour in hell so get it out of your system, get with us, yeah we did have this country music the boy said, I thought it was coming from the base, hey how do you get to the airport from here, have they bombed it yet, 'cause I gotta go, yeah I gotta he told Manuel's dad, them discotheques and nightclubs in

Lebanon, you ought to be ashamed of making money off our tears, off the arms and legs we . . . oh boy the poor kid's wigging out said Manuel's father, come and help me carry him so he can sit and rest in the lounge chair over there by the water, c'mon son that's it, he had to be looked after, saved thought Mai as she walked barefoot along the beach, skates in hand, we've got to save this kid, save him so he doesn't go to sleep tomorrow with his arms folded on top of those dead buddies of his and can't cry out Jesus I'm alive as he stares up at the torrid desert sun, Christ I'm alive, this blood on my face, it's okay, I'm alive. He saw Herman headed his way, this time in a wheelchair, and seeing him come down the street like this Yinn felt a twinge, damn this was bad, this, nah it's only for a few days Herman said, though he sounded furious, well at least you finally listened to your doctor said Yinn, now you're making sense, and he put his hand on Herman's bristly head, but he shook it off and yelled I don't want your pity Yinn, I'm not paralyzed in this goddamn chair, no no no no no, just resting my leg from the operation, then watch me dance and after that back on the tricycle and out into the street, cape and all, you did fix it didn't you Yinn, so why the hell aren't you inside sewing instead of fooling around out here with me, oh I was just waiting to buy you a drink Yinn replied, I'm not leaving you alone, damned if you have to wheel me into the bar in this thing Herman fumed, he'd even put on makeup and was all set to step onstage then and there, but the purplish colour along with the green eye-shadow was also meant to give him some camouflage, then enraged, he started wrestling with his wheels, from home to the street, then from the street to the bar where Yinn was in her low-cut dress waiting for the late show, no way, just till you can walk okay she repeated, I'm not leaving you alone Herman, you're too reckless, you're not going to get better that way she said as they entered the bar, and we all want what's best for you, Petites Cendres heard the charge of contained virility in Yinn's voice and saw the flash of renewed concern in his gaze, what's happening to us it seemed to say, Fatalité gone, that wound reopened again with a darkness and pain that made him want to weep though he had to hold that in for now, somehow his tall black wig and the dignity of his evening dress conspired to force a cool haughtiness he didn't feel at all, but the show must go on, as must his dancing and singing, not to miss a beat, not even to pick up Herman's wheelchair to take his attention off what absorbed him so much and coax a smile out from under that screen of makeup he was wearing, already the rush to the stairs to get into the show, greedy to see Yinn sing and dance as it said there under the bright yellow bulbs in the form of an arrow, but Petites Cendres didn't need it, this longing for retreat in Yinn's eyes, black curved lashes and delicate troubled features, what's happening to all our friends, first Fatalité, now Herman, sure he was laid up for only a few more days but what happens when one by one they're faced with some disaster or other, their days and their bodies suddenly ripped up Yinn thought as he looked at Herman, big strong Herman, who'd have thought they'd see him in a wheelchair, big, strong and incredibly vital not so long ago, and what happens when even the most attentive friend can't stop the threatened harm or just plain bad luck, uh-oh, revived by chugging a glass of vodka, Herman was up and out of his chair, standing on shaky legs, friends he said, a toast to getting stabbed in the back by life and let us never be afraid to take a chance on being happy, then finally Yinn saw the wan smile slide into Herman's tired lips, getting ready to wave goodbye to convalescence in a few short days though he already looked a little too worked up and unbridled despite his delicate condition, how about you sit down Yinn said, searching in vain for the face of My Captain in the smoke-filled bar, where's Captain Thomas, My Captain being a private name used only between the two of them, he's been out at sea on his boat with a bunch of tourists all day Robbie said, he's late because

he loves going night-diving alone after they're gone, right diving alone at night, sure said Yinn as he dialled the Captain on
his red cellphone, you don't just go diving alone at night in
the depths of the ocean he muttered, maybe he'd just like to
stay on the bottom, Christ he's as crazy as Herman, am I stuck
with a bunch of infants here, yep laughed Robbie, we're all
yours, just one big ragtag family, nutso, whatcha gonna do,
Yinn, putting his phone down on the bar, said right, not a
thing, what does he know about currents eh, he may be a
licensed captain, powerful currents in winter, sure, but it's
spring, okay time to drag the papier-mâché horse out into the
street said Herman, enough of the dockside processions,
orchids and roses on the water and all that, enough, enough's
enough said Herman, let's not overdo it eh Yinn, c'mon Mama
Samurai, life's for the living and to each his own, you know
Thomas is fine underwater, there's nothing anyone can teach
him, nothing said Robbie, Christ he's even got the sharks
tamed, Captain Thomas has nothing to learn from anyone and
you know it Yinn, Robbie called from the dance floor where
the tiny, pretty woman was dancing with him like a girl having
the time of her life, this was her night at the bar, every night
was, with applause for Robbie, letting him flirt with her during
intermission, this abstract yet so human love of his made her
feel bigger than any of them, a chaste love that made her
utterly radiant, all this time Yinn waited longer than he wanted
to for the scuffling of the Captain up the stairs and into their
cloud of smoke, right he'd show up just like that, stripped to
the waist, his white cap slanted over his brow and some
coloured fabric or other hanging down off it, just waiting to
be contemplated and admired in all his flamboyance like back
in the day, not long before, just a few years ago he'd been a
sexy international model you saw everywhere in the maga-
zines, travelled all round the world, got to know all kinds of
cultures, Yinn liked the fact that My Captain kept the same
insistence on elegance, that he received friends while lying in

his extravagant bed with champagne, surrounded by his collections of books and paintings, holding forth like a prince in his dressing gown, it annoyed Jason but delighted Yinn with its redolence of a life forever spent in dreams and fantasy, Jason seemed too down-to-earth with not enough openings to let the light shine in, just a little sprinkling of flashes in the night that he focused onstage from his little booth during a show or in rehearsals, where repetition corroded the enchantment of it all, then here was Yinn being distracted by the Next One, how on earth had Yinn been able to wrestle that dress, too dark by half, onto that body of his anyway, or maybe it was the Next One's lack of effort to hold himself in, perhaps it was the slumping shoulders that made him seem so awkward, you're some odd-looking girl you are said Yinn as he fixed the folds in the dress, you're gonna have to stand straighter than that, and for God's sake try to be a bit graceful, not like some college kid who's just had a bawling out, a real lady, I don't know how the Next One said, moving his body clumsily under that dress, honest I don't know how ladies do things, you've got a mother or a sister, haven't you Yinn replied, surely they've got some sort of beauty to inspire you, or do you just have nothing to go on at all, I can't believe it, I mean you're Chinese and that's what draws people to you, that difference, the shape and colour of your eyes, your skin colour too, plus your hair, I don't think this thing works for you, I'll have to find something else, something like a Chinese painting, yeah that would do it, we'll get inspiration from art, okay I'm on it said Yinn, pinning his handiwork as though he wanted to deflate the mannequin back in his sewing room, see that's better now, the piercings on your tongue and left earlobe are fine uh-huh, he brushed the Next One's ears gently with his hand though his thoughts were far away, he was preoccupied with My Captain deep in his ocean with night coming on, with him and with Fatalité's sister whom he'd rocked gently out there on the wharf, the wind blowing their

hair and the moment of implacable goodbyes upon them as
her brother's ashes settled in the water below them with faint
echoes of the Reverend Stone, dearly beloved, our friend has
rejoined his Creator, our lives here below not being given to
us but merely lent, this, dear friends, must never be forgotten
and on this day of bereavement, as bread from the loaf are
we separated from him, and a sister from her brother, Yinn
left her side to lean out over the floating orchids, their petals
rocked by the water, of course Herman had to yell enough
with the sadism Reverend, we've had it up to here, we all
damn well know life is only on loan, no point flogging it to
death, that's just twisting the knife, Rev, you wanna know
how many girls Yinn's had to hold like that because of a son
or brother gone eh, and there's got to be an end to it, an end
to the carnage of young lives, you men of God, spitting out
your stains of darkness, but Herman's words, like the Reverend
Stone's, got whisked away by the wind and fed to the grey
clouds and the gulls, the pelicans and the turtledoves perched
under the wooden beams of the terraces, still why dwell on
their farewell to Fatalité Yinn thought just as My Captain
appeared through the smoke with Petite and Oscar, his poo-
dle and boxer, in tow, or rather vice versa, cigarette in his
mouth and cap raked as always, checkered vest against the
chill, actually a shirt with jutting shoulders that Jason figured
he'd torn the sleeves off to show his tattoos and muscular
arms for Yinn, Jason was the landlubber and My Captain the
man of the sea, deep and impenetrable, that's when Petites
Cendres saw Yinn's long arms open to his friend, and something new this time, Yinn dragging him out of the bar, still
waltzing to the time he'd just kept onstage, c'mon and tell me
some more about China, what was it like Yinn asked his captain, well I was in this kind of water-house in Beijing, I mean
right there in the residence was this spa and water everywhere, water beneath the plants, a tree right up to the ceiling,
it was a place for therapeutic tea taking, the house of an

emperor of the Qing Dynasty, My Captain told it all, told about the incredible luxury of his early life until he hit thirty, then they didn't want him anymore and everyone forgot the sculptured body he said laughing, what, Shanghai Yinn asked with shining eyes, Shanghai yes Shanghai, but he wasn't even listening anymore as the Captain launched into an account of spit-roasted duck in an apricot and almond sauce, then on to his first years in Thailand, born while his father was stationed in Bangkok, Yinn thought of his own childhood, not really all that poor at first, almost comfortable he thought, his father had hit on the idea of selling chewing gum, sure, gum, why not you know Yinn said, laziness taught my father all sorts of creative tricks, then bang there we were, the best-dressed family in the neighbourhood with plenty to eat, now if he'd come back to America with us we'd probably be broke, what with his passion for adventure, women, passionate yes, but then Yinn fell into silent thought, the Qing Dynasty and its descendants he murmured, tell me some more about them, ah when a man has his dogs and his boat what more does he need, the Captain steered Yinn away from thoughts of exile, love on top of that would almost be too much eh Yinn, what do you say, you with no boat but the most faithful man in the world, dear Jason, still even his irony couldn't bring Yinn back from the far-off continent of his memories, the sky low over the rice fields and canals, he was saying and our unsteady little place, you had to get there over a gangplank, my dad built me a little balcony, kind of a tiny theatre, that's where I could dance and sing, and he would bring over all the village kids, enticing them with mint-flavoured gum, just you wait he'd say, my son Yinn's going to be an actor, he wanted anything for his sons but a military career, he wanted us to have more choices than he did, and oh how proud my mother was to see us in the oriental suits she made for us, they were still a solid couple in those days, Yinn lowered his eyes, and I was very young but I remember, then all of a sudden we were

uprooted and whisked off somewhere else, my adventurous
father wanted a woman from his own race, first one and then
another, he got used to it and we lost it all so I became the
head of the family, words which defined Yinn well and to
which My Captain replied but you are still head of the family
my friend, and how could it be any other way, you know I
don't regret the years of poverty without my father Yinn went
on, I sure learned some hard lessons, and that's something
new I'd have missed, that's what gets the spirit simmering till
we become who we're supposed to be, the Captain put his
arms around Yinn's shoulders, how about one more drink,
they strolled over to the bar, I don't like the gloom on that
handsome face, at least that is what he would have said if he'd
said anything at all, the Mekong, as it runs down from the
glaciers of Tibet, spreads through the dry forests of Laos,
Cambodia, and Thailand Yinn continued, but all our natural
resources have been crushed, no more Asian elephants, no
more Mekong dolphin, all of this huge area on the brink, and
Petites Cendres wondered what on earth they could be talking
about as they went back inside while he found himself entangled with a man and a woman who wanted to take him home,
but he wasn't interested, look, get this the man was saying,
my wife and I both want a man for the night, we both like the
same things, so hey why not have some fun, all of us together,
why not loosen up a little, we are, so let's get it on, uh actually
I'm waiting for some friends said Petites Cendres, besides I
don't go in for that stuff, and he was moving away from them
and trying to shorten his distance from Yinn and the Captain,
so this is what he might have waiting for him he thought,
disappointed that Yinn only had eyes for My Captain, not him,
slim pickings the couple who wanted to play with him instead
of a classy friend like that, a real man, he, like Yinn, fixated
on the affectionate arm round his shoulders, yep that was it
for him, just a hop into bed with this charmless couple, not
even a bit of flirtation, nothing, trivial and banal, I deserve

better than this he thought, his heart felt strangulated inside him, humiliation by pleasure, that's all they had for him, hey said Robbie standing next to him, if you need a place to crash you're welcome anytime, just us girls, all of us at Yinn's place, he said gently you can't spend your life on the Porte du Baiser sofa you know, that red thing will throw your back out, fine, no really I'm fine thanks Petites Cendres mumbled but he shuddered with a happiness that was taboo for him, just think-ing about Robbie being that close, Yinn's house but also Robbie's, when he visited his room, okay now he could hear what the Captain was saying to Yinn, look to tell you the truth I wasn't exactly following along like all the others during the ceremony, I didn't dump any ashes into the sea, in fact they're still on my boat, tomorrow I'll go for a long dive, maybe all the way down, and put them on a piece of coral so Fatalité can be truly free, free of all those chains life slaps on us, yeah that way he can roam the ocean, way off with the sea turtles and catfish forever, forever and afar, then he sensed Yinn was hurt by this separation of Fatalité's remains, how could you do that Thomas, we were supposed to all do it together, now where's he going to find himself, My Captain's answer was when I'm diving and I see a sea creature tangled in the line from a boat I set it free, that's Fatalité, now he's free, the seas and oceans are all his with the whales and the dolphins, how-ever few there may be left, Fatalité was an endangered species too and he's back where he belongs, Yinn was still upset at this, that's not how it was supposed to be, all the ashes were supposed to be under the bed of roses, I thought you knew that Thomas, look sometimes you need to bend the rules came the answer, we can't always be sticklers like you Yinn, oh Christ how stubborn you can be he snapped, step into the washroom, I need to talk to you, so how is this wrong eh, tell me how, because you've got to have the one-size-fits-all rule for everything, is that it, well the instinct for freedom out-weighs all your rules, but Petites Cendres figured what Yinn wasn't saying was he had a bad feeling about his friend diving down so deep with his bagful of ashes, Fatalité loved fresh air and sunlight, he loved the surface where he could see the sky and clouds, it's just not right was all he repeated, still I guess I have to respect what you're going to do anyway because you really believe in it, convinced by the Captain's determination, just then they were mobbed by some girls coming in from the street to offer condolences, geez poor girl, poor Fatalité, and they hugged the two of them tight, girls or boys it was all one, so talented, what a shame, beyond the hugs and embraces so customary in the bar anyway, and they did feel a little bit fortified by it all, now the two were looking toward the little balcony near where the bar opened out onto the street, and there was Jason with the musicians backed by the pale outline of the horse standing out against the red velvet curtains as it waited for Herman to haul it outside for spring later, when his leg was up to it, for now he had enough to deal with getting home in his wheelchair, nasty piece of crap he said, such crap, while My Captain and Yinn both tried wordlessly to hide their sadness as they watched Jason and the start of the late show, as his modulated voice spilled forth *he wasn't heavy, he was my brother, no not heavy*, I carried him sometimes, yet now he's gone I feel like I've been crushed by a falling tree, okay said Yinn, we're all set for this evening, the show's off to a good start, and with a quick kiss on the lips for the Captain before he left for his boat, not a word to encourage the foreboding, Yinn ran for the stairs, then up as if in flight to the dressing room. C'mon Tammy said, taking Mai by the hand, he's asleep in his lounge chair, who's this boy you were talking to, kinda crude isn't he, look at him snoring away while everyone is dancing around him, Manuel's father had lit lanterns to mark out his territory and also to get rid of the mosquitoes, quite a place eh Mai, geez I just got a text from my mom, they always seem to know where I am, and if they don't they message me or call my cell, even when they're at one of their writers' conferences or whatever, harassing me all the damn time, oh now don't you go thinking I had too many martinis, no no no no no, been smoking though, way better, hey what were you doing talking to him all the time Manuel was waiting to dance with you, he's in love with you, you know, your parents don't want you seeing him, mine are like that too, tough 'cause we're girls, my brothers now, they can do whatever they want but I get persecuted, do I look fat to you Mai, my breasts, around the hips maybe, I gotta lose weight but I gotta keep eating, like tonight, Christ what I put away, fish, steak, ice cream, as much as that boy over there, maybe I should go over to the bushes and stick my finger down my throat, I'm so scared of getting fat I can't keep anything down anyway, hips, it's the hips, no really I gotta be thin like Mom, she's skinny and beautiful and all, in school too, I'm having trouble in school, they almost think I'm retarded, it gets so I empty the fridge whenever they're not around, not too bright eh, see what I mean Mai, hey you listening to me, why's the kid in the khaki shirt so fascinating, he's really not your type and what would your family say, your mother even phoned, she's always on the phone to my mom, girls, that's why, aren't you worried what your folks'll say, geez why can't they leave us alone, you know what, they're thinking about sending me off someplace else so I can study better, just ship me off like some package or other, Christ it sucks being a girl and having mother hens for parents, north, they want to send me north, I'm telling you I'll just die, wintertime and the torches are lit on the beach, no mosquitoes, and Manuel's dad wants us all to know how rich he is, no need to crack a book for that, he sure didn't, that's what Mom says, besides she says his business or whatever it is isn't even legal and Dad says he's a bad influence on kids like us, yeah like we're all so innocent and we don't even know anything, oh I'm gonna throw up, see they come here without a cent and then get rich the crooked, easy way, oh geez my stomach it hurts, me in these sexy skin-tight shorts Mom just got me and I got them all dirty too, she's gonna have a fit, she said Tammy you're just gonna have to lose some weight, look your age, so she takes me for the special weight-control sessions at the hospital, nope that's not my real problem though I could stand to lose some, it's my mom telling me to be more normal, she says I'm the skinny type but I'm not, oh damn, now I've really gone and gotten them dirty, I can just hear what they'll say now, Mom wouldn't love me as much if she knew how fat I feel, she wouldn't say it as much, if they love you too much it's like you're their prey, and if you're big, fat, and ugly, but you aren't all of that Mai said, you're just like all the girls, and she wondered how Tammy would be able to go home after this with vomit all over her T-shirt and shorts, you never should've drunk all those coffee martinis, Manuel's gonna have to drive you home, oh no he can't do that Tammy said, they'll see his Mercedes then it'll be all over again, plus they'll find out I put my finger down my throat to stay thin, they mustn't find out, and I don't want some kind of special deal at the hospital either, it's like they want to humiliate me in front of all the nurses, you're lucky you can relax Mai, how do you do it, just skate along Atlantic Boulevard like you're sailing, not a care in the world, God I wish I could skate like that but I'm just too chunky, what I really like is to just stay shut up in my room with some rap music and dead people, what dead people said Mai, well not my family, I mean my own dead people, I wonder where they go, where they are now, what sort of Eden or whatever, you know like when they don't wake up anymore, I mean I always do wake up don't I, even my parents say they worry about me losing it and overdosing or something, so the hospital stuff's supposed to help prevent that too, they think it helps but nothing helps, it's a dream that they're trying to put me in, I know that, but in the dream I like how I look and I feel better, but you know when the dream doesn't look like anything, then it's dead people and everyone forgets about them, not me, I try to imagine what their last breakfast was like, who they had it with, their kids maybe, Mueslix and milk say in some manor or other where they can get up late and terribly, awfully alone, maybe even rehearsing all night, they're like gods then suddenly they're forgotten, not me though, I don't forget them, at home like they were in a hotel with AIDS and a cook, still horribly alone, a feeling of doom maybe, then one day they just can't wake up, cool rappers, people forget but I don't, nope they're mine these dead people, their eyes like deer's, they see me at night, then some quiet morning they don't wake up and there's crying, the kids are crying Papa, Papa, crying because they really do understand, their prince is in bed asleep, not breathing, the medics give up, but I don't forget about them, no not me said Tammy, I've still got their music all night and all day, no matter if everyone tells them to get up and open their eyes, they've decided sleeping is better, peaceful, so why get upset about them, behind those pale, transparent eyelids they're dreaming and they look so cool, so attractive, the whole world's seen them dance their way into ecstasy, now they get to sleep, no heavy feelings anymore, that's what makes it so easy to hurt and excite them when they're awake, pop stars or rapper kings, I can feel their music in my temples night and day, then no more oxygen in theirs, thick sleep, no way they're going to wake up, I see them though I really do, and hear them too, dancing in black jeans and jackets in my videos, dancing and singing forever and ever, damn my stomach's at it again, my parents say I'm anorexic, more visits to the hospital, special stuff, God I'm sick of it, all those dead-looking boys and girls, so sad, 'specially when I'm this fat, you've noticed it too, hips, boobs, when all I really want to do is look like those rappers, like just a heart with some flesh and skin around it, just out there singing away, but you're the same as every other girl Mai cut in, no way you're fat or ugly, hey lookit if you don't want a ride home with Manuel's parents, follow me on my skates, she knew it was going to be hard dragging Tammy all the way home, then there was the way she looked, that was going to raise eyebrows too, though maybe they wouldn't even be there, could be off at some conference or seminar or something, Tammy's pleading voice grated in her ear, on edge, begging, please you've gotta get me out of here Mai, really, far, I mean far, far away from here, Mère said who's there, who's trying to get into my room, Marie-Sylvie is it my friend Justin, his parents are missionaries in China, that's where he was born and brought up, he is here now, is it him she asked, is he back for a little jazz street parade, I'm not crazy about the drum though, Justin, it has to be Justin in that hat and linen suit of his, and complexion to match, so young-looking and stepping lively as he comes this way, oh do let him in Marie-Sylvie, go on, what are you waiting for, but Marie-Sylvie de la Toussaint groused that there was no one and Mère had better get to sleep, no one, really no one, besides do you really think I'm going to let any old stranger in here said Marie-Sylvie de la Toussaint, Mélanie would fire me you know that, no, no strangers in here, you're probably thirsty, here have this, so the little devil hadn't been in to kiss her grandmother goodnight after all, that's something she'll regret, I always knew that kid was no good, Vincent'll come Esther, just a few more days, maybe hours, now that's a loving grandson, even more than his mother, oh I knew to watch over that one, my child said Marie-Sylvie de la Toussaint, mine every bit as much as Mélanie's, Vincent, Vincent, that girl now and the delinquents she hangs out with, well isn't it just like her not to come, we knew it, not to come kiss her dying grandmother, brainless don't you think, but said Esther, sitting up in bed, I'm not dying, but then again she said nothing of the sort, not out loud at least, she was sure though that the servant had stolen her jewels, precious gifts that Mélanie had given her, maybe this woman was just as deranged as her brother He-Who-Never-Sleeps, deranged to have him in this very house, thieving maniacs both of them, for ages they'd both been fed and clothed by the family, now if Justin comes you're to let him straight in Mère commanded, we've always been close, so close, he the philosopher to my humanist, oh we still have so much to talk about, and Mélanie says Augustino's come back from India 'specially to see me, she says he writes so much about Calcutta, I'm thinking of that music Franz wrote for the church way off in Finisterre, it struck me as a requiem but Franz said it wasn't, you know Esther I just can't write music of desperation, a cantata of course, with melodies and recitatives, but the choruses are very down-to-earth, that was how Franz put it, a cantata, a celebration like the one for my grandson Yehudi, recently I wrote a cantata on the piano for the child I had with young Rachel, Wolfgang that's his name, can't you just hear the kids chattering and playing outside your door, what have you done with your specialization in music Esther, nothing she said, I'd completely forgotten till now that I had any gift, as each child arrived I forgot little by little, so your aim dear Franz is to populate the planet with hordes of musical angels, is that it, oh it's so like you, nothing in moderation, first Yehudi and now Wolfgang already sitting on your knee and stretching his little fingers over the keyboard, that's you through and through Franz, an unbridled will to impose joy all around you, but it's not my will dear friend, remember the day my grandson Vincent was born and some of your friends asked me what I thought of the black notations in Beethoven and I didn't know, I was upset at my own ignorance, dark notes filled with mourning, well I can still see them and I understand them better now, exuding anger, indignation, and frustration at his deafness, that is the despair that we all want to fend off, you above all Franz, illegible and sloping, screams of impotence, raging for a life not steeped in degradation at the end, tell me dear friend, isn't that what they really tell us, I'm certain of it now you know and that's what you remind me of by bringing

up my music specialization, gone for nought, oh for so long
I dreamed that my family was the be-all and end-all of my life,
then I came to fear being rejected from artists' circles like
Daniel and Mélanie's, contempt for her intelligence, that's a
woman's greatest fear, especially when it comes from her own
children, so what about you Franz, what do you say to that
manuscript blotted by black, swollen, and angry ciphers, are
they buoyed up by hope, is that what your overriding optimism tells you, she got up from her bed and walked to the
window and there she saw Wolfgang and Yehudi running
around with Franz beneath the trees outside, overarched with
the yellow of the frangipanis, may they always be so thought
Mère, just playing in the garden near my little place on the
lawn, the very day though, the very day Vincent came into
the world, Julio warned Mère that the White Knights had
arrived at the port, run, you've got to run, they know you and
your children are part of an anti-fascist group he said, they're
everywhere, waiting at the entrances to the hotels your friends
stay in, at the marina, oh they're here all right, the White
Knights are in town, that was Julio's warning, and the Nazi
insignia was there on the hull of Samuel's boat for all to see,
get out, you've got to get out, they're everywhere, faces and
eyes hidden by white masks, though Mère had warned Julio
not to get so upset over nothing, this was Vincent's first day
among us, they can't really be back again can they, hanging
round the door where Wolfgang and Yehudi played or Franz
went walking with the kids perched on his shoulder, look at
this Esther, my cantata, and even better, look at Wolfgang and
Yehudi, so much better than any music, no now that has to
be my best accomplishment yet, that's something worth cel-
ebrating isn't it, and Mère smiled at him from the window and
said oh do please come back to see me as often as you can,
so are they really as precocious as you were, truly, I mean as
prodigious as you were at their age, travelling all round the
world from one concert hall to another, isn't it still so infinitely

sad that one day they'll take your place as pianists or conductors while you lie beneath the earth simply to be no more, isn't there something truly sad in that Franz, your native optimism is so stunning but how can you answer that, oh look said Franz, a rainstorm, I'm afraid we're going to have to go my dear Esther, see you tomorrow my dear, there now we're soaked, they don't mind, they love the rain even when it storms, look at them laughing in it, especially when we're all drenched, come on kids, I'm going to have to put the top up on the car, get in, now wait for me, don't run so fast, innocent aren't they, they think I'm as young as they are, mind you sometimes I even believe it myself, then Franz hopped off with them under his arms all the way to the rickety old car, then put up the roof. Petites Cendres sensed the young man with thinning hair was watching him and smiling carnivorously, let's go up to my hotel room he said, just for an hour if you want, I've got powder and crystal, anything you like, actually I'm an anarchist just passing through and I feel lonely all of a sudden, everyone's having such a good time drinking and partying, so is this a gay bar, I couldn't help noticing your nails, you've got healing hands, just what my back needs, at the office I spend all day hunched over my drawings and plans, gives you cabin fever really, got a bunch of guys and gals working under me, God it's boring, you have no idea, you're all so wide open here, sure doesn't get boring does it, so your hands, I bet they're just loaded with talent, I never travel without my massage oils, 'nuff said, yeah I need those nails up and down my spine, never travel without getting massages at every stop, you for instance, I mean those hands and nails on my skin, wow, sure could forget the office with those, they all say I don't pay them enough, I've got all I need, okay so I'm just a little high right now, that's how come I'm talking to you like this, blacks, you gotta love them, though you don't seem all that black, 'specially those hands of yours, I was watching you over there with your friends and saying to myself that's what I need tonight, those hands, oh yeah, and goodbye to all my troubles, employees complaining all the time, it's too much, hey look I don't want to scare you off, I'm not looking for sex, just hands, your hands, your nails especially, say those guys singing, are they friends of yours, not too lonely are you, look if I seem a bit weird it's just because I'm high, right, so don't be alarmed, I'm really pretty tame, bored is all, so does stuff go on in that sauna, let's check it out, I wouldn't mind a bit of porn either as a matter of fact, so the other side of that saloon door, what goes on, yeah sauna, boy I can just feel the tiredness falling away, you have no idea, actually I get bored with sex pretty fast, it's got its limits you know, what I need is close contact you know, I'm from Ohio, so we going to the sauna you and me, I can get sort of marinated you know, these oils'll do it every time, hey you wanna stretch out along my spine, nimble fingers, what manna from heaven that would be, then Petites Cendres bummed a cigarette from him and sat there smoking, it had to be that carnivorous smile of his that did it, and Petites Cendres knew he wouldn't be going into the sauna with him, relieved that Robbie was still close by, Petites Cendres to the Captain's right, Fatalité should travel, she was a vagabond after all Robbie replied, and whatever you do, don't go any-where with that guy, see the way he's shaking, gotta be stoned, now I know why you like sleeping on the sofa so much, you get to see everything that's going on, and whatever you do don't go anywhere with him, Yinn's got no use for pushers here, he calls them cadre buyers because they have lots of money to flash around and nothing's off-limits for them, 'specially poor folks, which is just what Petites Cendres was thinking, Yinn's as honest as they come, so no way is anyone going to ruin his reputation or his image, even more because Petites Cendres' decline was so obvious even a per-verted architect could try and get him, not that his nails and hair weren't his strong points, they were, so why then didn't

Yinn respond to his charms, wrecked as they were, and no one knew that better than he did, Yinn had a way of sensing what was to come the way angels did, maybe he even took upon himself the weight of every destiny he tuned in to but felt powerless to lighten it, affording a brief gesture of consolation and nothing more, something immaterial and spiritual, barely noticed, that indefinable smile for instance, a distant and indifferent kiss on Petites Cendres' cheek perhaps, then all of a sudden between shows there was Yinn coming back down the wooden staircase with a short dress lapping at her knees, bare shouldered under the straps that Petites Cendres saw from behind out there in the street with Geisha, Vanquished Heart, oh how he admired the perfection of those shoulders, shoulder blades rippling with muscle as Yinn paced the street with the others, talking to customers as they passed, God how she'd like to avoid this Petites Cendres thought, but it came with the job and you had to boost attendance at the late show right up till dawn, Christ what kind of life is this said Geisha, getting in at five in the morning, sleeping for a couple hours, then yoga on the beach, then sleep some more till late in the afternoon, it was Fatalité's passing, that's what had everyone down, so who was there to get them juice in the mornings, Yinn's mother of course, Geisha said no one had the heart for anything now, crying alone in bed with pillows over their heads, yet here she was after them all to get up and have something to eat, sometimes she even brought breakfast on a tray, saying okay children enough is enough, it's been a bad week but there's always another one waiting, just like the new sun every morning, no matter how bad you feel, she knew her own son had the self-discipline to be at his sewing machine starting at ten and she was worried this one wasn't sleeping enough, especially around Jason, she'd been against their marriage from the start but Yinn just kept saying, not without a hint of arrogance, Mama remember how much you loved my dad, remember what it felt like to be in love, everybody was against that marriage too but that didn't stop you did it, parents, race, traditions, all that Mama, you remember don't you, and you always said love has to be stronger than two countries at war, love has to conquer anything and everything, so here was her Yinn with his modern ideas saying engagement and weddings were for everybody and just as sacred as his own with Jason, was she really so old-fashioned that she couldn't understand what came naturally nowadays, everyone's getting married in every town and country, what could her ancient customs possibly tell her about this and why wouldn't she see it, why not evolve with the times, because I was a woman and he was a man was her reply, now that I can understand, yeah well, like me you're an oriental woman who married a white man, what can I say, but she'd already heard his rationalizations and read him like a book, you know Jason already had a wife and three girls when you met him, where was it, Rome, and he said he'd never seen a woman as beautiful as you were, couldn't take his eyes off you, even when you undressed and he found out you were a boy, well Mama, that's love for you said Yinn, triumphant, what else can you call it, love's stronger than two countries at war right, you told me that when I was little and I never got it out of my head, and I, Yinn, was the result of that love, so strong, so irresistible, sure my Thai prince she replied, that you were and more, I don't deny it, and your brothers too, but why make this thing with Jason into some sort of political or social cause, isn't it enough just to be married to him, do you have to make it even more unbearable for your mother, you know he never helps me with shopping or anything, yesterday he thought he was hot stuff buying green bananas, green, at the grocery store, they're still on the kitchen table and they're never going to ripen either, there's your Jason for you, hubby, and what's it going to get you defending all those people, transexuals and the rest of them, marriage is a formal institution, it isn't for just anyone, geez Mama your ideas about sexuality haven't changed for the past hundred years, and all that time heroic men and women have come out of the ranks and overtaken you by generations, then Yinn reeled off their names, Del Martin partnered with Phyllis Lyon worked hard all their lives for equality and finally marriage in San Francisco City Hall, soon after that there were tons of others getting what they'd always missed, couples everywhere getting married, some of them waiting till old age, who doesn't need a stable relationship with the one they love Mama, why should so many people have to do without something so simple, we should be marching in the street, protesting the way Herman does, well that Herman can do as he likes his mother answered, he's not my son, you are, and I won't have you going around demonstrating in the streets out there in California, all kinds of horrible things could happen to you, anyway they're all going to end up married with or without you, good thing you keep busy in the sewing room, who knows where we'd be with all these modern ideas of yours, you off demonstrating like Herman and all, God what did I do to deserve this, son she lamented, so went their morning conversation said Robbie to Petites Cendres, the mother on her stool on the landing between the two stairways, but their tumultuous disputes did nothing to dim their respect for one another even if the volume mounted non-stop until Yinn ended up yelling oh go back to your room and leave me in peace Mama, there's really no point trying to teach you anything, you just won't change will you, and that Robbie said, was how Yinn began each and every day amid his sewing, agile fingers playing over cloth and fabric until Robbie himself showed up needing help adjusting his neckline and bust for the evening, plastic boobs, earrings, ingenue wig and with those same fingers running over him in caresses as spirited as they were impersonal, the hibiscus blossom in front, don't forget that Yinn told the yawning Robbie, then dressing him entirely and adjusting this and that for the evening, showing him how to hold himself onstage, and thus began their day in the household while Geisha, Cobra, and the others slept on and videos played continuously in various rooms, fond souvenirs of Fatalité dancing and singing in Robbie's, close-ups of her majestic dancing and singing, her Garbo-like beauty shining through the tears on the giant screen as Jason watched sitting on the edge of the bed in front of the computer, the hollow impression of Yinn's form still in the mattress, and he thought he could even feel the heat from it still as he placed his hand there. When he was small, Samuel, accompanied by his mother and grandmother, perhaps Jenny too watching over them all, skied down the glistening slopes under a blue sky, here in the Maritime Alps was where they came for winter sport every year, why on earth must you go down so fast, his grandmother, laughing and resplendently young-looking as were the other women in their ski outfits, all of them smelling of the snow and cold, and here was Samuel skiing well even at this early age, spoiled and loved as the firstborn his mother said, here with them for the very first time at this dizzying height, so impossibly loved and spoiled by all three of the women, Jenny still at home in those early days, oh why so fast his grandmother repeated, I'm just not as supple as you Samuel, and suddenly the sky turned grey and icy winds blew down from the silent, snow-covered peaks, then Grandmother lost a ski as she took one slope a little too fast and went off track, the swirling storm of fine, powdery snow, pale and blinding as a flame didn't help, and Samuel heard his own child voice calling for his mother and grandmother as well as Jenny, but nothing came back save the echo from the mountains, waking from this nightmare and coming to his senses with a racing heart, though the familiar foreheads of his wife Veronica and son Rudy were right there snuggled together beside him, he couldn't help wondering if his mother and grandmother were in danger, pulse still racing from wild alarm, he held his wife and child close, kissing them as they slept, he had to get up and reserve a flight for that evening so he could see Mélanie and Esther, an icy wind blew through the dark grey New York sky, now don't you worry Esther, I'll put your CD on again so you can listen to your sonata for piano and violin by Schubert once more, I'm surprised you're not tired of hearing it over and over again Esther, you know I don't like that blues they're playing out in the street with that fateful beat of the drum, this is the music I want, oh don't you listen to a single thing I say lectured Marie-Sylvie de la Toussaint to Mère sitting on her bed, her hands resting on a book so calm it shook up Marie-Sylvie badly, the sonata the governess "abheard" so much, what is it you're so keen on telling me that I don't already know eh, she seemed to say to the old woman, okay so you know I'm a thief who's stealing your jewellery, maybe even a madwoman as crazy as my brother He-Who-Never-Sleeps, the jewels are so I can escape from this house and never wait hand and foot on anyone ever again, besides if he is crazy it's because of those killers and that raft taking us down to the bottom with it, we were barely saved by some priest, yes I remember, and by your generosity when you opened your home to us, oh don't think I don't remember your kindness Esther, that priest even stopped them from cutting off our fingers and hands when we tumbled parched and hungry off the raft, those murderers wanted to cut his off too so he wouldn't climb on board with us, escaped convicts wanting to keep the number of passengers down, and once in a while a wave would carry someone off in the salt water that killed you if you swallowed it, that's how my brother went crazy and why I despise your family, Vincent no, not you dear child, not you, but can you at least under-stand the love between my brother and me, the same as you, Vincent you've come close to choking to death so many times, how many times have I rocked away your pain and his, right here in your villa and your gardens and garden shelter, how could you imagine, so what do a handful of jewels mean to you Esther, tell me, why in a few weeks, even days, you'll no longer be with us, oh I know how kind and charitable you are and I know you can find it in your heart to forgive me for the way I act toward you, and if you knew even more about why I do it, all the things that I have seen and undergone, all that happened on that disastrous crossing, just peasants the lot of us, goatherds out in the hills of Haiti, but the worst was yet to come, we could stay there in Cité du Soleil and be wiped out or leave, no one had any stomach for revolt against the tyrants, so leave it we did, and those with us on those floating heaps were killers and thieves too, fresh out of prison, not by the front door either, oh they'd've cut off our hands all right, and my brother couldn't swim anyhow and would never have made it back on board, though none of this was audible but Mère caught all of it from the close-up face of Marie-Sylvie as she fluffed the pillow and poured water from carafe to glass, brisk, rapid movements as Mère said to her I would have given them to you if you'd asked me, I probably would, the jewels were yours if you'd trusted me a little more, of course everything my daughter's given me is so precious, but the time has come to divest oneself of these things, so yes, probably they would have been yours, calm, oh so calm with her hands on her book, Mère continued listening to Schubert, not actually daring to sound these words out loud, perhaps later, yes later she would, more than just hoarsely whispering thank you, thank you for all you do for me, yes thank you. Herman told Yinn all the girls have to come with us when we parade the white horse through the streets, then dance onstage too, the last time for Fatalité's brothers and sisters, same as she did herself that night, tottering on high heels like stilts, the show must go on right to the very last, what guts that took, I'm gonna hunt them out of every nook and cranny, wherever the city has parked them, apartments, rooms, like some sort of leper colony, medicated to the gills, making them stuff down God knows how many pills every hour, even the

healthy ones, those barely left standing, youngsters in decaying, aged-looking carcasses, barely a breath left in them, idly
counting down the days left inside those poxy skins, maybe
fit for some medical experiment like lab rats, haggard and
waiting for the next one to die, no point going out or even to
the beach, a plague-ridden herd all of them, I'll round up
every single one to come sing and dance onstage just once
more, get 'em walking, parading through the streets, proud in
their old costumes, your costumes Yinn, yeah that's it, that's
what I'll do 'cause, hidden away or out in the open, they're
all still Fatalité's sisters, every one of us, majesty in the streets
with dresses, pendants and necklaces just like Fatalité herself,
no feeling tired or ashamed, just the honour of an artist to the
very end, princess-like and nothing less, I'm telling you Yinn,
there's no such thing as rotten love, no one deserves that
label, so Herman said, go get 'em Yinn anyplace you can find
'em, but some are in the hospice and they won't come out,
look I'll dress them as best I can Yinn said, dubious, but it
might be too late you know, still I'll do my best to get them
looking beautiful and young, fragile faded flowers, Herman
people think they're poisonous but they aren't are they, still
if they think that way themselves what can I do, walls cracking
apart on the outside, Jamie can help me with this, I can't do
it alone, it's too much for me Herman, you know there comes
a time when you can't push back the boundaries anymore,
our bodies aren't eternal, they can only do so much, not true
said Herman, the proof is that I'm here alive and kicking, see
that black flower blossoming on my leg, now the surgeon
would say bluntly that if you catch bone cancer soon enough,
yes, why not eternal if we want it, and those others out in the
parks, well now they don't want it, they've lost hope, they
can't feel anything anymore, well we've got to break them
out, every last one of them, that's what we've got to tell them,
not tonight, just for one night, unplugged from your tubes,
coughing up into hankies, shaken by pneumonia, injections

making you look like you're fly-bitten, enough pockmarked skin, as Yinn listened to Herman it made him think of the exultation of shipwreck survivors, but here in his friend there was the exaltation of redemption, maybe I need to pay more attention he thought, yet Yinn could imagine no spectacle more appalling than such a parade, whether in the street or onstage, multiple repeats of Fatalité all at once in the blue and mauve strobes from Jason's booth, when one, just one, Fatalité herself near death on that last night of her life, tore into him with hopeless violence and pain, and he said to Herman look you're asking too much, maybe if we got Jamie's white convertible, like for the evenings when we take the girls across town, that would look more dignified, then we could go find them wherever they are and maybe they'd go along with it and I could dress them and make them up, sure, just one short special night Yinn said, and Herman replied yeah a chance to get back some hope, after all Fatalité defied fate right up to the last instant didn't she, they've got to stand up and fight back, okay so an open invitation then said Yinn, to anyone who wants to be part of the show, voluntary, no one has to if they don't want to and Jamie will drive out and pick them up, but you can't fight nature, sickness has taken its toll and there's no denying that, you know that Herman, no but you can give them some armour, some sort of protection they haven't had for a while was Herman's answer, and Yinn had to wonder could he freeze the sickness in its tracks just for a few hours, beauty as an anesthetic for one and all, better than their decaying bodies hiding out to feed from tubes, barely breathing when the air outside was probably sweeter and the days longer, so Herman and Jamie sent out the call and bit by bit Yinn saw them make their way up to his dressing room, no longer men nor women either, shades perhaps, holding tight to the handrail so as not to tumble to destruction, and presto, Yinn upholstered the shadow bodies with flourishes of fabric, made up their pallid cheeks like pink carnations, veiled lumpy, skeletal heads with luxuriant wigs, though none of them wanted to sing or dance, just parade through the streets with Geisha, Cobra, Vanquished Heart, and Robbie, oh just like the old days when they were envied as artists, triumphant and insolent, oh yes the same as it was with Geisha, Cobra, Yinn, Vanquished Heart, Robbie, and the others, the unhoped for task of giving them new bodies with no trace of wounds or malady, Yinn recognized Fabian from dressing him and by his eyes, which were as beautiful as ever, the only one so young and beloved of Herman, but as he helped Fabian down into the street she knew Herman would never recognize him, she also thought it best to veil his yellowy features and the dark brown eyes that might give him away to Herman, Fabian had begged Yinn in a hushed whisper to spare him this, knowing Herman would no longer remember him lovingly if he saw him so emaciated, and Yinn had obliged by completing his disappearance inside just another unattractive boy or girl, if only for these few hours of celebration in the streets, one more shadow to add to those blended into one another like stars in the night sky, and Herman, applauding in his rumpled outfit as a droop-winged angel from the second show, never knew that Fabian was right there beside him just a few steps away, Yinn's disguise hiding the despair he would take to his grave but which was momentarily gone when he saw Herman once again, a one-sided reunion but at least he had seen him, and it softened his affliction almost as if Herman had embraced him and said quiet all of you, there is no such thing as pestilent love, here we have men hurt by the misunderstanding of others, nothing more, contaminated only by their disdain and icy indifference, and here among them is Fabian, vulnerable and broken, my friend now and forever, these were the unspoken words Fabian thought he heard, and they enlivened him as he raised his head to the stars while Yinn thought a line of ghosts, I see it but Herman doesn't, haunted vision of Goya's inexplicable ghosts in the night in bold colours and dark strokes, or else a night in blood, *The Destruction of War*, is this what I see beneath the coats and dresses and carnation-pink masks, the fleshy lips I drew on them, my stilt-walking Fatalités on parade, not one, not two but five of them in a procession of the dead, my princesses walking dead, is this what I'm seeing and Herman won't, this pitiable spectacle of dying spirits on the sidewalk with their backs hunched like Fatalité underneath their coats and their dresses with silver threads, where will they go when the last show is done, back to Dr. Dieudonné's clinic, back to some hospice on the outskirts of town, or like Fatalité will it be something grandiose, an apartment lit up all night and facing out onto the street, maybe back to their rooms and the yellow light cast on a bedside table where they get to choose between the bottle of sleeping pills and a needle to transport them to some otherwhere and a damp limbo of sleep, white, precise, and incurable, this was how Petites Cendres felt as he walked in the street deliberately steering clear of the procession and feeling Yinn's gaze fall suddenly on him, a long, hard gaze that settled on his back and shoulders, reminding him of the Haitian doctor's long-forgotten prognosis, a look of pity burning bright, either love or devouring pity from Yinn, indefinable to Petites Cendres yet it shook him, or was it just that Yinn, faced with this procession, didn't know how to define what he felt for the condemned, prisoners on parole from their dungeons for only a night, did he feel awkward all of a sudden, stumbling into someone else's nightmare, makeup, skilled prosthesis for the skin, distorted and innocent, was Yinn trying to win him over, trying to inject some vitality into his distress, a brief moment of hope and respite, for that's all it was for any of them, like Petites Cendres himself, walking free out under the starry sky, their own personal adventure, a moment lived to the fullest rather than the reverse, facing the expiry deadline that could not be cancelled or escaped, needing to dispel the morbidity of it all and relax, giving in to nothing but the joy of these girls as long as they kept to the streets, Yinn stared at Petites Cendres as though she were about to sneak up behind him and play a trick, he did that in the bar sometimes to accolades of surprise, then saying happy to see you Petites Cendres, welcome dear friend, and massaging his shoulder with firm fingers, only to disappear back into the streets again with all its billowing skirts, a balm on his soul that quickly vanished as Yinn fell back into her role as everyone's star, no, this wish was not to be, disconcerted perhaps but always serious about her job, the impersonal being that everyone else saw in her, including past and future audience members who'd seen the show, touching and prodding her to see if she was real, a lack of respect that drained her, hard as she tried not to feel any of its ambiguity, but majestic with barely a tilt of the head as though offended, while the girls, dolled up with plumed hats and brilliantly coloured dresses, yes while Yinn's haughty beauties, his own creations, flaunted themselves, Yinn summoned up last night's dream as he slept by Jason's side, in which Fatalité appeared as the bitchiest spectre of them all, furious, truly furious and saying why have you taken it upon yourself to disturb my sleep Yinn, why, to which she yelled back so I can be closer to you, no yelled back Fatalité, you mustn't see me, and at that moment Yinn realized the one held tight in her arms was not her Fatalité any more but a foreign shape dressed in ashes and an ugly outfit Yinn hadn't made, look what I've become, this horrible Fatalité, unbearable, with holes in my clothes and a body turned to ashes, why not just let me sleep in peace, cruel, you are so cruel, and with the sound of these words ringing in her ears Yinn woke up safe in her haven with Jason whispering into her neck sweetheart what's wrong, that's it go back to sleep, it was only a nightmare, you think so Yinn replied, you think it was only a dream, I really thought Fatalité was there, rising up out of the troubled waters of the dreams they live in, the same but not the same, someone else, not the one we all knew, and finally the dream dissipated into this one night in which life would triumph over all humiliation and adversity, in which the girls would be seen and admired as queens, and when Herman showed his pleasure at it all, which was rare, bravo Yinn, as Herman hugged her almost to suffocation, what a terrific procession, the people in the street were captivated and amazed and so am I, Yinn wanted to say she found it a bit like a carnival considering that for many of them it was the last gasp, then she looked at Herman in his curly angel outfit, that costume said Yinn, too many fringes drooping all over, I'll have to fix it, oh so that's the way it is, I'm an angel who's falling to bits mocked Herman, so just go wait for me over there in that dark corner of the bar, my tricycle, so I don't throw something out of joint on my way home, now listen here Yinn, in a couple of weeks I'll be walking on my own two feet all the way home, what you don't understand, Yinn, is that these people have to be shown just what their cowardice won't let them see, what if the black photographer Roy DeCarava, in the days when racism was a time-honoured tradition, had not recorded black dancers and musicians, the artist from Harlem pulled back the curtain the same way we're doing, what if he simply hadn't done it, then the world would never have known they even existed, but suddenly the photographer's personal experience became everybody's, behind that curtain were people, people who had to be seen, no longer hidden from those who wanted to know nothing of their lives, their songs and dances, their trumpet playing, an entire population which had been invisible for so long, d'you hear Yinn, what gets camouflaged by complacency needs to be seen out in the open, the unsaid needs to be said, and by revealing these black dancers in the streets of Harlem it's as though he was saying see, they do exist, here they are, you may not like their colour but still here they are, dancing under the neon lights, singing in the rain, playing their horns, someplace deep in this enclave where you couldn't reach they had the courage to live free behind the walls you made to keep them invisible, with the curtain gone these intimate scenes came to be known far and wide, no way now to deny their existence, but before that, long before dancers and musicians in the streets of Harlem, it all had to begin with a red and yellow sign that said STOP THE LYNCHING, STOP ALL OF IT, so you could know what those words meant and who was behind it, men, thousands of them, had to scream in revolt so you wouldn't forget over the years, yes they were still lynching less than a century ago, and remember it took open and visible pressure, even unbearable pressure, for human nature tends to forget its crimes, and listening to Herman, Yinn, now no longer listening, thought of My Captain out on his yacht as she went back over the nightmare night when Fatalité was so outraged and she was so grateful for Jason's lighting the lamp on her side of the bed before he went back to sleep, the wood-framed photograph of Yinn at twenty with the Captain's arm round her shoulder, and on the same shelf a recent picture of Jason in evening wear holding Yinn in one of her more eccentric dresses, all the more ironic for the fact that Jason had been unwilling to dress up for this publicity still for some holiday show, that's why Jason seemed to be sulking or feeling timid under the forced smile, his firm hand on Yinn's waist, two pictures in similar frames restore Yinn's faith in the future as well as confirming his present happiness, and although he and the Captain had been photographed together by Jason only ten years ago, he was struck by their youthfulness, a mere thirty or so, Yinn's hair down over her shoulders but the Captain's short, much as they still were now thought Yinn, yet what freshness in their gaze, sweetness freed of the longing for conquest, perhaps effaced or over-asserted on the Captain's part, a leftover from his days as a professional model, and Yinn's tanned features perhaps more oriental and refined then next to the pale pink face of the Captain, cheek to cheek with her, possibly exaggerating her tan and curved

forehead, the racial difference between the two was countered by their affection for one another, DEAR YINN, FOREVER
YOURS the Captain had written on the photo, and admittedly
their affection for one another compensated for it but still you
could see it thought Yinn, astonished to be suddenly aware
of it, and it was striking as he told his mother, love being
stronger than all else in his life, Jason, My Captain, and he
were serene and full of vitality, here and now enjoying their
existence while Fatalité no longer did, and out in the street
the near-death princesses paraded, his sisters, sisters and
friends, and there were no tears to be shed for life that went
on, My Captain, Jason, Geisha, Herman, and all the rest, no,
never a tear should be shed thought Yinn, for life's continuing
chain of reincarnations, and maybe these souls, wandering
through an imperfect world into another, less flawed and
knowing only this one, couldn't conceive of a better one to
come, still even in this one with its share of splendours, barring disaster one could partly be master of one's life, still be
able to metamorphose oneself as Yinn, My Captain, and Jason
had done, though Jason's discomfort in the clothing for the
photo reminded Yinn how he'd been mocked and jeered in
the schoolyard as Jason, fat Jason, and the photo almost made
it look as if those days had returned to haunt him in the
wooden frame, fat boy, fat boy, tormented as he was wearing
evening clothes when he was so used to bare arms, but he
had struggled into this unwanted layer just to please Yinn, fat
boy he could almost hear them saying once more, as though
right there at the photo session, hence the vague smile as if
waiting for the axe to fall, but in his transformation he had
also learned to fight just as Yinn had done among the L.A.
street gangs, and so dodge the insults and blows, and this was
how you lived, always preserving our right to change, to
transform oneself as surely as the Captain had stepped out of
his role as a revered model and turned wild out on the water,
where he was mostly alone though not always in need of that

much solitude he'd say, returning soon to his friends, but when exactly was it wondered Yinn, that the Captain had sensed this fissure opening in him as he prepared to start all over again, maybe it followed a fashion show or a visit to designers and couturiers in the villas of Brazil or the coastal region of Santa Catarina facing the lagoon and looking out to sea or at the beach, perhaps some chic villa with artists and intellectuals, adored and admired for his body at the non-stop billionaires' parties at home or at the club, when their jets flew in a short way from the fine and powdery sands of the beaches that made you want to languish for all eternity, as the Captain said, on these very private beaches at Ponta dos Ganchos, and adored all the while, loved for what he was not, explored by a man's hands, and there the Captain, Thomas, felt the loosening of the bonds tied round him for so long by lucre, a man's hand on his thigh shook him from the torpor into which he'd sunk for days on end in the sun, along with excess of alcohol and many other delights, the man said there remained about thirty more beaches to go and see, every one of them private, and as beach followed beach, depravation followed depravation, he'd become drunk on the paradises of the rich, sated and intoxicated till he found himself stumbling with shame, oh yes he said to Yinn, I suddenly felt I had to be reborn or else die in that rot of corruption, vanity, and adulation, even my body had had enough of it, not so thought Yinn, each of us is master of his own destiny, and like Fatalité, one bold, bitter stroke of fate, *my colours are blue, gilt, and green* sang Robbie, heading the parade with his wavy blonde wig over his broad forehead, dressed in a pleated robe that he hiked up just as far as he liked to show off his black satin jockeys, hmmm, too sexy for the time and place thought Yinn, but what can you do with him, Robbie with his tricks and jokes and teasing and droll indecencies, his way of suppressing pain he didn't need as though locking it away in someplace safe, and the tears held in with it of course thought Yinn, and sure enough here he was saying something that made Yinn laugh, you and your reincarnations Yinn, so what about Fatalité, when we asked her how she wanted to return, whimsically hesitant as usual, she said she didn't know and that had been her existential question always, which way to turn, what to learn, who to belong to, like some lost pup the way she always came back shamefacedly after leaving this kind of life, so Yinn, what do you say, do we change between incarnations, I mean is it really something completely different or would that be too disorienting if Fatalité, say, found herself living the life of a virtuous housewife all at once, boy what a shock that would be mocked Robbie, filling the surrounding night air, *yep my colours are green, gold, blue, and tenderness* he sang as the line of girls advanced through the night, Yinn remarked how orderly it all was, a truly fine procession, Herman deserves to be congratulated, really. The lights on the terrace added to the nighttime glow and Nora's self-portrait was nearly finished, though so huge one person could barely carry it, she herself being just able to but not without complaining loudly, the picture appeared to undulate as the night sky threatened to obliterate it with fog that was gathering bit by bit, absorbing both the oil marks and the liquidity of colours from the sky reflected in the pool, but perhaps it was overly dramatic around the eyes, especially Nora's, which were striking against the sky, above all in their expression, suddenly enlarged beneath the dark circles at her temples, yet the wrinkles and lines were unavoidable even though she'd painted this for her granddaughter as a memento to keep in her room, Greta had wanted it for her daughter while she grew up but Nora wondered if something so large and imposing was really the thing for Stephanie to have hanging over her bed, but of course it is Mama, Greta had said, Stephanie adores you, but it was probably more for Greta herself to remember her own mother by, she must be struck by her mother's approaching end to think about this, for she had always seen Nora as being still a young woman like herself, no, no time for such thoughts, focusing solely on the eyes, wouldn't that be a bit too intense for a child's room while the thirteen-year-old read or did her homework, awkward perhaps though at that age Nora herself had no longer been a child, she already wanted to be a surgeon like her father, that was when they were in Africa and already she went everywhere with him, caring for the sick, nowadays a woman just under sixty was still considered young, Greta would realize one day, Nora's hands often rough then, especially since she chewed her nails as she waited for him to pay attention to her, in the fall you'll go to boarding school in Europe with your brother, oh for just a thought, some attention from this gruff oracle perpetually irritated by us both, even when Mother served him his meal, always having to leave quickly and be useful, headed off again into the thorny bush, you will be, yes you will, a clever, learned girl, nevertheless pushing her and her skillful healing hands away, yes this is not for a woman, oh no, now for the facial expression to be so dramatic I must have overdone a line or a wrinkle somewhere, perhaps a little more white just here, muted, not too bright, perhaps I can just smooth it with my finger a bit, and on went her smock again, she knew she wasn't going to sleep after this, too many details streaming out of the portrait and demanding her attention, her smock, originally blue, was stained with so many coloured splotches and smears it looked like an abstract all by itself she thought, so stiffened by now there was no way to wash it, what joy it would have been to greet her husband at the airport tomorrow with the picture for Greta already finished, but she knew that wasn't going to happen, maybe he would understand her spending more time on it with her life dispersed into a thousand and one things to do, chores, shopping, one-way conversations with her children on the computer with their images appearing and dissolving again on the screen, their lives often just as closed off from her from living so far away, visiting several times a year of course and talking every day on their cellphones as well as seeing them on the screen, but still so far, not really there, each saying in turn sure everything's fine Mama, gotta go, the little one's got dance lessons, bye, talk to you tomorrow, yes everything's fine dear Mama, each one in turn, say how's your self-portrait coming, nearly finished, good, no they never had time to stop and hear what she had to say, they had their own lives, almost as if they weren't somehow part of hers, none of them being artistic like her, never mind the music schools, they hadn't kept up with it, yet for her it was the purpose in life along with her marriage to Christiensen, and now they'd enlarged the house and built another next door 'specially for them, but would they come any more often, she'd love to know what it was they did every hour of every day, nothing, nothing is so bewildering for a mother, losing control of everything, her own fate included, futile and maybe even useless, how could she make them understand that, or would they be indifferent just the same, well at least she'd got them all married, no, not exactly, well at least the girls had good husbands, but Hans, all right, a charming family when they managed some time together, but as flight attendants the father and son were both up there right now over different continents, oh Lord don't think about that, life was one long set of perils and some thoughts should just remain in the shadows, okay so a brush stroke here or else a smear of light blue with her fingers the way Georgia O'Keeffe used to do, she'd have completely changed the background though, a boiling stew of rainbow colours, not reality as it stood before her, Nora's face seemed too sunlit, eyes wide beneath blue circles or blue eyes under grey circles, what exactly was this, like Georgia O'Keeffe she'd launched herself into this world at twenty-seven, her world constructed from within using her palette, and when Nora couldn't reproduce what she saw around her, she managed at times to define her own inner reality instead when she painted the silhouettes of African women from memory, for instance they came out simply as dark lines against an orange sky, abrasively orange, and that was the day she knew, like O'Keeffe, that she was taking a leap into the void that might offer up a sort of absolute memory, African shapes lying dormant in her subconscious, the very treasures that O'Keeffe had looked for tirelessly, unknown or blank memory, but Nora stopped at that point, not wishing to plunge any further into whatever deranging unfathomable abyss her search for those forms and colours might lead her into, certainly a dangerous exploit taking her to lands and oceans of world-shaking upheaval, no, and knowing that O'Keeffe's work from the start was labelled as the work of a woman rather than a work of genius, much in O'Keeffe's work, rough reds and oranges, was as African as Nora's paintings had been for a long time, reds and oranges she carried with her in her very bloodstream, much as if she'd borne the world within her entrails of the same colours, oranges and reds that scorched her, in Nora's first paintings, before she feared going too far, conjured up the image of O'Keeffe portraying the red tides and the fertility of woman, and making her art nominally feminine reduced it as Nora would say to Christiensen when she saw him and ran to him with that straw hat of hers in the airport, yes at last it's finished, my self-portrait for Stephanie's room, I'm not crazy about the expression in the eyes though, too narrow, I don't know, something too introverted I think, the blue in them is good though, but something's still missing, perhaps they don't want to see or understand too much, they appear to be looking straight ahead, but aside from a fierce will to live I'm not sure what, a longing for speed, glancing too quickly hither and yon to the future, I don't want it to be overly volatile, too much white surrounding the bluish glance no doubt, I'll go back over it Christiensen, no it's far from finished, she had a way of disappointing those she loved, her thirst for life kept her spirit and actions forever at a feverish pace but her children found it too much, too tiring for her, yet that is how she was, but she needed time off to rest they said, when do you ever get a full night's sleep they asked, never they answered themselves, the inner pressure she bore created a constant atmosphere of urgency, all-consuming, and with it the allure of someone much younger, as her husband remarked, he enjoyed her tastes and the fact that she was almost eternally slim, discounting the time five years ago when their daughters on holiday had left their tops and jeans out to dry in the sun by the pool, then tried them all on for size, and how similar they all were, jeans just barely stretched over her stomach, and how the girls had laughed, see Mama you're as young as ever, not quite like five years ago, modelling for them in their intimacy, for children born of her flesh, Marianne the youngest had been a bit hesitant, no Mama you're going to stretch my jeans too much, they're not right for you, oh I'm bigger than you are, so she gave up the game as just a little too competitive and vain, they also told her she'd been out in the sun too long, that she was drying out her skin, she needed to feel its warmth all day long, rushing around doing a hundred things at once she was unaware of its boiling intensity, but she was aware of disappointing her children and she told them so, whether it was her painting or one of her charities in town or buying too many presents for her grandchildren, she knew they were let down, and no one as much as herself, now Mélanie and Daniel wanted her to come and visit Esther, what a comfort it would be, Christiensen had already been a few times before he went off to the Republic of Niger, but alone, Nora had refrained for exactly that reason: she was afraid of falling short somehow, how could Esther know what a disappointment she was, very overrated, as a mother too of course, at Esther's birthday party given by Chuan and Olivier, Nora had promised Esther she'd go back to Africa, promised repeatedly, Chuan's son was the DJ that night and Olivier complained about the deafening volume, Rwanda is staggering beneath the weight of its dead Nora told Mère, I will, I must go back and help heal and comfort them, just like my father, I know I just got back but I'm going again, not up to her promises and knowing it, judging herself harshly whenever she sought to help, she knew already that she wasn't going to do it, no she wouldn't go, too much to do right here, her children, then of course that portrait for Stephanie's room still not done, the children and chatting with them every single day on the computer, nothing spectacular, maybe not even worth it, but it was a duty that had its imperative, they must always know she was there for them, amid all this how could she just up and leave for such numbing struggles rather than lull herself in the tropical comfort of her garden, pool, two houses, one of them freshly done over, surely these would lure her children back home to her for longer holidays than usual, not a sure thing of course, but there were often friends who came for her exquisite dinners, always so hurried she barely had time to sit down with them, listening with one ear to their conversations while she laboured in the kitchen, such knowledgeable people her friends were, and sometimes not sure how to intervene, she injected a misplaced comment, or so her husband commented, loud and imposing he said, it just seemed to shoot out and stand on its own, she didn't talk as much when Christiensen was home, knowing he'd upbraid her for it in front of everyone, especially if she was off base or not quite focused, no no no it's not like that at all he'd say before bringing to bear his own superior knowledge, Nora would listen in silence, scolding herself once more for not keeping up with her friends' expectations, not as brilliant as them of course, this led her to resent them all, Christiensen and friends, all of them, no, no room for her despite the spectacular banquet she'd unveiled before them, no space of her own, never able to affirm herself, thus she'd decided not to visit Esther, why of course she was bound to let the venerable old lady down, but Mama is ailing badly

Mélanie would say, we count the seasons as we never used to before, that too scared her, the thought of seeing Mère no longer the woman she was, for now Nora was the healthy, dominant one, no, Nora couldn't bear to witness the decrepitude of one so dear to her, if one day they announced something like this to her she couldn't stand it, she'd defeated all kinds of torment when the children were young, no more now she thought, no, this was one of those disconcerting remarks she blurted out sometimes at home, sickness no, death no, she had another solution for them, a definitive one, of course they'd rush in to cut her off at such a thought, why how could she say or even think such a thing, and she found herself wondering if this was her way of testing her friendships, their abhorrence must surely be a testimonial to their love, provocation was her way of eliciting a reaction, shock them with something outlandish, in that case why bother weighing each word so carefully before uttering it, well no, after all Christiensen did weigh his words carefully, fine but why had she followed suit, to be heard and thought to be as brilliant as her husband, even more intuitive in fact, because after all she was an artist, she might not have his abilities, how could they not see that she above all deserved to have him by her side, an able economist and diplomat, of course that was his career, the untangling of human relations, whole countries, nations, with Nora in her perpetual modesty cocooning her children and home for so long as they wandered from country to country, quickly learning each new language, whether in Italy or Russia always quick to learn, never consenting to domestic help, just an au pair girl, her home so often open to her husband's African friends and their families, Nora, always modest, gradually learning the self-assurance of diplomats' wives, planning and organizing everyone's life, gradually daring to express herself more and more, it was she who kept things running, school for the kids, visits and receptions wherever they happened to be, knowing that the impact of everything she was doing with such quick enthusiasm would not last, no nothing would last except her love of painting, portraits, self-portraits, always with her and part of all she planned, and now she was finally settled and no longer trundling along behind her husband, the children grown up and married, yes finally here she was, everyone well set, so why now all was in its place was she so dissatisfied, like Christiensen she was growing old and soon the children would refer to them as ageing parents, that would be unbearable, now on the edge of a maturity not built around their offspring or Christiensen's travels but around themselves, their own leisure and rest, though Christiensen hated the thought of it, never stopping, and why would he want to he wondered, only by remaining active can one transmit what one knows, Socrates never stopped teaching did he, still what did she know of Socrates, not learned like him, self-taught and caught up in the whirlwind of life from the day, the very day her father, the great surgeon in Africa, said yes you can try to study medicine but you won't finish, you're not decisive enough, it paralyzes you, and he underscored her fragile nature, and what if it were true, this indecisiveness, what exactly did he mean by it, that she hadn't the capacity of careful thought, that she was headlong, unable to maintain the pace, that she was worthless, fit only to be a woman, mother, and wife, was it insidious of him, even though he got on well with Christiensen were they complicit or duplicitous toward her, no it couldn't be, she must be wrong, so unfair, Christiensen had always urged her to put her paintings on show, worked hard at finding galleries, vaunted his wife's talents, and he was adamant that she not go for too long without painting, but how could he know how disappointed she felt recently, all the worse for its being so sudden, 'specially now they'd been so happy organizing this and planning that, for that is how her life was built yet she didn't feel that way anymore, her enthusiasm giving way to bitterness, so that was it . . . growing old, it had seemed a promising time, he renowned for the remarkable efficacy of his work, with more to come, while she felt herself slide backward into dreamy artistic contemplation, poring over her paintings and feeling as she did now when she thought about O'Keeffe, incapable of doing that well and not content with being an imitator of something she found too free-form, Nora recalled a moment amid deafening music in the garden at Chuan and Olivier's when Esther expressed faith in her, you'll go back of course you will Nora dear, I'm so sorry your malaria's causing you so much discomfort, but such is the strength of a woman that even in a weakened state you never stopped looking after those poor kids with AIDS, why you saved quite a few didn't you, and they'll go on living a long time yet, think about that now, she replied you know down there, looking after other people's children, holding them, washing, changing, and caring for them, that was when I felt as though I were in full flight, not all disappointed in myself, or others for that matter, though we're all agnostics in our family it's as if some god or other were guiding me in a single language anyone could understand, and it was the same everywhere for everyone, live without apprehension or afterthought, even without knowing who, that was the pinnacle of light in my life, when everything inside me kicked in at once Nora said, really absolutely everything within me as resolute as it's ever been, none of the anxiety or feeling torn by indecision that my father used to pounce on, and who's to say he wasn't right after all, this though, this was the most exalted moment of my life, yes of course it weakened me so I couldn't stay, and this was the Esther, mother to Mélanie, that Nora refused to go and see, crippled by the fear of disappointing her, what was she to say that wouldn't turn out gauche, sure she would have gone on for a while about her kids, still hanging on to their marriages with the help of therapists and psychologists, Marianne of course had waited too long to get married, well her work came first, and Greta was on her second marriage while Stephanie swung between two parents in two countries, but these days it was practically the norm she noted, still, why so many attachments or marriages broken by divorce, now Nora had always been faithful to one man, wasn't that just the right thing to do when a woman was beloved of a man, but was this equally true for Christiensen the non-stop traveller, probably some things were better left in the dark, the beginnings of doubt could shake you to your roots and you never felt safe after that again, I have total confidence in my husband asserted Nora to her friends, never suspecting a single infidelity on his part, true to her as he was to everyone, Greta too, she's finally found her man for the ages, and with this Nora became acerbic and aggressive in her speech, yes always and always, and any doubt about Greta's marriage vanished, or probably should, erased from everyone's mind, sure there was the occasional argument or two with her new partner, I mean she's got a strong personality hasn't she, impulsive like her mother, nothing in life ever happened fast or well enough did it, and he was every bit as loving as she was, Christiensen, on the other hand, was calm, collected, and thoughtful, funny how mother and daughter made the same choices, had the same behaviour, now why would Nora confide her worries about the children to Esther, who was not very long for this world, what comfort could she possibly be, there was nothing she could say, she had reached the end and old age is its own relentless horror that picks us off one by one, but here Nora was still alive and strong, busy stitching up holes in her daughters' lives, patching the mix-ups between her son and his wife, come now my darlings everything's going to be just fine, and they all said she did them good every time and everywhere, but Esther now, Esther put her on a pedestal and she'd fallen short, not knowing what to say, not measuring up to the idealized portrait of herself, well you had to admit her trip to Africa had been a flop and that's exactly what she'd have said to the

old lady, what galls us women so much is the certainty of
failure in practically everything but motherhood, and as they
wandered the garden paths lined with red roses, of course
Mère would say no dear, you're wrong there, really you are,
for heaven's sake love yourself a little, I just don't understand,
Nora though would not delve into her father's rejection, cowardly no doubt, so her only reply would be but I paint, yes I
do, you know that don't you Esther, O'Keeffe now, she would
know how to make the wild and dangerous leap into abstrac-
tion, but me, well I'm obsessed with faces, bodies, portraits
of myself and of others, something clearly defined, think of
Georgia O'Keeffe, they only ever show her in old age, hair
and features taut, austere and sexually neutral, was she rising
to a challenge when she let them take her picture, as indefinite as Rembrandt grown old, willing to show only the quintessential beauty of a forehead too large, her sexually indefinite
body which once had been sensual and desirable, even provocative to her husband and lovers, the determined pursing
of her lips, the austerity in her face far outstripped by her art,
a face sparer than the art praised by men, I paint you see, I
really do paint she would say to Mère, and yet I am so dissatisfied with myself as I am, only to be told but why, my
child, do you have so little self-love, with a look Nora could
absolutely not have borne, the vitreous and distant look of
those about to die, no that was why Nora would not go to see
her, having known Mélanie's mother in her prime, solid and
dominant, running the whole household, yet now on the
threshold, no she would not risk this ominous visit with Esther,
well a few days more and maybe she would after all, um, that
white on the canvas, lighten the face and the whole picture,
make the eyes less charged and a little smaller under the bluish white lids, that's it she thought, now perhaps her husband
would approve. Herman said it really was time to roll the
horse out onto the sidewalk speckled with golden stars like
Christmastime, what a setting for it, and Robbie already

yanking on the reins, as he felt Yinn's gaze on his neck and shoulders Petites Cendres also noticed it scanning the marchers with concern, as though afraid someone's overflow of delight would make them break ranks, tempt fate and maybe disrupt things like the group of Fatalités gathered round the horse, symbol of spring and resurrection, perhaps she was afraid that their fragile health, plus the ample supply of rum Jamie and Herman had provided, would suddenly have them all running for the toilets and getting their dresses and robes all stained and dirty, then again maybe it was just sadness at the thought of My Captain making his descent into the ocean depths with Fatalité's ashes gently to be placed among the pink shells, coral reefs, and spectacular fish, a tiny bag quickly tugged by the water till its contents scattered like so many seeds of life, the last fiery cinders before eternal rest amid the undersea vegetation, Fatalité, a sadness Yinn knew he wouldn't give in to, no here she was dragging the Mexican Philippo into the street weeping over his drink, c'mon you're going to celebrate with the rest of us, five gins, that's it for you my friend, I'm mourning Fatalité, Philippo said, okay I'm also feeling sorry for myself because my sixty-five-year-old hubby mistreated me at his Christmas party, no Latinos allowed here he said, too noisy, whites only, no Latinos, now look at me Yinn, I'm good-looking ain't I, nice fleshy lips, hot for a man's body, here look at this, thirty years old, course he's good-looking too, works out and all, the gym and journalism, that's his life, never stops writing either, always in the first-class section flying off to some story or another, he bought me a house you know, over on Bahama, always comes to see me when he's out this way, not that often though, usually it's Brazil or Spain or wherever, my job's not much, I clean the streets and fix windows the kids have busted, yeah he knows and he said when I'm legal to travel he'll take me with him, but still street-cleaning isn't much of a job, I know that Yinn, see he keeps me in nice clothes and I've got all I need, yep I love that old hubby of mine, even if he says no Latinos in here, sometimes I think about shopping around, I mean hey, look at me, I got a nice face, I'm honest, and see my big lips, they're definitely going to look good to someone aren't they, somebody who won't say no Latinos in here, they're too noisy, yeah poor old Fatalité, I mourn her, I do, but I mourn for me too, poor li'l Philippo, I mean a good guy who gets no respect from his hubby, just pain and insults, y'understand Yinn, insults, hell it's no fun being a street-cleaner either with all that crap and stuff, leaning on my broom every day from sunup, I don't have to work, in fact he doesn't want me to, he can take care of me, but I want him to know I'm proud, even if I am only a street-cleaner, people in my country are proud and honest and I'm independent, okay now you can buy me a gin and tonic, I think I deserve it, geez poor Fatalité, and poor li'l Philippo insulted by his hubby, poor me he lamented as Yinn dragged him outside in the direction of Herman, Robbie, and the rest as they pulled on the reins of the white papier-mâché horse, Yinn gradually shaking off his sadness as if he realized, even without Fatalité and all the other Fatalités taking to the street, as Petites Cendres thought, he was still bound to lose all of them, oh they'd proudly go on working of course, just like Philippo, always standing up for each and every one of them wherever they worked, whether they lived or died, Yinn would personify the unbreakable chain of life to a better and evolving future, that's what he believed, and Yinn the Prince or Princess of New Year's, photographed over and over as she cautiously approached in stilettos and on a boat rocking on the waves, the first wave of each new tide being the roughest and the January 1 cold being the sharpest so soon after the last warm days of December, cracking the first bottle of the year in the frigid air and yelling Happy New Year to everyone, of course thought Petites Cendres, that's why everyone wanted her as page or maid of honour when two women got married, even if it was in secret with just an exchange of kisses, it dismayed Yinn's mother though that she was part of such off-the-wall weddings, as if same-sex marriages were perfectly natural, oh this boy with his new-fangled ideas, sometimes it was all just too much for a mother, really, those were times the house broke into an uproar said Robbie, huge fights erupted between Yinn and his mother, still not enough to wake up Geisha or Cobra smothered in their pillows though, not even the old dog sighing away under Jason and Yinn's bedcovers he told Petites Cendres, so now she said her son was depraved even if he was a good boy, well-mannered most of the time, well, when he wasn't pirouetting and rather crudely lifting his dress on Decadent Fridays in the Porte du Baiser Saloon, no she didn't like that, sure it was a way of bringing in customers, especially during weekdays when business was slow, no need to show off that frilly string of yours, they can see way up to your belly button, Yinn had inherited her delicate features but definitely not the benign dissipation, nor the erotic dances tinged with languor and ennui, no her child did not get enough sleep in there with his bed partner Jason, always kept awake and busy or dealing with some crisis or other, that's what led him to those street dances outside the saloon on Decadent Fridays with the other transvestites, then the nonchalant, soporific solo dances when he was really bored and down and he practically slept upright while he danced, yes despite his mother's refined contribution he had certainly got more from his dissolute father, although he didn't much like it, nice but depraved with all these modern ideas, that's how Yinn was like his father, and now to top it off he was page or maid of honour in these forbidden weddings, what next she wondered aloud to Robbie, really what next, he was sure to come up with something to torment her with, her patience had to be a lot more than she let on to her son, she somehow enjoyed scolding him in the home they shared with the others like this, the sermons delivered from the stool weren't enough, she needed to see more of him, and she actually had to let him have it at least once a month, it brought her closer to him and actually allowed her to rule the roost here. And this is my room said Tammy, take off your skates Mai, the floor was just waxed yesterday, oh and your mother phoned again, see the message light is flashing, it's not even midnight so why on earth do they keep calling Mai said, hearing the water from Tammy's shower already splashing on the tiles, I'd better get going as soon as you're out of there, see Tammy said, emerging in one of her father's white shirts that just about covered her completely, they won't notice a thing and I feel better already, oh don't go right away, I want to show you my room, say why don't you ever come see me, I need to get drunk for you to show up, the library's got books my parents wrote, they say Mum writes with a scalpel but I don't want to read those, my dad doesn't, he's a historian and I'm not afraid to read his, but Mum's are there just the same, see I don't even want to know what she thinks of me, no, no way, Tammy ran her fingers over the books as though afraid to dwell on them, do you read the books your dad writes she asked Mai, I wouldn't if I were you, his friend Adrien is a critic and he's often hard on your dad's books, they're sort of over-the-top he says, obscure, hard to figure out, oh my head's spinning but at least I'm all cleaned up now, they won't notice a thing, look my parents have already called several times looking for me Tammy, hey don't forget to get home before midnight, your father doesn't like it when you get in early in the morning Tammy said, he says it's too late when the fog's thick on Atlantic Boulevard, he says you should take a taxi or he can come and get you, but don't go right away, you never come over here, I mean we go to the same school and all, girls who don't smoke hash don't hang out with me 'cause I do but I was sure you and Manuel, well I thought you still like Emilio best but how do you manage to see him, his parents sent him to the Spanish Catholic school, and Mum says if I don't change

I'll wind up with the Catholics too, I'm hungry, aren't you Mai, so the marine, the kid in khaki, what were you doing with him, he was repulsive all covered in chili sauce and scary, I've got to forget about the fridge or I'll get even fatter, just look at my hips, then Mai said no, she looked all skinny in her father's shirt like that, if you're hungry why don't you just eat, you really are too thin, no I'm wide all over Tammy said, I get hashish on the beach from Manuel's dad to forget, when we're alone of course, absolutely no one must see us, in her books Mum complains about having a daughter like me, she doesn't know what to think of kids nowadays, 'specially my brother and me, so I'm never going to read her books, I don't want to know what she thinks of us, Mai looked at Tammy sitting on the bed in her father's billowy shirt, when it opened revealing her swimsuit with ROCK STAR written in sequined letters, hey I told you take off your skates, her pointed breasts moved under her swimsuit, Mum's just waxed the floors, if I ate something I wouldn't be able to keep it down anyway, and tomorrow I'm going for special counselling with Mum, they'll force me to eat, they don't see that I'm fat, that I shouldn't eat another thing, boy you should see those girls in special counselling, real skeletons, they hardly weigh anything, Mum says it's a tragedy, now Tammy she says, you don't want to end up like them do you, no I hate her voice when it sounds like that, and on the way home in the car I wind up crying, then I know she'll stop, see here on the wall and recorded in the videos are my idols, friends, look at that one, he never stops playing and dancing, he looks so cool, black jeans, and look at him dancing with that black hat over those big, soft dark eyes, see what I wrote on this poster, LOVE YOU FOREVER MIKE, now Tammy seemed ethereal, almost non-existent, shadow dancing on the walls of her music-filled room, a bubble, just a bubble thought Mai, meanwhile outside the window lush and vibrant vegetation climbed the walls of the house amid the suffocating humidity, and inside the cellphones went unheard surrounded by the cacophony, just two flashing red lights as Mai repeated that she really should go, she still had a few blocks to skate along Atlantic Boulevard and she might even make it in time to give her grandmother a goodnight kiss, the finger of light from her flashlight would point the way through the fog, it was close enough and her father wasn't one to lock the door at midnight, see he never stops dancing, isn't it great said Tammy, and look at these idols on the wall, they're my heroes from Columbine, guns and all, and on the twentieth day of April they will kill schoolkids like you and me, then kill themselves too, they're my heroes because no one else feels sorry for them, see the circle of blood round their faces, I put it there, no, no one's sorry they're going to kill themselves, my mother says it's not healthy, those faces, the pictures, the guns, the red circles like blood for April 20, I shouldn't be fascinated with Eric and Dylan's faces 'cause it's sick, awful, gone off on their own all alone, like gods on the day before the massacre, judging that the world they lived in was a hole, just one big absurd hole, really gods until they got too depressed, they wanted power and control, so depressed and their parents never even knew it, then they made their own power and control, picked up their guns and there it was, so easy, they could gun down girls like you and me, boys, I told Mum that kind of fury and rage could get into anyone, just like Eric and Dylan, say, who's sorry for them anyway, and she said I don't want my daughter worshipping criminals, I'm going to tear down those pictures of yours, but I said they were kids before they turned into criminals, just like my brother and me, so take a good long look at them, beg pity and pardon for them, pity that they turned into this and had to die so soon, a gun straight to the heart, the ultimate vengeance, no danger of their ever setting foot on another campus again, if their depression isn't absolved they could come back tonight, and that's what I told my mum, they're my icons to remember them by Tammy explained to Mai while the cellphones kept on blinking with messages, before they thought of themselves as gods they were just like you and me, nobody knew what Eric and Dylan were thinking, too bad they were friends, too bad they ever met, and the first day they met was the first day of their apocalypse, Mai saw she had other pictures on her wall too but much less obsessive and sinister than these, almost sweet in comparison, one was an Amur leopard, another was a giant panda licking its baby, but under her pictures Tammy had written THERE ARE ONLY A FEW OF US LEFT ON THE PLANET and WHO WILL ADOPT US, nearby her Prince Rock sang and danced on the screen with eternal grace, and though his moves were so disturbing she always fell asleep to them, awoke to them, listened all day with her earphones, and she told Mai it sometimes felt as though he were dancing all over her body and soul and it would always be that way, yet when her parents came home during the night her room had to be silent, like her brother's, no quieter than hers otherwise, no matter, she always had her earphones, an eternal dance thought Mai, there were pictures nearby of a boy in short white overalls and a black and blue striped sweater in his father's arms, beatifically smiling at one another, then another photo taken only a few months later of the boy, one of the same boy, now immortal as Tammy put it, next to his father's hearse, assailed by a sadness he could not express and obliged to stand up straight, hand saluting, face tilted and struggling to cry but prevented, a prince whose courage all had admired for this, her room was a shrine to her icons and princes, sheltered and immortalized, freed of all restraint and weeping in peace, a son whose father had been assassinated, a little king whose uncle would be too, how many times would he have to be here, unable to cry, always the same salute, Tammy's room had become the receptacle for all these tears Mai thought, tears Tammy couldn't allow herself, not any more than the royal boy in the photograph. Mère recalled the dream, something like Christmastime at Charles and Frédéric's, just seconds ago, the green garden gate was open and there they were to greet everyone: Caroline, Jean-Mathieu, Mère, Justin, Jacques with his friend Tanjou, Adrien and Suzanne, what a mix she thought, a young version of Frédéric, who always had a discreetly seductive draw for Mère that she couldn't resist, he must have been the one playing the piano for his friends, and Charles was accompanied by Cyril in the days when they were still in love and fresh back from India, Cyril still as jealous as ever of Frédéric though, even when he was their host, a good season for love and passion and for smoothing over quarrels thought Mère, a time for reconciliation and the joy of simply living, such light in Charles and Frédéric's house, and this is what convinced Mère to come, all that light and the green gate wide open, the voices of friends rising from the street as they made their way, all of them calling evening Esther, good evening, so nice to see you, Caroline the first to take her by the arm, I've missed you so she always said, you know Jean-Mathieu talks about you every single day, you know we went to England for our book on the British poets so I could photograph them don't you, you remember one of them, oh dear I'm so sorry, I can still see him with the pencil dangling between his fingers, and Mère listened to Caroline's high-pitched voice, oh yes that was certainly Caroline wearing such lovely clothes and a old-fashioned hat, all of them were there of course, Justin with his wife Laura and the children, and Mère finally blurted out what she'd been holding on to for so long, you know, about your book on Hiroshima you were right, it's not that Caroline doesn't understand your beliefs, she was never a pacifist like you and never will be, of course she is, or used to be, a woman of power, at least she'd have liked to be, and that's why she'd never agree with you, I just wanted to explain, just then Caroline came in through the wooden doorway, painted the same muted green, and kissed Jean-Mathieu, lifting up his red scarf, how I like this scarf you bought in Italy, yes Mère could still hear that high voice next to the low voice of Jean-Mathieu, who was saying it rained so hard my shoes are soaking wet, the streets are overflowing and the presents are all wet too, as Mère thought it is raining so hard outside and it is so luminous inside, this was when she was outside on the path wondering if she should go all the way up to the house, she felt moved by the sight of a rusted green bicycle Charles only ever used on Sundays still leaning against a fence of the same rusted green, Frédéric said Charles wrote his best poems on that Sunday bike, head in the clouds, forever having near misses in the street, that was how he wrote *Ash-Corroded World* Frederic said, he'd recite the poem right there on the bike, same as he would Dante or Blake for Adrien and Suzanne, that acrobat-poet's going to fall and break his neck one of these days, adding that Charles was the greatest misunderstood poet of his generation, oh come on now he's not all that misunderstood cut in Adrien, even if he hasn't been a poet laureate yet like me, sure it's an honour, a title but nothing to be vain about, I mean he's been publishing since he was fifteen and won the highest honours, he's got absolutely nothing to complain about, oh but he never does complain said Frédéric, he's rather ascetic after all and lack of interest in those things is his virtue, was this really true thought Mère as she ran these conversations through her mind, half-forgotten words from the past exchanged beneath the shining chandeliers before they gathered round the table laden with acacias and mimosas outside under the bower, the perfumes of flowers bending trees with their weight, can it really be that she is back there now breathing them all over again in such serene exaltation and all of them saying but why on earth are you standing there in the middle of the path Esther, come, come inside where the lights are on, come and join us won't you, and just as Jean-Mathieu took off his shoes right there on the parquet floor, Caroline screamed a scorpion and he's headed straight for you, well that little thing is parched from the dry season said Jean-Mathieu, and I'm a lot bigger than he is, just set him down outside with a broom, so Eduardo brought a broom in from the garden but too late, Caroline had already squashed it with the sole of her sandal and Jean-Mathieu regretted that, now why did you do it Caroline, he seemed to be facing off against an utterly different woman, not the goddess Caroline he knew but a creature of unwarranted cruelty, how could you he said again, a huge creature like me has the right to kill a little thing like that, tiny and thirsty too, he was probably attracted to the water in my shoes, Mère heard all this of course, oh that was them all right, nothing ever changes with them, same voices, same attitudes as they approached her saying welcome Esther, nice to see you, a dazzling brilliance surrounded them as they came closer, urging her to come closer too and join them under the sparkling chandeliers in Charles and Fédéric's house with everyone she knew and loved, such a fine mix of people from whom she could never be separated ever again, so much like old times with the rusted green bike up against the rusted green fence waiting to be used on Sunday for Charles to compose his poems out loud without writing them down, in the perfumed air, head lifted toward the sky as though Mère were there with him, listening as he cycled through the deserted streets early on a Sunday morning. Do you see the way Yinn's looking at my back and shoulders like he's designing something for me, see said Petites Cendres to Robbie, still tugging on the bridle of the white papier-mâché horse, see Robbie, boy this horse is heavy came the answer, look at the way he's staring at my back and shoulders Petites Cendres cut in again, but Robbie set him straight, it's not you he's looking at, somewhere in the line of girls a faint cough was heard and that had Yinn worried, her gaze hardened, where was this ghost of a cough coming from like a shudder of fright rippling through them all, her gaze was fixed now, and for her eyes to turn this chilly and pale she had to be either furious or unnerved that My

Captain was not present, his renegade scattering of some of
Fatalité's ashes still rankled, Robbie saying that he must be
about to cast anchor at this moment of sunset, maybe he'd
had a last minute's hesitation with the light package in his lap
before he went down in his wetsuit to the depths violated by
the debris of dead birds with wings sliced by boats racing over
the surface, the graveyard of marine mammals tangled in
ropes, the thought of their agony as the green eyes closed
forever, clandestine and captive, the damage done to the coral
reefs, the multitude of fish laid waste beneath this piracy, he
did hesitate all at once, it is our fault that all this has to die,
coral, animals, and all on this pink clay bottom, he'd rather
have found a less funereal place than this charnel house of
plastic and glass, animals buried in ropes stained with oil and
lead, so many traps they couldn't escape in this pink fog of
water, he'd have preferred to release Fatalité someplace
deeper amid the sparkle of silvery fish where the currents are
clear and crystalline, that would've been the place to say
goodbye old friend, sure Robbie said, and he did hesitate,
Jamie said he had some long coats for the girls who were cold
and there was the white limo for them to warm up in too as
they drove around town, though they'd rather stand up in it
with Jamie driving, but Yinn had to catch the sound of that
cough, faint but unmistakeable, and the night was barely
begun, there was that look on Yinn's face Robbie said, though
Petites Cendres was still convinced it was meant for him,
standing off to the side Petites Cendres had just the merest
cough, and Robbie insisted it wasn't him but one of the girls
in the line in front of the bar, so muffled you'd wonder how
Yinn could possibly hear it, really you would. Lou did hear
her father's voice above-deck saying the girls were asleep on
the folding bed below, like two little angels was how he put
it, telling Noémie in the triumphant, seductive voice he used
with her, thus thought Lou, never for her mother, just for
Noémie, he knew Ingrid would have caught the false note

straight off and disliked it the same as her daughter when it was used on someone else, so that's what he thought, that the girls Lou and Rosie were asleep while the boat bobbed in the foggy marina, not true, only Rosie was sleeping thought Lou, putting her hand on Rosie's inert shoulder, right she would be asleep after being used to turning in every evening at eight, the same time as her brother, just a baby really after all, hair netted over her face like feathers, just a little baby chick, like in the Christmas parade with the whole class of blue and red chicks in the truck, Lou never let them dress her up that way, the cocks were in a separate truck with the lambs, Rosie and the chicks being the smallest, even in the annual school ballet recital Rosie would wind up as a chick with other chicks following behind, course she was in kindergarten then and they all slept like babies, Lou thought about what her father had said, sometimes going to sleep for an hour then waking up to spy on him, listening in on what Ari said to Noémie on his cellphone, every word of it, well some she caught and some she didn't when he murmured or whispered, the slightest breeze carried his words away, words that it would pain her to hear in any case, in fact Ari was saying into the phone that he didn't know what to do with Lou if she insisted on carrying on this way, rude and still hating her father's loving someone beside her mother, really he told Noémie, I don't know what to do, honestly I don't, what do you think, does she need some serious discipline, sure I know, reining in, but I still don't know what to do, of course he'd never ever punished her, and Lou, tugging at her eyelids to stay awake, wondered about this, Ari was a man for suggestions, proposals, but he never disciplined her, not for her manners or her pulling faces, he always praised her grades in Italian and Spanish, piling even more courses onto an already heavy load with swimming, riding at her grandmother's, violin and piano, no wonder she didn't sleep at night with days like that, they were just too short, Ingrid was right, he had too many things to suggest or propose till her mother said it was too much, the little girl was not a machine or a computer and her father was some sort of unfeeling programmer, yes Mama's right Lou thought, now here he was insinuating to her Lou, my little Marie-Louise, how about a week at Mama's and a week in New York with Noémie and me, I have a piece of sculpture to finish in the park and that way you can spend more time with me, what do you say Lou? This was no time to mess things up, she had to sift through what he proposed and try not to hurt her mother's feelings, Ari's ideas were always comfortable and limitless but at her mother's there were three of them crammed into a small apartment, Ari's house was spacious and airy just the way he'd designed it, he was expansive like that about everything, his computer monitor was the biggest, Lou's room too, living comfortably was no sin he said but it didn't seem fair to Mama, whose place was the exact opposite and she shared a room with her brother Julien, Ingrid herself seemed to do without for the sake of her kids, hmmm better think carefully about what he's saying, and now he wanted to live in New York to top it all off, with Noémie as well, who knows, maybe he was even thinking about having a baby with her, that's what her mother said, who knows what these two jerks are thinking and what was in store for her under shifting roofs like those, no her mother said, you're better off with me, you should be with your mother, so Lou tugged at her eyelids and planned to stay awake although total silence had just descended on the cabin and on the bridge, her father's voice and the words that should have shamed him, really Noémie I just don't know what I'm going to do with my daughter, all she does is buck all the time, even awake, Lou didn't hear this part, I'll just go to sleep with my hand on Rosie's shoulder and that's it, Rosie her very own baby chick. With even strides Mai skated along Atlantic Boulevard with the yellow beam from her flashlight slicing through the sea fog, it had gathered all along her way and seemed to stick to her skin, you can barely even hear the waves she thought, and Tammy's music, "Billy Jean" and "Thriller," thumped through her head and the man with the black hat and black shades and the sexiest look, the sexiest moves, danced on for her, on and on Tammy said, night and day, and when her parents came home from one of their nights out on the town drinking with friends she heard the same arguments and fights, always ending the same way, too many kids, at least the oldest ones, Tammy and her teenage brother were already trying heroin, Mom had confiscated needles from her brother's room, then Tammy and her hash and her anorexia, his fault, the father's, for making her have too many kids, but the father shot back they're our kids, we have them and how can we not love them, never a thought about me though said her mother, I just wanted a family not a bunch of deadbeats like these last two, I'm just a mother as far as you're concerned, not a writer, and I can't get a minute's peace, never, just Tammy and her brother, they drain me completely, look it's just a phase her father replied, we have to stand by them, we were young, just students when we had them, we have no one to blame but ourselves, too much in love to think straight, and so they went on for hours, weighing in against one another Tammy said, our births, our lives, never should've been born, they both knew it and my mother said it, just parasites is all the two of us were, never gonna come to any good, my mother the writer didn't even dare show us to anybody, cruddy, that's all we were, and Dad going on that we were kids and deserved their affection and support, no way were we parasites but good kids, disturbed and insecure maybe, still needing to spend more time with them, I'm worried that you might be having another breakdown he said to his wife, we overdo it and you get depressed, that's what bothering those kids, can't you see he said to her, you think they've pushed us too far, and my mother would end up saying she was going to, he was welcome to us, throwaway kids, never should've been born, on and on it went all night long,

Mai was lucky said Tammy, to have parents who appreciated her, tomorrow Tammy'd be back at Manuel's private beach unless his father got busted first, but he was a smart pusher, careful Manuel said, and life on the beach was good, nothing to do but hang in the sun, swim, take it easy till the day Manuel and his dad got led away, but hey no that wouldn't happen, they were too smart for that, look at my prince dance and sing, he'll never ever stop, watch him even when you think he's asleep in some make-believe forever, just look how hot he is Mai, his looks, his moves, his hat and sunglasses, and the music in Tammy's room seemed to batter at Mai's temples even when she was skating, regular strides behind the yellow beam of the flashlight in the sea fog, not that late really, not even midnight, but what on earth was Marie-Sylvie de la Toussaint doing in her grandmother's place at this hour, lately she'd even been spending whole nights there and she hung in so that Mélanie couldn't get her to leave, Grandmother had some sort of unshakeable trust in her Mai thought, or was she just plain gullible, imposed on by the governess, Mélanie's own candour leading her into feelings of guilt toward poorer people every single time, anyway what on earth was that woman doing in grandmother's room, so Philippo's hubby showed up at the bar in a winter coat and telling Robbie he'd just got back from an assignment in colder climes and here's Philippo complaining about me, so you're all invited to my party Robbie, all of you, it's just that he drinks too much Robbie and I don't want his drunken friends sitting at my table in my nice clean house slobbering beer all over my embroidered tablecloths, I mean really I've done everything for him and all he does is complain, look you know me Robbie, I love Philippo and his brothers and sisters and his mother too, and I've helped that whole family, but does he show any gratitude, hell no, just goes on whining and moaning, he's a pain, Robbie said that's gotta be his seventh gin, you'll find him back there somewhere all teary-eyed and looking for a second hubby, no secret about that, he's been telling everyone hey look at my sweet face and plump lips, I gotta get him home said the hubby, he's always making a mess, dirty fingers all over my white tablecloth, him and his drunken slob friends, but his Latino friends are welcome in my place just the same, he's so damned spoiled, how can he say things like that about me, hey boys has anyone seen my Philippo, over that way in the sauna pointed Robbie, then turning toward Petites Cendres he said no you're wrong, Yinn's not looking at you, one of the girls coughed and it worried her, though you could barely hear it, one had a sudden fever, who knows which one it was, and they sat her down in the limo, couldn't stand up straight at all, probably the haughtiest one, the coyest, never mind which, and Yinn asked who but no one said anything, okay, everything's okay, and they went on with the tour, one of them said thanks to Yinn, what an enchanted night, what stars, Jamie's given us coats so we're not cold anymore, they chatted on about other bright nights on the sidewalks and in the cabaret, nights forever shining on their insomnia, almost wrinkle-free thanks to the makeup, so much like the good old days and almost as young-looking without the ravages of illness showing through Robbie said, still talented dancers and singers, maybe a hint of wear and tear in the voices but as bold and daring as ever, bold and daring as Fatalité, one, probably the coyest and proudest one, said to Yinn say remember when you ran out of red velvet one Christmas and all we had on were bows like ribbons over our private parts, some bikini Christmas that was, boy how we laughed, maybe a cloud over our heads, yeah hoods, remember that Yinn, but were we ever cold underneath, I mean it was December, right, never mind, we were good enough to eat Robbie added, oh yeah so much like the old days, flirty talk, painted smiles and laughs, lots of laughs, the only difference is what's eating away at them down inside, weird, unreal, not something you can touch or see, better not to think about it, why spoil the fun and laughs, perfect the way it is, a tragedy of happiness the way Yinn wanted it, Jamie the owner of the place too, both of them coming from poverty and making their way with a taste for the charming and fantastic, the bar, the sidewalks to the seafront and the jetty where Yinn stepped onto a boat every New Year's in almost full-length boots and a red silk dress all ready for the fantasy show meticulously created out of flesh and blood, a feast for the senses of one and all Robbie told Petites Cendres, who envisioned Yinn as depicted on those Christmas nights, his body glossy beneath the red velvet bow with an unaccustomed quiver, a chill, as if he were sur- faced in marble all of a sudden, such a vision, so icy it set Petites Cendres ablaze, Yinn looking so theatrical in the streets, detached under the golden glitter of a bikini or a red bow, steadily forward, a gift, a gift Petites Cendres only had to reach out and take for his own, or getting into the boat, what could be more incendiary out on the water, riding the waves under the night's unreal illumination, evanescent silver globes, luminous necklaces and bracelets dangling from her as if set alight on the water by those same nocturnal fires and spells, as she herself lit and choreographed that same night with a fairy ballet inside the bar or out in the streets, though always watchful of his sprites, a ballet that was magical but perhaps just a little too slow, fatigue had taken a little some- thing from them all, and she watched it closely Robbie noted, Yinn said she remembered those Christmas nights, sure she did, when the red velvet and ribbons ran out, a time like this, then she'd come up with all these costumes and the Chinese silk ran out, what would she have done without her mother's cupboard full of hidden treasures to fall back on, here son, enough to keep the girls decent at least, I told you to watch how much you spent didn't I, that material is expensive and you're so free with it, at least that Jason of yours doesn't cost me because he only wears tees and Bermudas which he never changes except on New Year's, when he gets into a tux, he obviously does it out of respect for you with all those cameras on you, and he's right, so tell me, is it your father's influence that pushes you to let yourself be filmed getting into a boat nearly naked on New Year's Eve, must be, he's the fanciful kind too, plus you're going to catch cold son, well yes what would Yinn have done without her mother's instinct for collecting things, crazy Christmas nights said Yinn to the girls, crazy Christmas nights, and as she skated home Mai saw the blinking red light on her cellphone, a message from Tammy, she could read it later, she was still overcome by one of the girl's posters and now here she was herself, sweet and pitiful, but with all this she'd forgotten about her grandmother, hmmm not good, Mai loved order and Tammy's life was anything but that, you never knew though, like the June bride on the beach, in the middle of all Tammy's confusion some sort of beacon sought Mai out, maybe it was the anxiety in her eyes, standing there in front of the poster and wearing her father's ample shirt from head to toe over her rocker swimsuit, there was Tammy once again saying to Mai just look at my prince's flaming hair, still no concern on his face, even in the ambulance they couldn't get the white glove off him, that spell-binding, miracle-working hand of supernatural gifts, was there a red filter on the camera as it registered the dancing and singing or was his long hair suddenly afire, it was, he was ablaze with second- and third-degree burns, just look at his highness coming straight toward us, head in flames and yet he doesn't lose his cool, look Mai, look Tammy said, it's like he's in some deep, permanent sleep or lethargy or something, it's an illusion though, hey you going already, I'll text you, you know, about my brother and me, g'night Mai, aren't you worried about skating along Atlantic Boulevard on your own, I mean don't you ever get scared, Tammy standing there dancing in her father's shirt and rocker swimsuit, asking you really gotta go, that happened in Los Angeles and no one was expecting it, hair totally on fire, no sweat, no reaction, why you going so soon, and Mai's mind skipped from Tammy and her father's shirt to the poster of the burning man on a red screen, as if nailed to the sunset, her very own prince alone in her room with her, isolated beneath a jungle of palms and bougainvilleas, a damp jungle, nearly midnight, guess it's not really that late thought Mai, it's just all that fog on the ocean and along the boulevard clinging to her skin as she strode, skating along to her grandmother who might already be asleep, who was thinking that she'd have to ask her granddaughter about the jewellery, they were so close after all, understood each other so well, yes she must ask her about that, the medallions and all, Esther would say are they still in the box, you have no idea sweetheart all the bad dreams one has at my age, imaginings that leap out at you, our imaginations hold so many horrible things, you have no idea, you're young though, you're not just stepping into a pure world of the supernatural, it's got some very ugly ghosts you know, obsessively ugly, mediocre at best, phobias of enemies on every side, I must tell my granddaughter that's not all though, there they all were for me to see in Charles and Frédéric's house, Caroline was the first to come over to me, the lamps were shining so bright and I just headed over to them, oh they were everywhere, and tenderness, and do you know what Caroline said to me, oh nothing new you know, dear friend she said, the only thing is to struggle always to do better, really Esther all that's required of us is to move forward, but that's not so easy when you're hemmed in with old habits like pettiness, greed, and so on and that's what holds me up, most of all I can never match the generosity of Jean-Mathieu, he's been so good to me all these years, no, how can I ever make up for it all, I've used him so and only now am I aware of it, I've even humiliated him, me with my financial cushion on the side, listen well to what I'm saying Esther dear, nothing to be proud of, believe me, and nothing that isn't the true picture of me as I am, you knew I'd be the first to approach you, that's what Caroline said from beneath her antique hat, stepping on that hapless scorpion inside the house, a smash from the flat sole of her sandal, this was Caroline, vain and greedy, heedless of Jean-Mathieu's financial straits, you'll know me and say that's her all right, no surprise there with all her faults, there she was holding out her hand to me and saying come, come, don't be afraid, she wondered would Mai yell that the jewels, medallions, and priceless tokens of love from Mélanie were gone from the box, Mère would hear her rage against Marie-Sylvie de la Toussaint, I always said, didn't I, that she was no good, and Mère would say you have to make allowances for what she and her brother have been through, that's something you need to learn, how to empathize, you've never been there have you, adrift on the ocean on some makeshift raft, no country, no home, you must develop that ability Granddaughter, that's what Mère would have to say to her, probably in vain, she knew Mai just wasn't ready to understand that language, and she'd also tell her you know that box also contains letters I sent to Augustino just as I used to, although he's hardly written back to me these past months, although he's become a writer with his entire life before him so I can't hold it against him, still I truly do believe, sweet Mai, that generations can't separate true kindred spirits, no matter what family, that's how I feel about you and Augustino, and I always will my dearest, he even wrote me that once links like that are forged in life we have to fight, survive, and live with the same impulse, the same passion, and perhaps he might have added the same hopes for understanding despite the chasm of age, one age, one time for us all to cling to and better know one another, borrowed time we can't get back if we waste it, oh those letters I wrote for him are now yours, this Mère would tell her granddaughter, she could still hear the protests when Mai discovered the loss of the jewels and medallions from the box, inestimable tokens of Mélanie's love, I told you Grandmother, I told you how awful she was, thieving and nasty just like that brother of hers, He-Who-Never-Sleeps and kills animals in the cemetery, preying vulture I told you, didn't I tell you, no then, no Mère would not tell her about the missing gems, she wasn't entirely certain and couldn't accuse her guardian as long as she wavered like this, really not fair, and here she was, Marie-Sylvie, raising the cushions behind her in the bed and saying, as if to reassure her, here you'll be better like this when Adrien comes in to see you, though it wasn't certain he was there right now, Mère remembered him of course, the white trousers and navy blue blazer as though he were there in front of her and confessing he'd seen Charly at the tennis court that afternoon and been charmed into taking a ride in the car she chauffeured, the idea of him stepping gingerly and uncertainly into it tormented Mère, maybe because without Suzanne anymore he was defenceless as he was getting ready to sell his house and move in with the children in New York and had fallen prey to Charly's wiles, oh that golden couple's house, the past splendour of Suzanne and Adrien, one last look at that Chinese screen, such delicate shelter for Suzanne when she wrote and read, all those years, all those poems above all, only now being published, how bashful she'd been about that he told Mère, she never wanted them to become public, must be because of me, I didn't push her hard enough, oh selling this house of love, of books we wrote together, just a Chinese screen between us, such a terrible uprooting, it tore Adrien apart he told Mère one afternoon, of course my children will look after me for a while, years even, then I'll go to one of those homes to wait to die, where boredom probably does everyone in, I am not just an old man I am a poet and I know it sets me apart and strengthens me, of course it does my dear replied Mère, and you're still majestic, just as Suzanne was when she left for Switzerland, she knew of course the leukemia was progressing very rapidly and would soon deform her entirely, not one for resignation though and why would she be, Esther, when I wrote my poem

"Giving Account," that's what I said, never, never must one give up, what a terrible sin it is, and I'll have to render accounts, what if I did let myself fall under Charly's deadly spell of beauty and youth so capable of destruction, might that not be better than imposing myself on the children only to have them one day take me to one of those places so I can die of boredom, a place for lives to twinkle out like countless fading stars, when my life as a poet might be so enriched by life and love with Charly, what a story to tell, life sustaining itself by meeting another life, you see Esther dear, this is what I've been thinking, perhaps it's not very noble of me but it is what it is, Mère's response was well my friend, it means you want me to have to go on worrying about you, forever worrying wherever I travel, is that it, on top of all the concerns I have about my children and my grandchildren, that was when Adrien, sitting next to her on the bed, took her hands in his and said Esther dear, you know a poet like me, suddenly abject and useless without his Suzanne, first and forever a dreamer, wild nights, wild said Robbie to Petites Cendres, Christmas and all the others that disappointed Fatalité, that's what took him from us, bled him dry, that was when Petite Cendres saw the glimmer of a tear between two dark lashes, Robbie's nighttime lashes, a crown weighing on deep, wide eyes, it's true she gave herself too easily to anyone who asked, it was a relic from the prostitution days with her mother, who'd had to do it since childhood, deflowered, bought and sold for pennies, deep in debt till the day she died, singing in glory and pathos, poor Fatalité, hemorrhaging life right there onstage at the cabaret, anything for a bit of friendship, just a bit, and yet no one around her seemed to realize it was going on, wild nights, my Fatalité's wild nights Robbie said, and Petites Cendres recalled one Christmas night when he'd spotted his old parents hawking their Bibles on Esmeralda, then the old man suddenly got up to scrape shrilly away at his fiddle, a worn old toque on his head once trimmed with fur,

and greeted Petites Cendres with respect, not recognizing him
in women's clothes, good evening he said, good evening,
baring a mouth full of cavities, and Petites Cendres felt sorry
for him and his mother sitting on the bench like that, his kin,
his own poor folks, destitute on Christmas. Nora swam vigor-
ously across the pool thinking that if she painted all night
again instead of going to sleep, though she didn't sleep much
anyway, and her children let her know that wasn't good, as if
she was to blame for having tremulous nerves, then at least
she'd be able to finish this one before Christiensen got back,
yes it would be finished she decided as she splashed through
the iridescent green water illuminated by the garden lamps,
fingers and hands still stained from the work, she'd quickly
stripped off her pant-stiffened smock for an instant skinny-
dip, the gumbo rained huge leaves among the vines that wove
it to the other trees, she'd eaten its fruit long ago in Africa,
savouring smells, sounds, and an atmosphere rather like this,
why such a fog around the orange and banana trees though,
for days now she'd been sowing and planting in the mist and
mould, you either had to get up early or not sleep at all to
keep pruning away the unhealthy growth on her plants and
trees, and while her husband was away she decided to paint
the floors with patterns of her own design so they resembled
the real plants and trees, like the tall and powerful gumbo
she'd painted in Christiensen's office, now one could move
from house to garden amid the same serene vegetation, one
her own painted reproduction, the other voluptuous and
vibrant, hovering over the pool rich in aromas and perfumes,
paddling through the greenish water that undulated away
from her but did so much good, now she could see the painting much better, just now set upright against the wall, it felt
good to do things on her own though it was hard to carry, but
as long as she had the strength she'd ask no one for help, was
it too rough, too vast, yes looking at it from a distance like
this it did seem too broad and the shape of Nora's face

somewhat ample amid the spareness of the portrait that
seemed to fade into the distance, as though craning upward
to view herself from above, a lunar space, her own face and
head suspended in a void, a major defect she hadn't spotted
up close, the distended eye that stared back at her out of
proportion, the enlarged eyes were what drew her in, they
should be attentive and not fixed, Nora realized more than
ever she didn't have the mystical ability of a Van Gogh depict-
ing himself while in the hellish tumult of a fever yet calmed
just enough by the green of his suit that allowed the white
shirt and dangling collar to show, the rough, worn suit of a
poor man, a jumble of greenish flames, not blacks and reds,
a rough-edged green to calm the man in the picture condemned to madness, a damnation ready to emerge from his
own red-bearded mouth, closed perhaps but still on the point
of biting and howling through clenched teeth, in her awk-
wardness Nora thought she must have painted simply the
remaining fragments of all that had fallen away, of course
Christiensen would say she was wrong to underrate herself
like that, still she'd at least like to actually hear the cry burst
out of that Nora's mouth, not stifled like Van Gogh's, a woman's scream, a woman who had borne children, not inert and
censored, not necessarily one of pain either but one of victory, this painted mouth of hers uttered neither anyway, not
a trace of a voice and certainly not a howl of any kind, only
a mouth drying behind lips pinched in perplexed hesitation,
vacillating between criticism and remonstrance or possibly
some delayed expression of wonder, now surely that was
what she really intended, yes, to leave the lips slightly open
in a moment of enchantment or at least a longing for enchantment, not shut them so firmly, implying an ambivalent ferocity
perhaps about to give way to curses, to calumny, or to a frustration that was not warranted when one considered how
spoiled she was, Van Gogh would have had more courage
than this in his picture of self-mutilation, wearing bandage

and fur bonnet as he clenched his pipe, the pipe, his sole comfort amid the flaming reds, the greys, the black of his coat and fur, then the deathly white of his bandage, the terrifying pallor in his face, the disconsolate eyes, reddened eyelids perhaps contaminated by his own paints, lead, arsenic, his own poisons already absorbed into his membranes, the furious and self-mutilating vision he had of himself, barely able to scratch out his painting in pitiless strokes, yet when it came to his friend, he painted with such primitive kindness, practically joyous, with a hint of a smile on the mad friend's face that bordered on generous indulgence when he painted flowers, Nora instead fled her own portrait and swam to the far side of the pool, where she watched the raccoons on the brown picket fence knowing she would soon feed them, this would have to be the last time though before her husband came back, he wouldn't allow it, lightning leaps and bounds of fur between the trees, knowing that in a few moments she'd be calling them and speaking their language, holding out dishes for them to take in their paws as agile as human hands, bits of bread, now already calling to them from the pool, yes speaking their language and saying I've had enough of this self-portrait, time for food, no more painting and worrying about veracity, enough or not enough, she'd go on feeding them in fact, tomorrow and tomorrow, secretly though so her husband wouldn't see, it was on a foggy night like this when she and her brother were both children that he had lost his baby monkey in the bush, it had gone to bed with him under the mosquito netting, then by morning it was gone, he thought he'd heard the yelp of a hyena in the dark, yes something like it, the paint smelt of oil and lead, her fingers were still stained with colours when Nora climbed out of the pool refreshed but a bit agitated, Christiensen would be here in a few hours but she dare not go near the picture again for fear of ruining it, she'd done that many times before, broken, destroyed her work by degrees, no, this time she'd be reasonable, and she got ready to meet him at the airport, she intended to look fresh and exquisite in an irresistible dress and straw hat with African necklaces, though perhaps her hair was too short, barely a strand touching her ear, she should have chosen a dye somewhere between blonde and red, this one didn't quite work, why was she so worried anyway, was this really necessary, for every Saturday when he was home, Christiensen had breakfast alone with Valérie at the hotel by the sea anyway, what was this constant need for female friends, weren't she and the perfectly run household enough for him, he was away so much as it was, in Niger or elsewhere, why Valérie and all the other lady friends for breakfast by the sea then, except when the children were there of course, but why this devotion to Valérie, she was exceptional, yes, though Nora couldn't understand her philosophical writings and hardly read them, Christiensen said he admired how she had overcome so many obstacles but Nora too had done as much and was alone so often right here in the present, Valérie was resilient but again so was Nora, yet these Saturday breakfasts and this romantic feel to their relationship, why thought Nora, Valérie had an intellectual and loving husband of her own, widely read too, so what need had she of Nora's, very helpful of course but still he was Nora's husband and did they really think she was just a child, an irrepressible kid, slightly irresponsible, thoughtless even, did they consider her at all in their chats together on Saturdays, he always seems to need some female artist or writer apart from me, I mean look at all the languages I've learned on our travels, and mostly for him, going from country to country with the children in tow, she'd never dare ask him this, not even where he went at midday on Saturdays or with whom, in fact he confided in her quite sincerely I eat with Valérie, she's got a problem that needs solving you see, she worries a lot about other people, friends, kids, and so on, and she's awfully generous he said as though his wife were not, now that was bad, Valérie sees into the problems of our time so very well he went on, there's always going to be this cleavage between the U.S. and Europe, that's where her kids are and her husband's here with her, was it really that or was Christiensen the psychologist peering into Valérie's soul even though her own husband understood her so well, but Nora would say none of this, furious but silent, it's better that way because jealousy is an ugly and confused state to be in, this she often said to Marianne, it's nasty to be envious of your sister Greta, look at me, look at your mother, Papa's always away but is your Mama jealous of what might go on overseas, no she's not, besides, such feelings are hideous and disruptive, now dry your tears Marianne, you know I love you every bit as much as Greta, now you really mustn't feel like this my angel, really, perhaps what she felt toward Valérie was envy more than jealousy, envy of her analytic intelligence, not to mention her brunette beauty, of course it was pleasant for Christiensen to dine in her company, besides he was just as close to her husband Bernard and often ate with him too, Valérie was a hearty eater unlike Nora, not like Nora at all, who was always dashing here and there, more likely to be feeding others than herself, never sitting long at the table, these breakfasts by the sea were really unfair she thought, really unjust, so why didn't she give vent to her resentment, yes that would put an end to it, then stop thinking about it, so why not simply tell Christiensen tomorrow or tonight after they've made love, why indeed, but in the picture her mouth let not a single word escape its lips, not a cry, not a shout of victory for her art or for the children she'd borne, reticent in all it sulking perplexity somewhere between criticism and protest, no, no retouching this, otherwise she'd ruin it, she looked back at the portrait bitterly, still brooding about Christiensen and his breakfasts with Valérie, then later on Saturday, as independent as ever, he'd be visiting Mélanie's mother with the same serene affability, just the sort of thing she herself was incapable of, he would not see death encroaching on Mère's face as it nestled among the pillows, just a woman and mother still wanting to see those near her reconciled and reconciling, Augustino had written that he wouldn't be back since Adrien had scorched his first book, though his grandmother urged him to come back, to soften up, Adrien just couldn't keep from striking down young poets, novelists, and writers in general, even running on and repeating himself, perhaps he was jealous, frightened of Augustino's lucidity Nora thought, that must be the reason for her reticent mouth, her moody confusion, her hatred of Christiensen and Valérie's complicity, of Bernard, Esther, and anyone she could not control and command, even with his children Christiensen acted independently of her, each one elicited a different way of listening, of teaching, he was a mentor to Valérie, to all of them, recommending, guiding, inspiring, and it irritated Nora to be set aside like that, Christiensen said Nora was like one of his children, almost like Ibsen's Nora in *A Doll House*, how insulting to live this way, oh there'd be an occasional compliment on her youthfulness of course, but worse still some invisible conspiracy had brought him to resemble her father, and now she suffered to the point of confusing them, her husband and her arrogant father, two mentors who did her violence, wait, no not that, no this was her dismay talking, when she painted she was always subject to this senseless agitation, maybe akin to Van Gogh's painting himself in scratches and scrapes, ah of course that had to be it, and as for the tête-à-têtes over breakfast between Christiensen and Valérie, well there was nothing she could do about that, Christiensen would go on advising and guiding and she'd just go on worrying about his female writer friends, why one of them was so narcissistic she even mistreated her youngest children, what could Valérie possibly do to save these teens caught up in drugs and abandoned by parents so very much in love with themselves and their own success, who stayed out all night at the casino, how could the younger ones be saved Valérie asked Christiensen, so he reminded her about his own daughter Marianne, a social worker in the Washington ghettos confronted with similar delinquents, still these weren't ghetto kids Valérie said, they live like us in middle-class houses, Christiensen, it seemed, just couldn't understand his daughter's social vocation, not having delinquent children himself, far from it, they'd lived sheltered lives and gone to the best colleges and universities like hers in Europe, no this conversation could go on and on, searching for a way to deal with the rebellious children of a self-centred writer, better if Nora were spared this sort of discussion, she couldn't bear the subject, anything approaching violence unsettled her and she began to apprehend it everywhere around her, threatening, even in her home, no when it came to violent people, especially children, she lost it, there was a complete loss of bearings, at least her own children hadn't turned out that way even if Hans butted heads with her, quite often in fact, saying his grandparents and their parents had colonized Africa and all the continent's woes came down to that, this shocked Nora when she thought about all her father and grandfather had done, devotedly caring for lepers, operating on gangrene, and all she'd seen growing up with them, what did Hans know about the suffering of Africans anyway, it was an evil past and it was on white consciences, yes he said, all their wars and misfortunes still stem from this, oh how hurt Nora felt and she'd have liked to guide, shape, and control the things that came out of his mouth, she had no idea where this came from, what did he have to revolt against, he had everything, but he'd remind her of the little slave-girl who slept at the foot of his grandmother's bed right on the ground just like that with no covers or anything, the *boys*, as his grandparents called them, waited on both older generations far out in the bush, a nice, quiet European life that would shame them for generations to come said Hans, yet Nora had no idea why he spoke like that, her only son, it was so hard to bear, words coming out of his mouth she could neither suppress nor control, accusing her indirectly, and yet how alike they really were, mother and son, such a striking physical resemblance, so why treat her like this, why, better to forget about it now, she had to get dressed to go and meet Christiensen at the airport, think about him and nothing else, so handsome and so able in everything he did, what on earth would he think of her self-portrait though, especially leaning against the wall like that, would he stand in judgement on the straw hat, the billowy white dress, the African necklaces, better not think about it, just him, Christiensen, her husband, her own, tonight he would possess her, tonight and tomorrow she'd be by his side at last, at last she could sleep and rest, knowing that he once again ruled over the house, she too would rule over what was hers with no one to disturb them, no one. As Mai opened the gate her father had left unlocked, she saw lights go on all the way up the garden path perfumed with oleander, to her grandmother's one-room cottage, past a stone pool where the birds came to drink in the daytime, chirping and chattering while Mai's cats circled, though too well-fed to pounce, all of it so deliciously languid to her, then of course there was her swing beneath the trees, forever waiting as though she were a little girl again, gently rocked by warm sleepiness on summer afternoons, the breath of music and traces of fog that still hung over the island, her grandmother's shutters open to the night so the familiar music still filtered through, the same Schubert sonata for piano and violin she'd listened to so many times with Grandmother, leaving her skates on the swing Mai carefully stepped toward the little cabin while the red light signalling Tammy's message continually blinked on her cellphone, finally she couldn't put it off anymore and took the message, then another one, what was it she wanted to say, a pact, my brother and I have a pact, listen your name is borrowed from a girl who disappeared when she was eleven and they never found her, this second one set her heart to racing, then suddenly she felt breathless, we do too want to disappear, my brother and me, that's our pact, like the prince with the flames suddenly climbing up our hair, then nothing, we melt like wax, no sign of regret or surprise, just a white glove, reading these words Mai quickly replied no, don't do it Tammy, forget the pact, no I'll see you tomorrow, then she thought tomorrow's too late, her fingers trembled on the phone, you've got to wait Tammy, my grandmother, she's, no Tammy don't do it, your friend, your friend Mai, how strange it sounded to her, your friend, your friend, words she hardly ever used, no pact, you get that, no pact at least until I see you, my grandmother, my grand . . . I can't leave her tonight, she's, but the words weren't there any more, flown from beneath her fingers, what should she do first, go to her grandmother or to Tammy, then the sonata from her grandmother's room began again, she'd have to go via the veranda where, leaning against the living-room door, she'd bump into Marie-Sylvie de la Toussaint out for a smoke and looking bitter, Mai would have to get by her somehow because she'd be leaning hard on the door like some deranged vestal, priestess of evil, but Mai was as big as her brother Vincent now, no longer the slight young thing that Marie-Sylvie de la Toussaint could slap around when she didn't listen, those days as a victim of her sadism were gone and Mai was as athletic as ever her fragile brother was, in fact one would say he was the girl and she the boy, firm thighs and square shoulders, oh there you are said Marie-Sylvie de la Toussaint, emerging as though hidden behind a cloud of cigarette smoke, your parents are out in the car looking for you, there was the priestess of evil squarely before her in the middle of the veranda, then Mai felt the slap on her cheek, yes Marie-Sylvie de la Toussaint had done it, and why, what had Mai done exactly, it wasn't midnight yet but this sadist had slapped her anyway, Mai, as big as Vincent and bearing the name of a girl who had disappeared when she was eleven, Mai, this Mai knew that her friend Tammy, friend, what a strange word but that's how it had to be, her friend Tammy had sworn she'd go up in flames with her brother, no, that she could not let happen, but who to run to, her grandmother or Tammy, yet over all of it she resented the slap, slapped on the cheek the day her grandmother was, the night when she might be . . . then her mind switched back to Tammy and wondered what really struck her deepest, all this as she heard the sonata still playing through the open shutters out into the foggy night, a blessing, a blessing that her grandmother still lived and was listening to her music, whereas Tammy, who could possibly know, who could foresee, whatever few words she'd texted, your friend Mai, wait, forget the pact, no wait, your friend Mai, there was no way to know what was really happening to them. Each of them giving a tug in the direction of the party, the white papier-mâché horse slowly advanced, Robbie on one side and Herman in his fringed dress and beige boots on the other, the echo of the boots clicked loudly inside and out and Petites Cendres thought Robbie looked ecstatic and totally untrammelled, though it was really too bad Fatalité couldn't experience this night, right about now the Captain must have just left her to rest in the sand at the bottom of the sea with the wild fishes, the bag of ashes ripped open and the last grains of her existence pouring out, perhaps he'd hesitated awhile before doing that and sat through the sunset on the deck of his boat with the bag still on his knees, pretty foggy, not enough wind, he'd been waiting quite a while already in his white cap with gold trim before finally getting into his wetsuit and diving in, quite a while, Yinn was thinking about the same thing and about the Captain's mutinous decision to take some of the ashes and do it his way, to pay homage by planting them on the bottom, or maybe he was more worried about My Captain putting himself in danger on the slopes of a coral reef where currents were the strongest, Yinn's gaze settled on Herman's wheelchair ready to take him home later on, the operation had worked so he was stuck with his stroller as he laughingly called it for a few days longer, and now he was already up dancing and singing the night away, still his hollow and slightly livid cheeks were puzzling, so was his thinning neck, still Herman always demanded a lot of himself thought Yinn, maybe I should have told him to go home to rest, then go see someone, but you couldn't tell Herman anything could you, he'd just blow up, he didn't even admit to being treated, he just denied the whole thing, anticipating the concern in Yinn's expression, he yelled come and join us, why you looking so melancholy just now when the limo's gonna take us across town so the girls can get a round of applause and some admiration, looking serious, Yinn turned toward the door and took in the stairway, already crowded with customers waiting for the late show, she was the natural pole of attraction though she'd rather be out in the street sharing fun and regally greeting all the girls driving by on their way to zigzag the main streets in slow procession, lightly draped in winter fog and tinged with the smell of salt water, Yinn opened the door when they got back to the bar, bent down, and bestowed a glittering necklace on one of the girls, the same as they gave to prospective customers outside before the show, they seemed to her a bit like business cards, the ones she'd had made in a risqué pose that showed her long legs peeking out from under her flounced skirt, nevertheless chaste-looking, as the other necklaces and cards got trampled underfoot by those out walking into the dawn after the show was done and before the purple lights were turned off over the stairway and Petites Cendres headed for his spot on the red sofa, the beauty of Yinn and the mystery of her impenetrable languor in the poster were not yet crumpled in the street, the cards not yet pulverized by feet or scattered by the wind with the words COME SEE THE SPECTACULAR ARTIST YINN become just paper balled up and turned to garbage by indifferent crowds now feeling nothing in particular anymore, their thirst slaked for the moment, never knowing who she was under that libidinous pose, not even her face under the blue mascara and slanted eyes with lashes galore or even, thought Petites Cendres, lingering a little over this fleeting image held only for the night, Yinn's black hair falling over her shoulders, slenderness in skin-tight jeans or loose shorts like Jason's, he must be so very happy in the steady glow of a love that encouraged his art to grow and the sewing room where marvels were born every day and there was no crowd to be weaned of his poses, Petites Cendres mused, couples seeking the fruits of unconditional freedom through him, everywhere, they came from everywhere to see him, hear him, be near him, that pair of Muslim boys for instance walking straight toward him hand in hand and watching the show, seeking out Yinn's gaze as if to say at least with you we know we won't be persecuted, stand up for us Yinn, you know if we go home we'll be stoned to death or hanged or jailed and tortured to death, you know what they do in Iran, defend us Yinn, you are our only hope in this massacre of youth, often they need only do that, hold hands, a fraternal kiss, and they're dead, stoned, help us against this barbarism Yinn, don't forget about us, and every night Yinn's soul overflowed from this flood of laments, nothing he could do though, just seek consolation in the arms of Jason, the only one to carry this burden thought Petites Cendres, Jason was there for him, constant and reliable, that was certain, the hollow cheeks and neck of Herman, his denial, Petites Cendres' cough, all of these scatterings too much of a burden, too human, and in his extravagance Yinn bore all of it alone. Don't tell me you don't recognize him, it's Lazaro, the one who killed a student during a demonstration in Chicago, I know it, I saw him on TV and in the paper Olivier said, waking up his wife Chuan, you and Jermaine even heard the gun go off when it happened, hey it's after midnight and Jermaine's still out with his friends, so go back to sleep will you Chuan said, tenderly placing her hand on Olivier's forehead, she knew she wasn't reassuring him at all, so tormented was he by now that nothing would do, a dull, relentless feeling she couldn't put her finger on, he didn't seem like the man she had fallen in love with anymore than Jermaine saw a father in him, of course he dropped by on occasion quoting something from an article he had written long ago when he was a young black civil rights campaigner, the time of heroics in the streets, that must be what he was thinking about when he woke up like this in the middle of the night talking about those who still did what he no longer had the strength for, don't you remember Caridad's son Lazaro, he asked his wife, what a fanatical kid he was even before he grew up, of course you do, Chuan looked at this man, hers, so old and white-haired all of a sudden while she herself still felt so young and even closer to their son, he was touching but no longer reachable, crushed by the weight of a lifetime's inner and social pressures, first a young militant, then a rebellious journalist, then a senator, what repression and pressure he must have gone through and never saying anything to his family, just holding it in all those years, were it not for such extreme swings in his memory he surely would have been content in the house she'd designed 'specially for them right by the sea, Cuban architecture with ochre and yellow walls, red tiles cooked by the sun, their own house, their own shiny-coated dogs, how happy they should have been, their beloved and only son Jermaine, who had told his mother he wouldn't be going back to work on his film in California till his father was better, but his mother wondered when that would be, will he, will we ever find peace and happiness again, they tell me it's irreversible, maybe Olivier was right this time, could Lazaro, have committed the Chicago crime or was her husband simply confusing his face with one of many in the media after the protest against the punishment of a Muslim girl by her father and brothers, then there it was, the sudden intrusion of Lazaro all dressed in black, just as Chuan used to see him on his motorbike as he noisily circled their house and aggressively spied on them, and his mother complaining and worrying about him, he was evil she said, he'd inherited the violent behaviour from his father and uncles back in Egypt, his eruption amid the students, the explosion of a handgun, the girl crumpling into the arms of her friends, who knows, maybe this time Olivier wasn't having night delusions, if he was wrong about Lazaro she'd go out on the patio, wait for Jermaine and talk to him, and why was the sea fog lingering and surrounding the house, the garden, and the patio this way, yes she'd wait and talk to him, who knows, maybe this time he was right. Mère thought how sweet it would be if she could hear Franz talking to Yehudi and Wolfgang outside her window, sitting on the bench among the frangipanis, talking about his past and their future, Wolfgang may be gifted for the piano but he still lunges joyfully at Mai's swing, he'd still rather play than bend to Franz's discipline, stretching his finger over the keyboard, yes they'd both be virtuoso pianists as well as orchestra leaders he said, you see Papa Franz one day will be very old and not right now but later, no matter where he is, will be there to see you both doing your exercises in the conservatory, yes he'd see it all, and the same papa or grandpapa would see it all through a window carved in the clouds, yes all of it, the same Papa Franz or scarcely balding Grandpapa with a black and grey mane just the way you see it now or when I'm conducting the orchestra, you must grow with the musicians in suppleness and grace, that's how it will be, Yehudi and Wolfgang were still small of course but growing up they'd acquire a huge musical memory and would conduct complex works from that memory, just the way Franz did, but they still needed to work extremely hard regardless, and other musicians will do the work for me, but for now sol-fa lessons, my friends, sol-fa, and I know you hate it now both of you, oh how sweet it would be to overhear thought Mère, under the yellow frangipani blossoms as Wolfgang played on the swing and the cord squeaked in time to his delighted cries, where was this eccentric Franz anyway, and the boys where were they, his beauties and prodigies as he called them, had they all gone off in that rattletrap convertible of his in the rain and dense fog wondered Mère, how come she didn't see them anymore, such a charming group and so entertaining, or perhaps Franz had been busy with some new creation while she was sleeping, something by a new composer that the world simply had to hear, Japan it was, who could remain unmoved by that face ringed with a mane and never more alert than when bounding out onto the stage, whether it be in Japan or Brazil, oh they weren't out on the swing or beneath the yellow frangipanis anymore, Franz and the children, well his latest ones anyway, there were quite few after all, now all she could hear was the sound of voices outside on the veranda, it must be Mélanie and Daniel back with Mai, who knows what kids get up to, had Mère ever known for sure, there is nothing so sealed off as lives that no longer depend on us, that was Mai for you, despite her parents' watchful eye and the tight rules she was subjected to and why, from her bed Mère could see the shadow of Marie-Sylvie de la Toussaint projected onto the mosquito screen, hovering there, taunting her with its dissimulations and thefts and hostility, now she could hear Mai's voice, then Mélanie's and Daniel's on the doorstep confronting and arguing with her, Marie-Sylvie saying she forbade me to smoke in the house, though weakly, your mother orders me about, your grandmother too piles it all on me, do this and do that, you'd think she was the lady of the manor, do you really think I can put up with it, me Marie-Sylvie de la Toussaint, maybe she'd like to remind me how I herded goats with my brother on the hillside, always humiliating me, humiliating both of us, but Daniel and Mélanie would say no, just calm yourself Marie-Sylvie, none of that, our mother has the greatest respect for you and your brother, Esther showed that when she took you in, though whatever Mélanie or Daniel said it would never be enough for the ever insatiable Marie-Sylvie and the fathomless sense of humiliation that appeared to be a class trait, and she said as much, Jenny for instance had studied with the priests and was already a notch above her, now a member of Doctors Without Borders, she at least, she was able to go out on her own and grow while Marie-Sylvie could never be more than a lowly servant, not as humbled as my brother though, a reject, a larva, incessant and bottomless were her complaints Mère reflected, bile chewed over and over for their privations and abjectness, Marie-Sylvie and He-Who-Never-Sleeps, a shadow charged with murderous aggression just lying in wait, yes right there on that veranda while the toads croaked and the silhouette of Marie-Sylvie de la Toussaint rustled in the foliage around her, as they awoke on the nearby island Rosie and Lou were about to see the dolphins as Ari promised, and the white sands of the uninhabited beach would also show off its egrets and blue herons Lou's father told her, so can't we please make up now while we're in this lovely paradise, can we, have you thought at all about what I mentioned, you know, living part-time with me and Noémie in New York, or are you going to stay jealous just so you can hold it against me, you're not going to be my enemy are you Lou, are you still my sweet child, hmmm, while he'd thought she was sleeping below-decks he'd told Noémie on the cellphone he just couldn't understand how the child managed to be so headstrong with him, and regardless of Lou's hurt feelings Noémie had answered maybe it's just time to stop worrying so much about her and her mother, let's just think about us, I think that's the way to go, we have our own lives to live after all, don't we, and she's just a child, you know they get over disappointments like this pretty quickly, you're a grown man she went on, ever the seductress who disliked children or at least had little enough regard for Lou to understand her properly, Ari what on earth are you waiting for to live your life to the fullest like everyone else, you know you're going to live to regret always worrying about what Ingrid thinks, or Lou, it's really pretty dumb, I mean with me you're going to have everything you've always wanted or dreamed of, how many women are still going to want to be your lover eh, not many, with time they'd be indifferent to him even on this beach, what a charming liar she thought, then taking Rosie's hand she said let's go over on that rock in the shade of the palm tree, look I've got a DVD player in my backpack, we could watch a movie, just you and me, and little Rosie, almost an infant, would surely say no I don't want to, I want to be on the beach with you and your dad and see the dolphins and play with them, and the egrets and the blue herons, that's why we got off the boat, so Lou was going to have to pinch her just enough to hurt and whip her into line, nope you're coming with me, she'd punish Rosie and Rosie would cry, but that was the plan, then she'd dig in against her father tomorrow, not knowing that while they were playing with the dolphins he'd go right on phoning Noémie, she'd have to make a point of never leaving him in peace with her, she launched into the details, it was a film about alligators and I brought it 'specially for you she'd say charmingly to Rosie, a cartoon actually 'cause you're just a baby, but Rosie said, like Ari, she'd much rather see the real thing, live alligators and blue herons, that was Lou's plan though she wasn't yet sure if it would work, and despite the fact that her father was smooth and persuasive, Lou was determined to do this and mercilessly stonewall everything he said. Boy I'm really not much of a grandson am I Samuel thought as his plane came in for a night landing on the island, he'd been way too wrapped up in his choreography for *Venice in a Night*, this was typical of artists like himself, they didn't notice a thing going on around them, riveted to their passions and projects, however shattering the news might be about Grandmother's health, yet here he was still thinking about the dance, he had to phone his videographer about the two curved screens it would take to portray Venice with its houses and buildings crumbling beneath the sea, the terrified doves and white pigeons taking flight above them, both screens portraying glaciers and icebergs in one atonal conflagration, a sense of embracing chaos from the outset soon followed by sorrow, now as he closed the door on his wife and child still sleeping, he realized that anyone would prefer to feel that kind of warmth and security, huddled together instead of taking the plunge into suffering, and perhaps Samuel still felt the sadness of lost comfort, a comfort in believing his grandmother to be immortal, like Tanjou the young Pakistani student his family had befriended, immortal till Samuel saw him falling with the debris from one of the New York towers that cool autumn morning, had it even sunk in that he'd never see him again, anchored in him forever young and forever a friend to them all, and so too for his grandmother, neither of them had the right to just disappear like that, Grandmother so profoundly a part of him that no misfortune could tear that far into the tissue of his being, it just wouldn't be, it couldn't, and with his head leaned against the window of the plane he suddenly realized he had to warn the captain or the steward at once, for as they made their descent toward the runway he could just make out through the mist two other planes heading much too close, the way he'd seen them do in Moscow during a combat simulation, a mock battle of course but still terrifying, planes that practically grazed the rooftops of houses, the Academy of Science, universities and museums, there were regiments of tanks, cavalry with heavy machine guns, aren't they already deployed in the streets, where were these planes going down, on the Academy, on campuses or museums or theatres where the Bolshoi once danced, where, yes got to warn the steward or the captain, those must be warplanes over the city between us and the runway, then with his head still against the window the calm voice of the captain snapped him awake to announce that they were landing in a few minutes, they had to circle a bit till the fog over the runway dissipated, Samuel couldn't help repeating, as he took out his cellphone, I'm really not much of a grandson am I, not much of a man either, it devastated him that his grandmother was out of sorts, perhaps seriously ill, and as soon as they landed he really had to phone his videographer and dancers to make sure nothing would be overlooked in their mosaic of dance and song portraying the world's snowiest peaks melting, nothing left to chance, and as Ari paced the deck he turned off his cell for now, perhaps until tomorrow, weary maybe of helplessly living in wait of Noémie's voice and her often contradictory words, sometimes in virulent opposition to his daughter, which he disliked, why did he have to choose between them anyway, he loved them both of course, but was he so enthralled with this woman or had he become so incapable of thinking like a man or so negligent as a father, he picked up the damn phone again with all its temptations, but what would be the point, things would only change again tomorrow, so why not just sail off with the girls to the next island, Rosie on the other hand was really still a true child, not a hardening preteen like his daughter, and she was agog at the dolphins, whose trainer was a special contact of his since he was a constant mariner, so he could reserve them just for the kids' enjoyment, a whole aquatic park just to cater to Lou's morose moodiness, but what was the point if she was just going to snub him and head for her folding bunk and sulk below with Rosie in tow, oh well it was done now and the cellphone was turned off, he was all hers, perhaps it wasn't too late to turn back, take a short break from Noémie, but he still didn't understand why he as an adult had to bend to the whims of a little girl when he was in love with an exceptional woman, and who knows if he'd ever find any-one like her again, an art critic who could seize in a glance the essence of his sculptures in all their present-day complex-ity, too bad Lou was so badly brought up as Noémie put it, it irritated him, that was when he had the idea to surprise Lou, who so loved animals, he'd cover her walls with nature photos from the lithographs in Tom Mangelsen's *Peace Dances of the Wild Geese* as they migrated across a grey and misty sky, maybe that dance could represent the reconciliation of Ari and his daughter, a bridge to better days, if not then maybe the picture of the bear and cub or the fox and its kits, mother bear and mother fox by the same photographer, serious mothers with their young ones, the she-fox with muzzle pointed, eyes alert, and ears pricked in the direction of green fields where she'd let the little ones play, for now snuggled against her comforting fur as if asking permission and she wondering if the place was safe enough, the question lingering on her wise-looking face, so Ari would tell Lou see how this artful photographer was able to capture the most beautiful scenes that nature still has left, every March the cranes and wild geese in Nebraska hold a ritual called the Peace Dance and they fly off in their thousands from the fields where they've fed into the grey, misty sky, off toward Alaska and Siberia, just look at the hope for a long future reflected in these birds, every animal in the world in fact, there's such pure truth in these pictures and they're for you, the mother fox with her young, the mother bear beside her cub, serenely sniffing the air, we live in a time of disappearance and who knows how much longer we'll see these things, but Lou, though listening, would distance herself from her father right afterwards by lining up a video clip or DVD on her computer, already gone was the age when he could talk to her or have any influence over her, and this Peace Dance would not accomplish a thing, majestic birds or not, peace with her father wasn't what she wanted, it was just as cut and dried as that thought Ari, but he'd cover her walls with posters anyway if only for his own peace of mind, in fact though Lou didn't realize it, he himself was the maternal fox and bear, holding her for just a little bit longer here in this little fortress of a nest with him, nuzzling against his fur, soon enough she'd be off to some flowery field or broken-down road, the world in all the uncertainties it holds for all of us, and escape she would, though Ari tried to see far enough ahead to pick out the dangers that await all our children now, he must, surely he must write to Asoka her godfather to ask his help and spiritual guidance, but what sort of answer could he expect from the austere and saintly monk steeped in prayer and meditation in an Indian temple, the answer that Ari should renounce all pleasure, think only of his child, be a man and a father before all else, especially in such revolutionary times when temples burned and monks fought in the streets for the rights of the poor, all at once Ari was filled with fear for the life of the wandering monk in his saffron robe, he who in this very time of revolt himself fought in the streets while temples burst into flames, what shame Ari felt that his own personal battle was for his art, his art and Lou, what when she slipped away from him in the next few years and when his art no longer sufficed to ensure his future and hers, was it not a dishonour to be this way Ari thought, and on this night of fog out over the water, Chuan said to Jermaine, her son, as he appeared on the patio, let's not speak too loudly now your father's finally asleep, look I think he's right this time, Caridad's son is a killer, now how do you think a mother's supposed to deal with her son's crimes, Chuan stroked her son's face and hair, I mean what would it be like if it were you, Caridad told me herself on the quiet when I was buying some craft pieces in her store, it's as if she knew her son was in for some terrifying part of his life, there was some sort of abscessed hatred in Lazaro that had grown even as she carried him in her belly and her husband beat and abused her, she herself had borne this child, this vengeful abscess of hatred growing inside, oh yes all this before, and afterwards of course bursting into the bloodiest fury, beginning with Carlos his first sworn victim in a childhood quarrel over some shoes, Carlos discharging a stolen rifle he thought was empty when he was attacked by a Cuban cook, then ending up in jail for manslaughter, and all Lazaro could think of was wreaking vengeance on Carlos when he got out, it grew in the meantime, the abscess grew, this Caridad confided to Chuan, the arming of her son by degrees, then becoming more and more a loner, an armed bandit obsessed by killing, anyone and everyone but especially Carlos, filled to the brim with hatred and tortured in the womb by a father as brutal and bloody as he, as hateful of women, oh what can we do she said, when all of a sudden our sons turn bad and leave for Pakistan or elsewhere, who really knows what border village, for indoctrination, hate training, cultivating the poison that is already there inside them, sons cast off, cast loose somewhere in southern Asia or wherever to blow up a train and a station in the name of those wild religious principles, ready to kill hundreds, even thousands of people in the exploding fury of that bloody abscess of hatred, and what can a mother do when he is no longer her son, just another hideous barbarian in some guerilla unit even ready to kill their own mothers, what she asked, and Chuan stroked her own son's hair sitting next to him on the patio at night, she said if it were you what would I do? Robbie told everyone in the bar to listen to Eartha Kitt singing "Santa Baby" in that languid voice of hers, the purring of a feline underlaid with rebel cries, sure it would have been nice for her just to be the little kitten she looked like so she could get her black voice listened to, the black rage of South Carolina plantations where she'd been raped by a white farmer, that's what Robbie was going to sing tonight, "Santa Baby," she'd actually borrow that rage and become Eartha Kitt onstage, plus of course the languid feline moves he'd practised for so long now, the segregation of the fifties produced a lot like her, riding out the bigotry of customers who came up those stairs every day Robbie said, still yanking on the reins of the white papier-mâché horse, from under Jamie's cap came the remark that this was the coldest it had ever been in February, so a second limo had been ordered up to make it easier for the girls with those heavy coats on rolling through the chilly night, they were gorgeous, wow this was the best said Jamie, electrified as he scurried here and there to keep busy and warm, hey some cars I got for us, right I mean look at those fine leather seats, smooth streamlined bodies like birds' wings, c'mon girls get in, you're in for one helluva night, Geisha ya wanna get on the PA and announce tonight's show, we gotta wake these people up Herman chimed in at the top of his voice from atop a dress with transparent fringes but apparently not feeling the cold and still holding on to the reins, everything just the way you wanted it Yinn, he asked with a touch of irony you like our parade or is it more just some sort of folksy show for you, kinda like carnival night, Yinn said yes, it was terrific, just keep the noise down so the cops don't hassle us, but Herman could see her mind was somewhere else, almost as though surveying her queendom, what with Herman out of his wheel-chair, still in the shadow of the bar and barely noticeable, then again maybe she was wondering about Fatalité's ashes travel-ling down to the bottom with only My Captain to guide them, that's what Herman thought anyway, but it was time for some fun and you could hear the peals of laughter from the girls in the limos, then one of them stopped near Yinn, who opened the door for Cobra to get in, Cobra right now seemed the antithesis of Fatalité, a wholesome girl with just her pink, healthy face in a rainbow of colours fresh from the cold like skating out onto the ice in winter, her siren hair blowing in the wind, she was so deliciously rosy as Robbie put it, juicy and fit to take a bite out of, and Cobra climbed in jostling the others as if they weren't brittle-boned skeletons but just as healthy as her, just a touch too virile thought Yinn, and it made her shudder a bit when she suddenly pictured one of those carnival parades by the Belgian painter James Ensor, Yinn had often gone to his work for inspiration for her stage sets, a blurry nightmare whirl of faces and heads like his painting *Masks Mocking Death* in which he mocked death, the carnival scene might have been on the beach because all the skulls had sunglasses and the people were ready to stretch out in the sun, or was it the light filtering through the cracks in the chalky masks, maybe steeped in drunkenness, dancing a jig in the fading sunlight before relaxing on the wharf, maybe they were just devils aflame that the painter had invested with a deathly chill as they waltzed in a Dantesque procession that would be their last, was this what Yinn saw as the healthy, impatient, and vigorous Cobra joined the others in the car, all of them wearing the masks Yinn had nimbly made herself but now starting to come apart, the same cadaverous blur the painter had used in *Masks Mocking Death*, death beneath the bald crowns of the girls in this last walk through the town simply became even more devastating and unabashed for all that, and now here was Herman yelling to distract Yinn, look, stars, stars like Fatalité, boy would she have been proud of us all, let's give them a round of applause and some admiration, this is the tribute you wanted for them, right Yinn, look how the crowd's with them all, well us, hey by the way have you fixed my lace cape yet, I can't wait to get out there on my tricycle, but Herman's words melted into the bar music while Yinn waved to the girls as they drove past and escaped from his thoughts, concentrating on the good vibes of the moment there on the sidewalk with Cobra as she unleashed a shower of necklaces on Yinn, good night Yinn, good night sweet Thai prince. It's time you learned something about empathy Grandmother told Mai, by that I mean Marie-Sylvie de la Toussaint, but all this while Mai could still feel the slap and the insult laid on her, she'd stared at her aggressor long and hard thinking nope, I don't think I will empathize, besides what would things be like in a few hours when Vincent got back, Marie-Sylvie would be oh so sweet, and all this ill-feeling would disappear once her child was on the scene along with her nastiness toward that little tramp Mai, because that is just what she said when she slapped the girl, but under the shock of the moment Mai's thoughts had gone back to Tammy, her parents probably slapped her every single day, mortifying, that was why the pact with her brother, no it couldn't be, it had to be stopped, Mai'd be with her in a few hours but the disaster for now was being slapped by Marie-Sylvie and no longer being able to count on her bedridden grandmother just on the other side of the door to defend her, slapped by that horrible woman, okay a woman who'd been humiliated, as her grandmother would be the first to say, but still Mai had no intention of empathizing, not now, not ever, she'd just have to tell her father, surely he'd stand up for her though he'd never come out against any member of the household before, so he'd probably say look how many years she's been with us, when our son was sickly and she looked after him or when we spent so much time in hospitals with your brother's asthma and so on, but no she was not going to go out of her way, oh how sweet it was to hear Schubert drifting through the open blinds in Grandmother's room, she still felt the full humiliation of that slap and the music seemed to play for her alone, saying you see Granddaughter not everything here is so simple or homey, not even here listening to my Schubert just like yesterday and tomorrow, I live, I breathe, now do you feel a bit better, I know it hurts and I'm not able to get up and defend you from such unfairness my child, I know it's wrong, this was all the consolation her grandmother had to offer, and Mai thought about the kid with chili sauce all over his face that night at the party and where was he now, wandering through town in the fog, shifting from side to side drunk with despair, maybe yelling out that he was from the First Battalion, maybe going back to the beach to dig what he called his grave for the night, like digging a trench in Helmand Province, Afghanistan, for somewhere to grab fitful sleep, digging his nightly sepulchre by hand and wishing his buddies were there with him, each one in his own hole, lairs with hard

earth to sleep on, rocks and a bit of straw, the same spots
they'd use to shoot from after a few winks, sure he had a bed
waiting for him the boy said, a grave after six days' and nights'
march with backpacks and guns in the blazing heat, so yearn-
ing for sleep with machine gun clutched tight, water bottles
in a row next to his boots and cracked mud-caked socks,
packed earth for a resting place, lidless coffins thrown together
for an intermission in the terror, inserted head first into their
helmets perhaps, barefoot and ready for sleep as though
driven into the ground, fast asleep and snoring only moments
from the whistling shells like the chili-face boy digging himself into the beach, a grave-maker in the drifting sea fog, still
in one piece at least, as if howling and crying to Mai they were
all in one piece, all of them burying themselves for the night,
but they were all there, not in the clinic being fitted for new
hands or knees or some other part of themselves, out in those
farms that's what we did he told Mai, and surely he was doing
that now out on the beach, chili face and all, forgotten once
again by the partygoers and townspeople who'd seen him
wandering by, you're nothing but a little slut Marie-Sylvie had
told Mai, then the slap, both of them burnt into her, how glad
she was to hear her grandmother's music like a blessing,
remembering Fatalité while Yinn bathed and washed her, still
determined to show up at the cabaret for the evening show,
for sure she'd be here even if it turned out to be the last time,
no way she'd miss it, her apartment bathed in a glaring light
day and night while Yinn soaped and rinsed her with gloved
hands, she told Yinn see you go to the trouble of protecting
your hands, they're the instruments of your art, that's right my
friend, I'm the kid with the nasty African disease, see these
lesions under my eyes, my name's Rosinah Motshewwa and
there are thousands more like me and her, twenty-nine she
was, no I'm not Rosinah and she's not me, I just saw her in a
newspaper, thousands like us, and who would have imagined
seeing Fatalité sunk so low that Yinn would even have to pass

the hat for her funeral, Yinn could still hear her voice when she washed her, thousands, there are thousands of us, you ever think about that Yinn, then Yinn pictured thousands of white limousines filing through the streets, men, women, and children all passing in front of her house, like Rosinhah they wouldn't be in limos though, more like carts, Fatalité at the front of a line so long it stretched beyond the city limits, enough of them to fill the ocean, did anyone even have the strength left to dance or smile, rows on rows of them barely able to walk and some couldn't even do that, standing upright in carts, now no longer smiling and singing, that's when Herman said what's the matter Yinn, got yourself all tangled up in Cobra's necklaces, here let me help you out, so this was a good thing we did tonight wasn't it and Yinn's face suddenly shut down tight, though he said sure it was good, meanwhile Herman got her shoulders free and shook out the folds of her blue dress, still it saddens me to know Fatalité was so hard up that we had to pitch in for her funeral, I just can't get over it, then she remembered dreaming about Herman too, the same Herman who right now was here in front of her holding the horse's reins, in this dream the horse came to life, and on top, as white-fringed as the horse, was Herman riding straight across town like a conquering hero, hey what you need isn't a tricycle, it's a horse, suddenly more intimate and almost tender, she said that's it a horse, right, well in the meantime until I get my legs back, I've got this Herman said, pointing to his wheelchair, at least it gets me home at night, 'cause these evening shows just wear me out, you're kidding me Yinn aren't you, he cursed the thing standing by itself in the shadows, see here's my fiery steed champing at the bit, my stroller, that's not what I meant said Yinn, I had a dream of you winning out over all these problems, I am already said Herman, brushing it off like Fatalité, always will be he said again, and don't you forget it Yinn, don't you forget it, held close to her heart, the red roses still in their ribbon and cellophane were to be Nora's offering to Christiensen at the airport but now all of a sudden she wasn't so sure, some insane impulse made her dash them to the floor and trample them, hard leather boots grinding the petals, when she awoke in the dark she saw the garden lights on, still foggy, still night-time, she must have lain down on a deck chair by the pool dressed and ready to drive to the airport, straw hat and all, then fallen asleep under the gumbo tree, its blossoms sweetening the chill night air just before sunrise, just a quick nap and the nightmare of trampled roses and crushed wrapping clung to her perspiring skin like reality, Christiensen would have said maybe our dreams are cleverer than we are but she didn't agree, one had to beware the rough edges of the subconscious, such unholy disorder, the smashed flowers would be part of it from now on, let it go and never come back, now how did her painting look in the gentler light of garden lamps, hmmm, still that lunar space surrounding Nora's face, the bluish pallor beneath the eyes as though the model were about to take flight, that tight line of a mouth she didn't like either, practically a hint of greed or grasping, why not just tear the whole thing up before her husband got here, get rid of everything she didn't like about it, that reticent fold of the mouth, that face borne aloft in a lunar void, restrained eyes, quick, think about something else, phone the children in Europe and find out where they are and what they're doing, why didn't they tell her more about their lives, even the ones she was closest to, all she had was the camera on her laptop, faces still too blurry when they moved, she talked to them for hours every day, yes, but still they said so little about themselves, nothing to give her the reassuring sense of their being gathered around her, it had cost so much to renovate this place for them but when on earth would they show up, no not greed or grasping on that face but a lack of nuance and balance, though O'Keeffe would never have made a mistake like that would she, sitting in judgement of her model instead of simply portraying her, these forms were too well-defined, too stiff, not free, not alive and unshackled, lyric in a way Nora herself could not be, no this picture deserved to be trampled, squashed underfoot, same as the red roses of her dream she thought, now then what was she going to cook for Valérie's birthday dinner, a few days from now all her friends would be gathered round tables set in the garden, better forget about that godawful painting altogether, Bernard and Valérie were gourmets quite capable of appreciating the finer points of her cuisine, rabbit possibly, not like when her vegetarian kids showed up with all their complaints in tow, especially Marianne, who couldn't bear to put up with dead animals, think about it Mama little lambs and rabbits, just babies, and you're killing them, well I mean you're getting someone else to do it for you but think about those places where they torture them and chickens too, no there would be none of this from Bernard and Valérie, they knew good food and they always said hers was perfection, still that picture was another story, that moon-framed face and the dissatisfied corners of the mouth, what would they say, would they say anything at all, astonishing, that's what they'd say, they always did, astonishing as always Nora, unusual, bizarre even, no not that but genuinely astonishing and deeply moving, her father now he would have said unusual, no bizarre, no a failure perhaps, bitter and envious that way, he'd say it was a total failure, I honestly wonder why you even bother to paint, my girl, it's the same as when you decided to be a surgeon, surely you can see you haven't the talent or the ability for it, that was when Nora would weep for days on end, even when she and her brother were away at African convent schools she did, and now Marianne was the one who felt envious of her older sister, get rid of the horrible thing, poor child, still the social worker in her was extremely sensitive to others, the only one of her children who had this in her, perhaps a character flaw that made her a sponge to soak up all injustice and evil, too vulnerable to the crises of the marginalized kids in her care, that same sense of charity, even exaggeration, worried her mother, fortunately the others were more realistic and a little less empathetic, all of them married whereas Marianne never really saw it as a choice for her, of course she'd prefer the company of a man plus her work and her destitute clients Nora thought, but still she had finally convinced her daughter that marriage really would make her feel more secure and less fragile, besides was social work really what she wanted most, why not be a housewife like her mother, no Mama no way she would say, what's so wonderful about that, a housewife like you and you learned all those languages, even read Ibsen in the original and for what, so you could raise us, I feel bad for you Mama really I do, Marianne was so easily swayed and she fell for all those fashionable feminist theories, what ingratitude, as if I haven't given my children everything, they had all I had to give, but what encourages me is Greta the oldest, she said I was right and thought a bit the way I did though we disagreed sometimes about the importance she gave her professional life compared to her family, but I was always there for them all and their children too and I still am, every day we talk, okay so it's on that shimmering screen but I do talk and I go on talking till they have to listen to what I have to say, then they're gone, too much to get done they say, but why, why don't they tell me everything, I so want to know, why do they seem to be falling away one after the other, even Stéphanie the one I painted this for, why did she say again yesterday Grandmama I have classes, got to run, I can't talk now, I really have to go, tomorrow I'll talk to you, tomorrow or the day after, why did a woman's life have to be this way Nora wondered, this sudden sense of futility and uselessness in everything she did, this consuming vortex of obsessions had to be cleared away now, just the tiredness talking that's all it was, night after night without sleep, soon she'd be off to the airport and Christiensen would sweep her up in his arms, kiss her, and say darling my dearest darling, and she'd be fulfilled, she was all set to go, oh why all these wretched, devouring thoughts anyway, except for Marianne's deep humanity and her husband's passed on to their youngest even more than the others, no one realized the generosity she'd shown in Africa, almost as though it didn't fit with having children, no apart from Marianne and Christiensen none of them realized what those months of endurance and service had meant for Nora, for that brief time she was no longer just a housewife in a dollhouse, not her husband's Nora but a full-fledged woman in her own right, taking care of the AIDS-stricken like her father had, but probably better as a mother to them all, perhaps a better mother than she'd been to her own children, six-month-old Amos for instance, little N'zuzi, who but her looking desperately for a vein to transfuse just as their little eyes closed and the lids froze, just a vein to get this life-giving fluid into them, but too late, much too late she thought, that's what days without food had done to them, and whenever she thought about her family she saw them too, above all Amos and N'zuzi whom she'd bathed and tried to feed when they were no longer able, shooing flies away from the bottles, Ugandan and Rwandan children, Amos, N'zuzi, and so many others all dying the same way in countries she never should have left, she knew that now, but what on earth were all those voices on her doorstep thought Mère, Marie-Sylvie came in having forgotten to close the blinds, better if they all stayed outside because the room was now filled with fog and damp circling her bed and that wouldn't be good for Vincent's asthma, nothing mattered more to Mère than her grandson's health and future, what was it they were saying, Manuel's father had been arrested during the night for corrupting minors and the house was swarming with police, Manuel saw his father led away in handcuffs, at least Mélanie and Daniel's daughter was not drugged and asleep on the beach and what a relief that was, probably off with Tammy somewhere, no wait here she was on the veranda with them, back before midnight for her grandmother's goodnight kiss and now hugs from her parents too, not the scolding she'd get any other time, tears and kisses from them instead, still crying they went softly up the steps, her father holding her mother by the hand, okay I'll wait till tomorrow when you come Tammy had texted her, the pact's off thought Mai, the stoic and princely pair with flaming hair and a single white glove melting like wax were not for tonight, such horror averted thought Mai, Tammy's parents, not knowing their own children or even wanting to, had no conception of anything like this, their library, books, their whole house and maybe even themselves going up in flames with the children, there it was again, her grandmother's music drifting through the window as the fog wound its way through the trees, then the cocks crowing too reminding them of a daybreak like any other, soon the timid warmth of February would thin out this fog without dismissing the lingering chill, the tropical spring and riot of vegetation would have to wait just a bit longer, yes better for Vincent not to get too close thought Mère, it's so close in this room she might not even make him out anyway, not Vincent or Samuel or Mélanie or any of them, when oh when would it dissipate so she could see daylight Esther wondered, and when would her old familiar voice return so they'd know how very much she loved them, so very much, and now here's our very own muzhik yelled Herman as Robbie left the stage almost bowing under the weight of all his synthetic furs, you know what you need said Herman, you need Jamie to get his snow machine and have it come down on you from the roof in great big flakes, course on the sidewalk it sort of turns into dirty puddles we'd slip and slide in, then he went on to complain about the cold that wouldn't quit, that and the icy fog that wound its way along the contours of the shore, so rare that hardly anyone believed their eyes, and bit by bit the limos brought everyone back to the warmth of the smoky bar and Robbie's dark eyes sparkled beneath his fur hat and heavy lashes as he glad-handed all the girls, cautiously ushering them to the bar, okay girls he said, drink up, it's on me tonight, this was a relaxing time for Petites Cendres, just before dawn, he felt the comfort of all these friendly bodies pushed up against him, people he knew he could trust if he had to, bodies fighting any number of germs and viruses, no matter if some hid themselves beneath Yinn's makeup or tucked their chins into fur collars, barely able to breathe in coats way too big for them but big enough to cover the lesions like Petites Cendres, and what did their frailty or his own matter, right now for the moment they were together, alive and joyous, his and everyone's celebration thoughtfully put together by Yinn, and when the cocks raised a racket in the fog, he shepherded each of them home through it to their apartments or to Dr. Dieudonné's clinic, where they still tried to maintain some appearance of a normal life just as Fatalité had in his place that echoed all night long bathed in glaring light, Petites Cendres thought Herman still hadn't realized Fabian was part of their group as Jamie said later, so wrecked he could barely climb the stairs and Jamie almost took him in his arms and put him to bed but Fabian wanted none of it, he just worked away at it, holding on to the handrail with Jamie holding him as tight as he could and sighing adieu, adieu brother of mine, now not a word to dear Herman, all right adieu brother adieu, and that sent Jamie running back to the limo with tears running down his face and that was how the night ended for Fabian thought Petites Cendres, sad and how else could it be, the other girls lingered at the bar till dawn, their laughter thready and thin and Robbie by far the funniest in all those furs, his brother was in town from Puerto Rico so he'd let him have his room, he was a club singer too, and where are you going to sleep asked Herman, oh the sofa in the corridor at Yinn and Jason's, the warmest family I know, right said Herman, kind of your universal family aren't they, Yinn's utopia would be for everyone to sleep at their place, all between those yellow wooden walls, a warm inner sunshine for all those abandoned in the night Herman laughed, hey not only does she love Jason but she's sorry he can't have his two daughters with him, hey why not, why not, I bet if it weren't for Yinn's mother raising a fuss they'd all be there, but she threatened to join a convent if he did that, being an agnostic she sure surprised Yinn with that one, she's not even Buddhist like me he said, so what are you going to do in a convent, I mean isn't part of our tradition that parents not grow old alone but surrounded by their children Mama, well then I'll go live with your brothers she answered, besides she figures Yinn needs her as a moderating influence on those modern ideas of his, all this garbage about universal love, love without borders, nope Yinn needs her, besides she's a sewing whiz and he'd never get his costumes done on time without her, I mean think about it, 350 costumes a year, he'll wear his eyes out but what she really worries about is him wearing out his heart loving Jason and everyone else, no she's just gotta be there with that love of his spilling out all over the place in universal empathy, and now Robbie's got his brother there too and for how long, let him sleep out in the hall on that sofa no way, Robbie'd never sleep properly on that thing but neither was she going to give up her room, I mean there's quite a breeze out there in that hallway, yep Robbie told the girls at the bar, with Yinn and her mother, Jason, Geisha, and Cobra we've got a real family and that's what really counts in life, Petites Cendres overheard this and worried that Robbie would ask him where he spent the night, maybe he'd invite him in like the brother so close to Yinn it was a torment, but Robbie had to get back onstage for the closing show though it made him shiver just to think about taking off his furs to perform, already on the stairs he started to sing *I love gold and red and green* and the sweet, sweet air as the smoke piled up in the bar, and Petites Cendres longed for the night to end and for them all to leave

after that spectacular parade in Jamie's limos, now he was
ready to fall onto the red sofa and weave a web of dreams
but he'd have to wait till Andrés shut down the bar and settled
the ticket-counting with Yinn the star of the show who was
also fighting off the cold, by then he'd be a boy again in grey
pants and a jacket, simple elegance just like that, black shoulder-length hair and now just the odd-job man, humble as ever
like when Petites Cendres saw him bent under a black laundry
bag, somehow that stirred Petites Cendres even more, it was
both moving and tempting for, whether dressed to the nines
as a woman or in simple elegance as a man with something
woollen or leather to ward off the cold, the sweetness of her
went straight through Petites Cendres even though it was
impersonal and disinterested on Yinn's part, straight through
him like on those boiling nights at the bar or in the sauna at
the Porte du Baiser with the frenzied rise of sexual excitement
in the customers, was this really the rough and ready crowd
Yinn sang and danced for every night then left afterwards in
the early morning calm and blasé, even contemptuous of all
the promiscuity, oh yes Petites Cendres read it on her face in
the exhaustion of the night as she smoked and drank her
cocktails through a straw, dark hair let down over her shoulders, to Petites Cendres' eyes this was the languid Eurasian
woman that Jason had fallen for at first sight and told everyone so, was it all this nighttime rumba that made Yinn want
to retire at thirty-three, that's what Petites Cendres now overheard Yinn whispering to Andrés, and she'd say it to them
again tomorrow, prophesying that she was made for change,
made to adapt over and over, that's what an artist is first and
foremost, a living metamorphosis, a creature of revolution,
that's what he'd say to Petites Cendres tomorrow and it would
leave him ruthlessly alone, but now absorbed in the accounts
with Andrés in the Indian tunic and silk scarves that kept him
warm but saying nothing, even after the night's happening
thought Petites Cendres, nothing said, nothing foretold or

prophesied like a sentence brought down on Petites Cendres, none of that just yet. Let them leave me alone, those were Marie Curie's last words thought Mère, yes leave her alone, no one at her bedside, especially not Marie-Sylvie de la Toussaint spreading her shadow over the mosquito net, how many times had she asked if Mère wanted Justin your friend in the linen suit to come in, he'd never worn it before though nor the hat, to which Mère repeatedly answered that's not Justin, he never dresses like that and he isn't pallid like that either, but perhaps he's changed and you don't recognize him the servant retorted, he says he really must see you and he was in that street procession you watched from your window, the black group playing all those jazzy laments slow oh so slow, the drums remember them all the way to the cemetery, remember the drums, you didn't like those did you, the gentleman really does want to see you and he says you've known each other for years and years, your family too, should I let them all in, but Mère said no I don't want to see anyone in this dense fog and dampness, she'd forgotten about Justin and centred her mind solely on Augustino, would he come, oh what human misery he must have seen in Calcutta when he began his second book, his father hadn't approved of his going so far alone and no one knew what he was doing in that overcrowded and busy city, but Mère just kept on writing to him anyway though he never answered her, maybe he'd gone to ground somewhere, and what exactly was it he was searching for Mère wondered, some dawning light or revelation or was it maybe to lick his wounds after Adrien's devastating review of the first book, though Mère had told him this happened to the soul and thoughts of many men as they dried up, especially Adrien struggling with the loss of his wife and subsequent loneliness, above all Augustino should not take it personally, this was Adrien growing old and disillusioned and hateful, but he had told his friends no this was unacceptable, it made Adrien feel better when he delivered terse condemnations of young writers, not just Augustino, they were all targets of his tight-lipped sarcasm and he'd done it for years Mère wrote to her grandson, surely he knew that as men age they get worse not better most of the time, what had overtaken Adrien was a repressed mean streak triggered by the loss of the woman he loved, yet he was still handsome and easily drawn to younger women, which might prove dangerous to him laughing and enjoying himself every day at the tennis court, did he even remember being offensive to Augustino, of course not she wrote, of course not with all these distractions and amusements, and so it was that his spirit dried up in him, and as for Justin no that wasn't him, she was sure of it, no he was far different, a peaceful friend and son of a minister, brought up in China and now a prolific writer himself, he'd certainly respect her wish for peace and quiet, so who might this stranger be that Marie-Sylvie was talking about, linen suit and pale-looking skin under a white hat with upturned brim, oh she'd probably end up telling her to show him in anyway, besides surely daylight would work its way through the mist sooner or later, how nice that would be to see the window with the first rays of sun shining through the palms onto the frangipanis, the orange trees, and the lemon trees, Nora saw the red and purple line across the water on the horizon, it was early and no one would see her driving too fast as usual undeterred by all the tickets she'd got, a young Cuban fellow had stopped her once when Christiensen touched base at home, but I have no papers on me, my husband has them all, and she felt a bit ashamed at having consigned all trace of her identity to her husband mostly because of the way the young officer frowned at her, a muddled sense of shame at virtually admitting she'd been a man's possession even to the point of not wanting her own chequebook, not even for household expenses, with a certain detachment she would have said it's not my role, that's what she'd tell Christiensen as if ransoming her freedom and letting him take everything bothersome off her shoulders, material things just didn't interest her, unlike other women who didn't disdain to know how much their husbands earned, in fact it repelled her, still a muddled sense of shame she thought as she drove faster and faster along the deserted highway while pelicans and ibises took to the sky around her and out over the misty ocean, past it all that reddish purple horizon as the sun rose, faster she had to see him as soon as she could and feel him swing her up into the air, at last we're together again my darling, my love. As he held the wheel and navigated toward the neighbouring island Ari hoped the egrets and blue herons would help soften Lou's disposition and bring her closer to him, maybe even to say Papa love whoever you want, I'm a big girl now, in these pink shorts you can see how long my legs have grown like Mama's, I can look out for myself now Ari, and he'd stretch out his arm and stroke the two heads in front of him, Rosie and Lou both fast asleep in the canvas chair near the rudder while the mist moistened their hair with droplets as though they'd just climbed out of the bathtub, oh if only things could always be like this Ari thought, Lou always my sweet little girl not bent on tormenting him, hey almost time for the Peace Dance, this time between father and daughter as the blue herons took off with the pelicans for the neighbouring island and did their own dance, and while he dreamed of peace with his daughter she opened her eyes under fog-entwined hair wondering what if he's brought us here to some isolated beach to dump us on the dock so he can go and join that Noémie as fast as he can, what'll we do alone on a strange beach Rosie and me, oh the waves are gently rocking the boat, better just go back to sleep and stop thinking about him, tomorrow she could sound him out before he tried to get her to pardon him once more by launching into that tired old story about the wild geese and their Peace Dance, better just sleep, he knew the sea and what he was doing and wouldn't get them lost and he probably still loved his daughter too much to abandon her on some far-off beach, too much to just leave her there on the white sands of an island where no one lived except dolphins, blue herons, and pelicans, who knows if Ari . . . but she fell asleep as Mère saw Charles and Fréderic's house once more shining in the night from chandeliers already visible from the porch, sounds of the party too with the stilted voice of Caroline at her elbow saying come my dear, you know this house all too well don't you, here take my arm, they're all waiting for you, and Mère would have gone along with her but she felt the dry hand of Marie-Sylvie burning hot on hers, should I let in the strange man that calls himself your friend Justin she asked, you know the linen suit and white hat, but Mère said this apparition sounds too pallid to be the real one, oh the day is dawning and at last I can see the sunlight on the trees in my garden, please Marie-Sylvie do let him in, I'm ready now the fog's lifting, yes let him in, maybe this mysterious stranger is Justin after all, hmmm even pale-looking in a linen suit and white hat. And outside Yinn was shivering from the cold in a blue fur coat fitted at the waist as she leaned against the outside of the bar while Petites Cendres watched, from her demeanour she was obviously fed up and not at all in the mood to be on show for passersby to ogle and prod as if she were somehow unreal, not so of course, not even onstage a few minutes later in a brilliant yellow bikini, always alone deep down whether on show for publicity's sake or going over the top for the audience, always alone thought Petites Cendres but reachable when someone young came close as though in a way she were the offspring of the entire world, the joyous groups at the foot of the stairs that led to the show, especially the young boys and girls come to share her great gift for understanding, harmony, and relaxation, a genuine tenderness for all that were different, especially when they came from places where sexual outsiders were never at home, always condemned, sometimes to death, Yinn knew this thought Petites Cendres with a wonderful lightness of spirit as the happy gangs of kids climbed the stairs and ran toward Yinn to be greeted always with a smile celestial in its androgynous ambiguity, affectionate though in a way that might seem a little distant but still a kind of whirlpool for reconciliation, was there a place for Petites Cendres in all of this, was there somehow a way in like the apostle John on Jesus's shoulder in so many paintings, John whose love could never be more than forlorn, not to him did the master raise his eyes as the blood of redemption seeped through the cloth and out of his angry face beneath the crown of thorns he could feel breeching his skull and executioner's nails through his skin, how could he manage a thought for the lovelorn John, lovelorn Petites Cendres forever hanging on his shoulder, almost lying in the folds of his tunic even at the Last Supper, John who in all candour could not know the extent of his suffering that night and the next day when that shoulder and tunic were taken from him, too innocent to know thought Petites Cendres, still this same place was his, and now as some of them drifted out of the bar and others drifted in, he saw the Next One, Robert the Martiniquan from Decadent Friday still dressed for the night and splaying wide the sheepskin jacket he wore over his underwear, causing Yinn to remark with the knowing air of a specialist well nature certainly did right by you didn't she but you might be a wee bit cold, her hand brushing the Next One's cheek and his green locks, Yinn's connoisseur finger tracing the arch of his eyebrows and appraising the young Asian face, your brow needs to be a bit higher she said, I'll show you tomorrow, the brow's our way of showing pride in ourselves, especially us Asians Yinn told the fervent young disciple he would soon teach to sing and dance onstage, then Yinn kissed his forehead with that arm's-length neutrality of hers as though they were two children, then bade them all goodnight and headed off toward Jason before he finished turning off all the lights and bright-coloured spots, Petites Cendres noticed the rounded shoulders and tattooed arms under his sleeveless shirt as Yinn looked on, attentive and tender as though they were already alone and asleep in a tight embrace while the poster of Greta Garbo looked on as if watching from a giant screen, and Robbie too watching his own screen as Fatalité danced all night without ever growing tired, this Fatalité was never going to die alone in his apartment, an apartment that still burned in a cruel glare day and night, no never going to die again said Robbie, not all the lights though, Jason left the red night light on over the sofa where Petites Cendres would soon stretch out in the shadowy alcove where no one could see, Yinn would be last to leave while Jason waited outside under a street lamp with a suitcase full of electronic instruments at his feet, Petites Cendres could make out the white-toothed smile and curled lip as he stretched out on the red sofa, now he wanted nothing but for Yinn to pass by just a little too close in his simple young-man elegance, grey pants and jacket for a wintertime that would soon give way to ten months of summer in a red sleeveless vest and cargo Bermudas like Jason's, pass by but not before leaning over and taking Petites Cendres in his arms, just a man-hug you understand, like brothers, with Yinn saying are you crazy sleeping on this sofa when I've got a houseful of rooms, honest you really are crazy, then Petites Cendres would close his eyes and pretend to be asleep he was that happy, but it got darker away from the night light, and Yinn took a few steps toward the door, stopped and looked around, then seeing Petites Cendres sliding toward the red sofa, gave him a tender wave and disappeared.

Acknowledgements

With thanks to Kelly Joseph, a fine editor, and much appreciation for the confidence and fond support of Marie-Claire Blais, my sons Antoine and Olivier, and Jocelyne Brûlé.

— Nigel Spencer

About the Author

MARIE-CLAIRE BLAIS is the world-renowned author of more than twenty-five books. She is a four-time winner of the Governor General's Literary Award for Fiction and has also been awarded the Athanase-David Prize, the Gilles-Corbeil Prize, the Blue Metropolis Achievement Award, the Molson Prize, and several Guggenheim Fellowships. She is also the patroness of a recently initiated prize for young authors as part of a Québec-France exchange. She resides principally in Florida and travels extensively.

About the Translator

NIGEL SPENCER has won the Governor General's Literary Award for Translation with two consecutive novels in this cycle: *Thunder and Light* and *Augustino and the Choir of Destruction*. He has translated numerous other works and films by and about Marie-Claire Blais, Poet Laureate Pauline Michel, Evelyne de la Chenelière, and others. He is also a film-subtitler, editor, and actor now living in Montréal.